W9-BTL-924

DEATH AND HONESTY

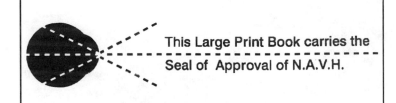

This Large Print Book carries the
Seal of Approval of N.A.V.H.

DEATH AND HONESTY

CYNTHIA RIGGS

WHEELER PUBLISHING
A part of Gale, Cengage Learning

GALE
CENGAGE Learning·

Detroit • New York • San Francisco • New Haven, Conn • Waterville, Maine • London

GALE
CENGAGE Learning

LIBRARY OF CONGRESS CATALOGING-IN-PUBLICATION DATA

Riggs, Cynthia.
    Death and honesty / by Cynthia Riggs.
        p. cm. — (A Martha's Vineyard mystery)
    ISBN-13: 978-1-4104-1806-7 (hardcover : alk. paper)
    ISBN-10: 1-4104-1806-5 (hardcover : alk. paper)
    1. Trumbull, Victoria (Fictitious character)—Fiction. 2. Older women—Fiction. 3. Murder—Investigation—Fiction. 4. Real estate appraisers—Fiction. 5. Rich people—Fiction. 6. Martha's Vineyard (Mass.)—Fiction. 7. Large type books. I. Title.
    PS3618.I394D45 2009b
    813'.6—dc22   2009021647

Published in 2009 by arrangement with St. Martin's Press, LLC.

Printed in the United States of America
1 2 3 4 5 6 7 13 12 11 10 09

FOR
DIONIS COFFIN RIGGS
POET
1898–1997

ACKNOWLEDGMENTS

Thanks to all of you who have become friends of Victoria Trumbull through libraries, bookstores, and borrowing from fellow readers. I love getting your letters and e-mails. Victoria is very much alive to me, and I gather she is to you, too. She'll stay ninety-two forever, which she claims is her best year so far.

Jonathan Revere continues to feed me ideas for writing my way out of the outrageous situations Victoria gets herself into. And, if it weren't for Arlene Silva and the Vermont College MFA program, Victoria would never have realized her sleuthing talent.

It's become a tradition to put up for auction to fund scholarships at Vermont College a weekend at the Cleaveland House bed-and-breakfast, plus having one's name in the next Victoria Trumbull book. Mindy LePere won the honor this time, and makes an appearance as a nurse. She had no choice about her character. At least she's not a villain.

Little did Jordan Ronson know when he first sat at the cookroom table and shared his woes with me about a neighbor's psychotic rooster, that he and the rooster would become an integral part of the book. Thanks to both you and Chickee, whose name has been changed to protect the innocent.

Here are some of the many people who've helped me with my writing, researching, editing, critiquing, and hand-holding. From the Howes House writers there are longtime members Jackie Sexton, Shirley Mayhew, Jeanne Hewett, and Ethel Sherman. There's poet and birder Sally Williams, photographer/publisher Valerie Sonnenthal, author Ernie Weiss — read his cliff-hanging escape book *Out of Vienna* — Nelson Potter, computer genius Ed Housman, Gerry Jackman Dean, Rabbi Carla Theodore, artist Barbara Moment, and musician Charles Blank. From the Sunday Night Writers there's Carolyn O'Daly, whose essays are sure to be picked up by National Public Radio, Rev. Bonna-Whitten Stovall, who writes of Mississippi and Southern Baptists, Rev. Judy Campbell, working on her third mystery, sailor and company starter-upper

Geoff Parkhurst, and Elissa Lash, who makes the life of an ecdysiast both poignant and hilarious. I hope I haven't forgotten any of you.

Thanks to Alvida and Ralph Jones and to Ann and Bill Fielder who've gone over every one of my manuscripts.

Most of all, thanks to Nancy Love, my agent; and Ruth Cavin, Editor, and Toni Plummer, Associate Editor, who work long and patient hours at Thomas Dunne Books, St. Martin's Press.

Thank you all.

An explanation may be needed. Martha's Vineyard is one of eleven islands in the County of Dukes County. Redundant, I know, but that's the way it is. Hence we have the County Sheriff of the County of Dukes County.

CHAPTER 1

The fickle Island weather turned raw and chilly, and a cold April rain slashed against the west windows of Victoria Trumbull's house. Her granddaughter, Elizabeth, lighted an oak fire in the parlor, and Victoria settled into her mouse-colored wing chair with a book of Robert Frost's poetry for a comfortable evening of reading.

When the phone rang, Elizabeth answered. "For you, Gram. The chief."

"Am I getting you at a bad time, Victoria?"

"What can I do for you, Casey?"

The call was from Mary Kathleen O'Neill, also known as Casey, the town's police chief. She had appointed Victoria her deputy after realizing how much the ninety-two-year-old poet knew about the Island and its inhabitants. In fact, Victoria was related to most of them.

"Have you seen Ellen Meadows lately?" Casey asked.

Victoria marked her place with a slip of paper and set her book aside. "Not for several days. Why?"

"She's disappeared."

"How long has she been missing?"

"She didn't show up this noon for a lunch date with Selena and Ocypete, the other assessors. How do you pronounce her name, anyway?"

"She pronounces it 'Oh-SIP-i-tee,' " said Victoria.

Casey paused. "Wait a sec, Victoria. Someone's on the other line."

Victoria heard a slight click as Casey put her on hold. While she waited, she held up her glass in a toast to her granddaughter.

Elizabeth lifted hers, too. "To you, Gram. Thanks!"

It seemed only a short time ago that Elizabeth, going through a divorce, had invited herself for a couple of weeks. Now, Victoria couldn't imagine life without her sunny granddaughter.

Casey came back on the line. "Sorry, Victoria. Thought it might be news of Ellen, but it was Jordan Rivers complaining about Lambert Willoughby's rooster. Where was I?"

"You were saying Ellen didn't show up for luncheon with the other two assessors."

"Right. They went to Ellen's house earlier this evening, before it started to rain. She wasn't there. At least they didn't see her. Adolph hadn't been fed or let out, so the animal control officer took him home with her. I don't know that anyone's cleaned up the mess."

"Is Ellen's car in her driveway?"

"The two said it wasn't."

"I don't know Ellen well," said Victoria. "In fact, I don't know any of the three assessors well. I have no idea where Ellen is likely to be."

"It's not a police matter yet, but if she's fallen or had a stroke or something . . . She's in her seventies. At her age, you know . . ."

"No, I don't know," Victoria said firmly.

"I asked Junior Norton to stop by while he was making his police rounds. No one answered his knock."

"I'm sure her door's not locked."

"We police . . ." Casey paused. "*I* can't enter her house without her invitation." She emphasized the word "I."

Victoria waited.

Casey said, "The woman who bought the old Hammond place had an argument with Ellen about her assessment."

"She's not the only person in town to have

13

argued with Ellen. I've had some heated discussions with her myself," said Victoria.

"You know I can't authorize you to enter her house on official business. However, as a friend and neighbor. Or at least, neighbor . . ."

"All right," said Victoria, getting out of her comfortable chair. "I'll ask Howland to take me there." She disconnected and immediately dialed Howland Atherton, her friend and a semiretired drug enforcement agent.

"I know Ellen only by sight," Howland said after Victoria explained about the missing assessor. "Enough to keep out of her way. What's on your mind, Victoria?"

"I need to check her house."

"Now? I'll be glad to take you, but it's pouring."

"The sooner the better. Casey is worried about her."

"Okay. I'll be there in ten minutes."

"I can take you, Gram," Elizabeth said.

"Keep the fire going. I won't be long."

When Howland showed up, rain was pouring off the main roof of Victoria's old house, overflowing the wooden gutters and gurgling through the metal drainpipes. Howland parked as close as he could to the west steps, but even in his short dash to the entry, his yellow slicker was drenched. He tossed back his hood, exposing silver hair that curled artistically around his forehead and ears.

"I'm wet," he said. "I'll wait out here in the entry."

She shrugged into her faded tan raincoat and tugged her rubber gardening boots over her stocking feet, wincing as the boot rubbed against her sore toe. The wind blew rain into the open entry door and whistled through the cracked pane in the kitchen window.

As she was buttoning the raincoat, Victoria said, "Casey won't go into Ellen's house without a warrant. She wants me to check, as long as it's unofficial."

Howland nodded. "An adult missing for less than twenty-four hours doesn't give the police probable cause."

Elizabeth appeared, holding a musty black silk umbrella. "I found this in the attic, Gram. It'll help keep some of the rain off." She escorted Victoria to the car, then dashed back into the shelter of the entry.

Ellen's house was only a half mile from Victoria's, but the rain made it seem farther. The windshield wipers slashed back and forth, moving curtains of water without making much difference in visibility.

Ellen's house was dark. Howland parked close to the side entrance. Across the road, Alley's General Store was closed for the night, the porch regulars long gone.

As they went up the steps to the kitchen door, lilac branches heavy with tight buds slapped them wetly. Victoria knocked, waited, then cupped her hands against the glass pane and peered in. When there was no answer, she pushed the door open and they stepped inside. Howland switched on the lights and sniffed. "Something smells bad."

Victoria agreed. "No one let her dog out."

Nothing seemed out of order in the kitchen. Victoria noticed several cardboard file boxes on the dining room table and stopped to look.

"Forget those for now," Howland said.

They checked the front hall. The parlor seemed almost too neat. Obviously not used regularly. Nothing was out of order in the two upstairs bedrooms or the bath, so they returned to the kitchen, where the smell was strongest.

Victoria looked around. "Someone cleaned up whatever dog mess there was. We haven't checked the pantry."

The pantry door was partly hidden by the refrigerator. Howland lifted the latch and tugged the door open.

Victoria's first impression was the stench. The second was the buzzing of flies. Only then did she focus on the woman lying on the floor, a chubby woman, her eyes open, her face a purplish color, a scarf knotted so tightly around her throat that it sank into her flabby flesh. In her death throes, she had soiled herself.

Victoria backed out of the pantry. "Call Casey, will you, Howland? It's not Ellen."

CHAPTER 2

Victoria and Howland waited in the dining room for the police, sitting at the table far from the open pantry door.

"Could you tell who the victim was, Victoria?"

"I believe it's Lucy Pease, Ellen's neighbor. I didn't want to look too closely."

"Hell of a crime scene," said Howland, rubbing his nose with the back of his hand. "No telling how many people have tramped through the house looking for Ellen, including the two of us. In cleaning up the dog's mess someone incidentally cleaned up any nearby evidence."

Victoria could think of nothing to say. The sight in the pantry was too horrible. She had no desire to write, her way to pass time, and no desire to talk. She'd known Lucy Pease only slightly, enough to greet her at the post office. Lucy was a pleasant enough widow with two grown boys who lived off

Island and a married daughter who lived in West Tisbury. Victoria had never sat with Lucy at the senior center luncheons, never played Scrabble with her.

Howland ran his hand over his face and rubbed his nose again. He crossed his arms and tapped his foot.

"Perhaps Ellen is off Island," Victoria said.

Howland stopped tapping his foot.

"What was Lucy doing here?" Victoria continued. "Why would anyone kill her? A burglary gone wrong? The house is so tidy, it didn't look as though anything was disturbed."

Howland said nothing.

"Did the killer think Lucy was Ellen? The two weren't at all alike. Lucy was short, plump, and white-haired. Ellen was, or is, medium height, muscular, and colors her hair. Black."

She stared absently around the room, at the glass-fronted cabinet with tennis trophies, at a framed photo of Ellen in military uniform accepting an award from some dignitary, at the blue jardiniere with long-stemmed silk poppies. Her glance stopped at the stacks of cards next to the cardboard file boxes patterned in a mottled black and white, like the school composition books her daughters had used. Each box was about the size of a shoe box. She reached for one of the stacks and drew it toward her.

Howland leaned back in his chair and watched, arms still crossed. Victoria scanned the top card, then picked up the one below and examined it, and then the next. She frowned as she looked at still another card.

Howland leaned forward. "What have you found?"

She held up one of the cards. "These are property cards that describe each and every piece of property in the township. Our taxes are based on this information." Victoria's frown deepened. Wrinkles on her forehead and around her mouth formed angles of disapproval. "They belong in Town Hall, not here."

"I suppose the assessors were working with them."

"The records belong in Town Hall," Victoria repeated. "The assessors have an office in Town Hall. They have no business working in a private home where citizens can't know what the assessors are plotting."

" 'Plotting'?" Howland laughed.

"There's nothing funny about this." Victoria held up the pile she had looked through and slapped it. "The cards in this stack represent the highest-assessed properties in town. What were the assessors doing with them?"

She laid the stack of cards on the table, pushed her chair back, and began to say something more, but at that moment the police arrived, Casey and Junior Norton from West Tisbury, and Sergeant Smalley and Trooper Tim Eldredge from the state police barracks in Oak Bluffs. Before they could exchange greetings, an engine roared into the driveway and stopped. Doc Jeffers, the medical examiner, had arrived on his Harley.

The doc shucked off his oilskins and helmet and hung them, dripping, on a hook beside the kitchen door. He nodded at Victoria, then fished around in his black leather bag and pulled out a pair of latex gloves, which he snapped on, and went about his business of examining the body in the pantry.

Tim Eldredge hung his own foul-weather jacket next to the doc's, conferred with Sergeant Smalley, then took a notebook and pen from his shirt pocket and joined Victoria and Howland at the dining room table.

"Sorry, Mr. Atherton, sir, and Mrs. Trumbull, ma'am. I'm supposed to take down your statements."

Howland nodded. Victoria said, "Of course."

While Tim was asking questions and taking notes, Victoria could hear Casey and Junior Norton discuss with Sergeant Smalley the placement of yellow crime scene tape. When that was done, Smalley came over to the table and waited for Victoria to finish talking.

"When you've given your statement to Tim, Mrs. Trumbull, there's no need for you to stick around. You, too, Mr. Atherton. We know where to find you."

Victoria got up from the hard chair with relief. The rain drummed steadily on the kitchen roof.

"Wait inside," Howland suggested. "I'll get the car."

A few moments later he pulled up close to the door and helped Victoria into the passenger seat.

"I could use a stiff drink," he said. "You don't happen to have any scotch, do you?"

"I do. Enough for both of us. I hope Elizabeth kept the fire going."

The next morning was bright and fresh with a hint of spring. A soft breeze shook rainbow mist off the cedars in the pasture.

The night before, Elizabeth went to bed before Victoria and Howland returned, leaving soup warming on the stove. Victoria hadn't felt like eating supper. After two stiff drinks with Howland, who'd had only one, she turned off the burner under the soup and went straight to bed.

This morning she made up for not eating supper, and tucked into her usual hearty breakfast of shredded wheat and sliced banana. There was a knock on the door and Casey entered.

"Morning, Victoria. Are you okay? Sorry I put you up to it. Awful, finding Mrs. Pease like that."

Victoria pushed her empty cereal bowl aside. "Has anyone notified her daughter and sons?"

"Junior called them last night. The sons are on the eight-fifteen ferry from Woods Hole. Annie, her daughter, will meet them." Casey checked her watch. "They should be here any minute, and I need to be over there to talk to them. Before I go, though, I have something to show you."

"Help yourself to coffee," said Victoria. "You know where everything is."

Casey took her mug into the cookroom, a small room off the kitchen where Victoria liked to write, and set it on the table, then spread open a manila folder and shuffled through the contents. "Here's a photocopy of a note Sergeant Smalley found in Lucy's pocket. From Ellen to Lucy saying she had to go off Island for an emergency dental appointment and would be away overnight. She asked Lucy to feed Adolph and let him out."

"That answers a couple of questions," said Victoria.

Casey sat down and stirred two spoonfuls of sugar into her coffee. "I'd never have recognized her, Victoria. Not a nice sight." She continued to stir. "The forensic guys came over last night on the late boat."

"Were they able to find anything?"

"Too many people in and out. They collected what they could. There may be some trace evidence."

Victoria was silent.

"Doesn't seem like a robbery," Casey went on. "Burglars usually don't kill unless they're surprised, and then they most likely smack the victim on the head without intending to kill. This was deliberate. A scarf knotted around her neck."

"I suppose we can assume Ellen was the intended victim," Victoria said.

"Possibly."

"If so, the killer was someone who didn't know either woman."

Casey pushed her chair away from the table. "I'm glad the state police are handling

24

this. Gotta go, Victoria. Thanks for the coffee. Take care. And please," she studied Victoria, who had a certain determined look about her, "please, Victoria, don't get involved this time."

After Casey left, Victoria brushed crumbs off the table and set up her typewriter to work on her weekly column for the *Island Enquirer*. She wrote for some time, trying to word the news of Lucy's death sensitively. At one point she took a lunch break, then worked in her garden for an hour before she went back to her writing.

Finally, she got up stiffly, bent her knees a couple of times to make sure they still worked, and went up the step from the cookroom into the kitchen. As she did, she heard a car drive up.

Howland's battered white station wagon pulled up by the steps and he got out. A large shaggy dog took up most of the area behind the backseat.

"I'm on my way to the vet's, Victoria. I can't stay. Fluffy ate something that didn't agree with her."

"Not serious, I hope?"

"Who knows. She likes to roll in dead fish she finds on the beach. I passed Casey on the way, and she asked me to tell you that Ellen Meadows returned to the Island on the ten-fifteen boat this morning."

"Was anyone at her house to break the news of Lucy's death?"

"Junior Norton's been there all night. The forensics team left around dawn. Casey had Kerry Scott's cleaning crew in. They've come and gone."

Victoria heard a sharp bark from Howland's car.

"I've got to go," said Howland. "Fluffy can't wait much longer."

Victoria continued writing. She finished around four and was drinking her tea when a white car that seemed as long as Packer's Oil delivery truck pulled up by her kitchen door. Surely the driver had taken a wrong turn. But the limousine stopped and a uniformed chauffeur went around to the passenger side and opened the door.

CHAPTER 3

Victoria had seen a great variety of life-forms during her ninety-two years. Few things astonished her. But the woman who exited from the chauffeur-driven limousine came close. One shapely leg after another emerged from the backseat, feet clad in high-heeled sandals with thin gold straps. The legs went on for such a long time, Victoria thought at first the woman must be naked. The gold shorts she wore were more appropriate for a warmer day. This was early April, after all.

The woman came up the stone steps, holding the railing as if it were a stage prop. She was as tall as Victoria, taller, in fact, with those sandals. Flaming red hair tumbled to her shoulders and her enormous bosom intruded on Victoria's space.

Victoria stepped back. "May I help you?"

"Mrs. Trumbull?"

"Yes. And you are . . . ?"

27

"I'm Delilah Sampson."

Victoria said nothing.

"I'm sure you've seen me on TV? On *The Straight and Narrow Path*?"

"I don't have television," Victoria said, and waited.

"Oh, dear!"

When Victoria still said nothing, the woman added, "I bought the old Hammond place on the North Shore."

"Of course," said Victoria. "I understand you had an encounter with one of the assessors the other day. Come in." She led the way into the kitchen.

"I guess there are no secrets in this town," Delilah said, and glanced at one of the gray-painted chairs.

"That seat will be a bit cool on the backs of your legs," said Victoria. "I'll put a towel down."

"I'm fine."

But Victoria could see that the woman was not fine. The problem seemed to be more than legs sticking to a cold seat. Her face was drawn and under her eyes were dark circles. She was older than Victoria had first thought, but Victoria was not good at guessing ages. Maybe forty or fifty. The brilliant hair seemed at odds with her face.

Victoria felt a sudden stir of sympathy.

"Would you like a cup of tea?"

"Yes, please," and at that, Delilah burst into tears. "Howland Atherton suggested I talk to you, Mrs. Trumbull."

Victoria ripped a paper towel from the roll under the cupboard and handed it to her. "Howland is a good friend." She turned on the stove under the kettle to reheat the water, then sat facing Delilah. "How can I help?"

"It's that dreadful assessor."

"Ellen Meadows?" Victoria thought of the three women, Ellen, Selena, and Ocypete, the one they called Petey. Then she thought about Ellen arriving home to find her neighbor murdered in her home. That would have to be difficult.

"No, not her. That man. Oliver Ashpine."

"He's the assessors' clerk, not an assessor. I've had a problem or two with him myself. He's not what most people would consider a people person."

Delilah sniffed. "You heard I got into an argument with that woman who looks like a prison guard?"

"That would be Ellen Meadows. Chair of the assessors. Yes, I did hear about that. Go on."

"She told me to come back this morning, so I went to Town Hall, like she said, and she wasn't there."

"Ellen had an emergency appointment off Island."

"Well, they told me to return later, so I went back this afternoon. I've just come from there."

"You met with Ellen?" Victoria looked away, not sure Delilah had heard about the body in Ellen's house.

"She seemed to have something on her mind."

"Yes," said Victoria. "She would."

"When I bought my property, the house was a wreck."

"It was a historic building, more than two hundred years old. I understand you had it torn down."

Delilah patted her nose with the paper towel. "Mrs. Trumbull, I want to pay my fair share of taxes. I never even look at the bills. But I don't want some second-rate assessor taking advantage of me."

Victoria wondered how Ellen had managed to do any business at all today. "You haven't explained what the trouble is. The old Hammond place can't be worth a great deal. It's rocky old farmland, swampy and overgrown with brambles and locust trees."

Delilah blotted her eyes, careful not to

smear her mascara. "I bought it for two million."

"Dollars?" Victoria said in astonishment.

"Yes. After I built my house and had the view cleared, the assessed value went up. Doubled from last year."

"That wasn't Oliver's decision," said Victoria. "The three assessors determine what our properties are worth."

Delilah didn't appear to be listening. "The assessment went from the two million I paid to four million after I built my house, then seven the next year, then eleven last year. This year, it's twenty."

"Million? Twenty million dollars?" Victoria pushed her chair away from the table. "You can't be serious!"

"Ms. Meadows gave me a copy of the tax bill she said had been sent. For ninety-two thousand and something."

"You were billed for ninety-two thousand dollars?"

"But the bill I got in the mail was for over one hundred and two thousand."

"Good heavens! Well, that can be settled easily. Tell Oliver Ashpine to correct the mistake."

"You don't understand, Mrs. Trumbull. The assessment isn't the only problem."

"Then what is?"

Delilah dabbed her eyes again. "Howland told me I could trust you."

"I certainly hope so," said Victoria.

"He threatened me."

"Who threatened you?"

"Mr. Ashpine. Oliver."

"How?"

Delilah held the towel to her eyes. "With my past."

Victoria stood up, outraged. "Demand that your bill be corrected. He can't threaten you like that. You have nothing to hide."

"But I do. Before Henry and I were married — Sampson is my stage name, his name is True — I served," she twisted the damp paper towel, "as an escort."

"What's so terrible about that?"

"For an escort service."

"Well?"

The sobs were louder now. "Call girl, Mrs. Trumbull. Ten years ago. Actually twenty. I was one of the most exclusive call girls in Minneapolis." She looked up at Victoria, her eyes magnified by tears.

When Victoria looked puzzled, Delilah said, "Prostitute, Mrs. Trumbull. I was a prostitute."

"Yes, I know what a call girl is," said Victoria, sitting down again. "But this *is* the twenty-first century."

"When Henry met me, I was singing alto in the church choir. He said he loved how sweet I looked in my red robe and lace collar, and I didn't want to disappoint him."

"Where is Henry now?" Victoria asked.

"At my place. He spends most of his time in Zebulon. Church business, you know."

"Zebulon?"

"West Virginia. He flew in yesterday. He's staying in the guesthouse." She hid a smile behind her damp paper towel. "We had a little disagreement he hopes to patch up."

"Then explain your past to Henry, right now."

"Henry would never understand. He's a clergyman."

"Clergymen accept people's foibles."

"Not Henry." Delilah blotted her nose again. "There's something else I haven't told him." She shifted in the chair, and the backs of her bare legs made a squeaking sound. "I'm filing for divorce. Before that clerk tells Henry about my past career, I've got to do something to protect my assets so Henry can't touch them."

Victoria didn't hear the last part of Delilah's sentence. What registered was the hint of blackmail. "Don't you dare allow anyone to blackmail you."

"If Mr. Ashpine tells Henry about me,

Henry will take everything I own."

"Assets from your television career?"

"From two of my ex-husbands. Henry produces my TV program for the church, and naturally, it doesn't pay what a commercial show would."

"Surely he can't take money you've inherited."

"My lawyers say if the divorce goes through before I can protect myself, Henry is entitled to half of everything I own. And if that assessor . . ."

"Assessors' clerk," Victoria corrected.

". . . if that clerk tells Henry about my former career, Henry will make sure the church lawyers wipe me out."

"Surely a clergyman wouldn't do that."

"Fundamentalist."

"Oh," said Victoria. "I suppose the church is opposed to divorce?"

"The church isn't. He is." Delilah balled up the soggy paper towel. "When I married him, I didn't realize what sort of person he is."

"In what way?"

"When I met him, he flew around in corporate jets and courted me on a huge yacht with captain and crew. It all belonged to the church. He's on salary. A clergyman's salary." Delilah's mouth turned down and her voice had an edge to it. "He married me for my money, and all the time I thought I was marrying him for his."

Victoria got up, ripped off another paper towel, and handed it to her.

"Thanks, Mrs. Trumbull. He's already gone through almost two million dollars of my money."

"How long have you been married?"

"Three years."

"He spent two million dollars in only three years?"

"He likes nice things. Clothes."

Victoria, who got most of her clothing from the Thrift Shop, whistled softly. "What is it that you want from me?"

CHAPTER 4

"I've got to put my financial plan in action before Oliver Ashpine talks to Henry," Delilah continued.

"What sort of financial plan?"

A dazzling smile broke through Delilah's tears. "A farm." Her voice shifted down from shrill. "That way I can get an agricultural restriction and lower my assessment."

"A farm," Victoria repeated. "What sort of farm?"

"I'm going to raise chickens and goats. And I'm getting a yellow tractor. I tried it out at a Deere store off Island. The man there really was a darling. I'm going to order overalls and a straw hat with a red bandanna." Delilah swept her mane of bright hair on top of her head and held it there with both arms.

Victoria felt strangely surreal. "What do you know about farming? Chickens? Tractors? Goats?"

"I've ordered two dozen baby chicks. They should arrive within the next couple of days."

"And the goats?"

"Lambert Willoughby is building a goat pen for me. He works at Town Hall, you know."

"I know who he is." Victoria looked away. Lambert Willoughby's mother-in-law was Lucy Pease. His wife must be in shock over her mother's murder last night.

Delilah apparently didn't notice Victoria's distracted look, because she went on. "I've ordered six fainting goats from a place in Minnesota called Billy-Goat Bluff."

"Fainting . . . what?" said Victoria.

"Goats. They're this tall." Delilah held her hand about three feet off the ground. "You can't believe how cute they are, Mrs. Trumbull. When you say 'Boo!' like that, they fall over in a faint with their legs straight up in the air."

"But . . ." Victoria said again, and blotted her forehead with a paper napkin she tugged out of her pocket.

"Girls, we have a problem." Ellen Meadows slipped off her reading glasses and scowled at the two women sitting across from her at her dining room table, Selena Moon and

Ocypete Rotch. All three women were well into their seventies, and had served together as town assessors for a combined total of nearly a century.

"We're so sorry about Lucy," said Selena in the soft southern drawl she'd affected since high school. She smoothed her pleated gray skirt and plucked at the buttons of her pink sweater. "Such a darlin' sweet person. What a dreadful thing for you to come home to."

"Your own house!" Ocypete put her hand up to her breast. "Murdered. I can't begin to imagine how you must feel." Ocypete's layers of chiffon, tie-dyed in pale shades of orange, lavender, and green, quivered at the thought. "Awful. Simply awful."

"Yes," Ellen agreed. "Awful. But we have a problem, girls, and we have to deal with it immediately."

Selena glanced toward the pantry door. "You must be terrified to be in your very own home knowin' someone was murdered here. Someone you knew!"

"I can't think about that right now, Selena." Ellen tapped her pen on the oak tabletop. "As you know, we've been setting aside a modest percentage of, you know what, for years. As a result of our being careful, very few taxpayers have complained about the small increases on their tax bills. Very few."

"Yes, indeed," said Selena. "Less than one percent."

None of the three could now recall exactly how the "setting aside" began, but it involved some incorrect paperwork coupled with an accidental overpayment of taxes. The assessors conscientiously opened a separate account for the overpayment, but in their own names. Should a taxpayer question the error, the refund would be available. But a taxpayer never did.

Over the years, a few select taxpayers received erroneously higher bills, and usually paid without question. The overpayment went into the setting-aside account and was ready in case a taxpayer filed a claim for a refund, which rarely happened. By the time the three assessors retired from their respective nine-to-five jobs in the army, the post office, and the bank, the setting-aside account had ballooned into a considerable amount. Enough to supplement their fixed pensions. They invested most of the nest egg in a promising new film company.

"You said we had a problem, Ellen," said Ocypete.

"I hope the problem isn't something I

did," drawled Selena. "I worry so . . ." She patted her blond curls. "I mean, I don't think we're greedy, do you-all? I think we've been entirely fair."

"Who's trying to be fair?" Ocypete flipped the hem of her diaphanous skirt over her broad thighs.

Selena coughed. "Petey dear, I hate to mention this . . . it's not that I don't like perfume . . . but patchouli, I, well . . ." She fanned herself with her scented hanky.

"Don't care much for your scent, either," snapped Ocypete, tossing her long white hair over her shoulder.

"Girls! Please!" Ellen rapped her knuckles on the table. "Our problem is Oliver."

The two turned away from each other and looked at Ellen. The property cards from the mottled black-and-white file box that Victoria Trumbull had examined the night before were spread out like a hand of bridge on Ellen's dining room table.

"I'm afraid Oliver isn't much of an improvement over Tillie, after all," said Selena.

Ocypete nodded. "Has anyone ever questioned what happened to Tillie?"

"Villagers assume Tillie ran off with a married man she'd been seeing." Ellen straightened the pencils in front of her and repeated, "The problem, as I said, is not

Tillie, it's Oliver. He's triple-dipping."

"What can you mean?" asked Selena.

"This afternoon I met with Delilah Sampson . . ."

"Poor Ellen. Coming home to, um, your house and . . ."

Ellen went on, louder. "Delilah Sampson, as you know, confronted me the day before yesterday, quite upset."

Selena murmured, "I knew it. I've always felt that woman was trouble."

"I suggested she come to Town Hall this morning when she'd calmed down, but, of course, I had to go off Island."

"Of course," from both Selena and Ocypete.

"I'm surprised you met with her this afternoon, considering," added Ocypete.

Ellen bowed her head and murmured, "Mrs. Danvers in Town Hall evidently hadn't heard about Lucy's death, and told Miss Sampson to return this afternoon, when she thought I might be back. Fortunately, I did meet with her. If I hadn't, we might never have learned about Oliver."

"What was Miss Sampson's problem?" Ocypete asked.

"Her property assessment is too high, according to her. Much too high."

Ocypete gathered up the property cards

in front of her, tapped the edges on the table, and dealt them out into tidy stacks again. "Well, of course it is," she said.

"She does pay rather a lot in taxes," murmured Selena. "I mean, we assessed her property at fifteen million . . ."

"Don't forget, we had to add a bit for the setting-aside account." Ocypete swept her arms out in a gesture that indicated abundance.

Selena quickly put her hanky to her nose again.

"Oh, stop it," snapped Ocypete.

Selena dropped the hanky. "I don't think eighteen million is unreasonable for a hundred acres of waterfront property and a rather large house."

"Rather large!" Ocypete chortled. "Eight bedrooms, five baths, a whirlpool spa, six fireplaces, a movie theater, a koi pond, tennis court, swimming pool . . ."

"Girls!" Ellen rapped her knuckles on the table again. "Miss Sampson claims we'd assessed her property at twenty million, not the eighteen million we decided upon. Certainly not the fifteen million on the town records."

Selena and Ocypete stared at her.

"But we didn't," said Ocypete finally. "The bill she received from us was something like ninety-two thousand dollars based on our eighteen-million-dollar assessment."

"That's right," agreed Selena. "We visited her property on a rainy day last March. I was wearin' my Wellies, I recall . . ."

"Selena!" Ellen barked.

"Go on, Ellen," said Ocypete. "What about Oliver?"

"I told Miss Sampson to take a seat and went upstairs to check the discrepancy with Oliver. He wasn't at his desk."

"He's supposed to be working," grumbled Ocypete.

"He does have quite a lot to do," Selena said, "since he's both the tax collector and our clerk." Selena turned to Ellen. "Maybe he stepped out for a minute . . ."

"We *know* he's the tax collector, Selena," said Ellen. "After Tillie left, we made sure he was appointed tax collector in her place. Surely you haven't forgotten all the lobbying we did with the selectmen."

"He's the only person in town, besides the three of us, who knows about the setting-aside account." Selena looked down at her hands. "And, of course, Tillie knew."

"And Lambert Willoughby, her brother. He knows, of course." Ocypete turned to Ellen. "Oliver wasn't at his desk, you said."

"Since he wasn't there," Ellen stopped

drumming her fingers on the table, "I looked up the Sampson tax bill, and, as we thought, the *official* bill for the town records was based on a fifteen-million-dollar assessment. The bill Miss Sampson should, of course, have received was based on the eighteen million we agreed upon." Ellen paused and the other two stared at her. "The bill she actually received was based on a twenty-million-dollar assessment."

"How . . . ? Who . . . ?" Selena began.

Ellen interrupted. "I assumed Oliver used separate file drawers for the town records and for the setting-aside account, the way Tillie did. The bottom drawer of his filing cabinet was locked, so I used the key Tillie had taped to the bottom of the bookshelf."

"Really, Ellen . . . !" said Selena.

"I found the bill based on the eighteen million we'd decided on, copied it, and took it down to Miss Sampson."

"And?" Ocypete adjusted her skirt.

"She claimed it was not the same bill she received."

"Oh?" said Ocypete.

"As I said before, the bill she showed me was based on a twenty-million-dollar assessment. Not eighteen."

Selena and Ocypete gaped at her.

Ellen held her glasses case by its chain

and swung it back and forth. "I told Miss Sampson that Oliver had made a mistake and we'd speak to him. After she left, I went to the office and found a copy of a third bill, the one she received."

"Based on twenty million!" gasped Selena.

"Three different bills." Ellen paused and glanced first at Selena, then at Ocypete and repeated, "Three different bills."

Ocypete picked up a stack of the property cards, plucked one out at random, and laid it down on the table. "He's tax collector."

Ellen nodded. "Right."

"Taxpayers mail checks to him."

"Right."

"He deposits the checks into the town account."

Ellen agreed. "With a certain portion going into the setting-aside account, of course."

Ocypete nodded. "Does Oliver have a separate private account?"

"It would seem so," said Ellen.

Ocypete glanced at her cards and plucked out another one. "Tillie's beginning to look better all the time."

"A bit late, isn't it," said Ellen.

"Oliver can't do that," Selena cried. "Changing the assessment without our ap-

45

proval. That's not," she hesitated, "legal. He simply has to go."

Ocypete snorted.

Ellen smiled. "The selectmen appointed him. They're the only ones who can fire him. Talk to Denny."

"Oliver is Denny Rhodes's cousin," said Ocypete.

"No, no," corrected Selena. "Denny's *wife* is Oliver's cousin."

"How much in taxes are we talking about?" asked Ocypete.

"A lot." Ellen jotted some figures on the scratch pad in front of her.

"I don't understand," said Selena.

"What don't you understand?" Ocypete muttered. "He's a greedy bastard."

Ellen held up her notes. "His bill to Delilah Sampson, based on a property assessment of twenty million dollars, was around one hundred thousand. If she had paid without question, as she always has, the town would get a little over seventy-five thousand. Fifteen thousand would have gone into the setting-aside account. The remaining ten thousand is not accounted for."

"He's spoiled everything," muttered Ocypete. "Who else has he overbilled?"

"You mean . . . ?" murmured Selena.

Ocypete turned on her. "Ellen means, Selena dear, that a small difference in assessment of a mere two million dollars has broken the camel's back."

"What shall we do?" Selena wrung her hands. "Perhaps we can call it a terrible misunderstanding?"

Ellen set her elbows on the table and leaned forward. "We need to have a little talk with Oliver."

"Soon," agreed Ocypete.

CHAPTER 5

By the time Delilah emerged from the bathroom with the tear-stained damage to her face repaired, Victoria had made up her mind. "I'll talk to Oliver Ashpine about your assessment. Will you give me a ride to Town Hall?" She glanced down at the knees of her gray corduroy slacks, stained from kneeling by her flower borders earlier that afternoon, and brushed off what dirt she could.

"Thank you, Mrs. Trumbull. You won't tell him what I said? I mean, about my farm and divorce?"

"You needn't worry about that."

"Darcy can drop you off at Town Hall and bring you home again."

McCavity, Victoria's marmalade cat, rubbed up against her. She gave him some fresh cat chow and filled his water bowl. She then left a note for Elizabeth, who was at work.

Once they were outside, the chauffeur held the limousine door for them. Victoria could see only his mouth, set in a faint, crooked smile. His visored cap shaded his face. Something about him was familiar. Where had she seen him before? She climbed into the backseat, sank into the soft leather upholstery, and stretched out her long legs.

Delilah slid in next to her. "Town Hall, Darcy."

The car wafted them away. Victoria could scarcely feel the ruts and bumps in her driveway. Delilah chattered, but Victoria heard only the rich hum of the car's engine.

As they passed the West Tisbury police station, she saw the police Bronco out front. Casey was at work and Victoria felt a pang of regret. She hadn't ridden shotgun with Casey for more than a week.

At Town Hall, the chauffeur opened the door and offered Victoria his arm.

Delilah leaned toward her. "Thanks, Mrs. Trumbull."

What was now Town Hall had been Victoria's school when she was a girl. The downstairs didn't look much different. There were no desks or slate blackboards, of course. But iron posts still rose from floor to ceiling and the floor was painted the same scuffed green she remembered.

She climbed the stairs to the second floor. Oliver Ashpine, the assessors' clerk, had office space in the far corner of the building overlooking Music Street. Padded cloth screens divided his area from the rest of the room. He was hunched over his computer, his back to her. She could see the screen, which seemed to be showing a movie.

"Oliver!" Victoria announced.

He started, then tapped a key that darkened the screen and swiveled to face her. "Back again, I see. Is there something else you want?"

"I need to look at property cards." Victoria settled herself into the visitor's chair that faced Oliver's tidy desk. The top was clear except for a cup holding pencils and pens, a calendar pad with appointments penciled in, and a white pasteboard candy box. She folded her hands over the top of her stick and waited.

Oliver shoved a pad of yellow forms toward her. "I'm in the midst of something and can't help you now. You'll have to fill out a request."

"Whatever you're watching on your computer can wait while you get the property cards for me."

Oliver stood and removed his glasses. He was a short, plump man. His black hair was slicked down as if it were painted on his scalp. He swung his glasses by one temple, leaned a hand on the desk, and glared at Victoria through pale blue eyes.

Victoria waited.

At last he said, "Why do you want the cards?"

"I don't care to tell you why. As I'm sure you know, Massachusetts law says you have no business asking me."

"Does this have to do with your house?"

Victoria gazed at him.

He put his glasses back on and stood up straight. "The cards are not available."

"Then I'll wait until they are."

"I believe the assessors are going over them."

Victoria looked around the empty room and thought of the black-and-white file box on Ellen Meadows's dining room table and the property cards spread around. "I assume the assessors haven't taken those cards out of Town Hall?"

"I'm busy, Mrs. Trumbull."

"I think not."

"Assessing properties is complex."

"Perhaps you will explain it to me, then," and Victoria smiled.

"Mrs. Trumbull, I'll have the cards ready for you tomorrow. Which properties are you interested in?"

"Everything west of the airport and east of Tea Lane. You can exclude the properties in the very center."

"You want the whole town of West Tisbury, is that it? You're asking for more than two hundred cards."

"I want all of the properties I just mentioned. I'll wait until you bring them to me."

"You'll have to examine the property cards here," said Oliver, pointing to the floor.

"Fine. I'll photocopy what I need."

"That's fifty cents a copy," said Oliver.

"Ridiculous. By law, it's twenty cents a copy."

"Twenty-five, then," said Oliver.

Victoria took out her checkbook. "Twenty."

"No checks."

"You'll take mine." Victoria filled out the check, leaving the amount blank. "Where do you keep the cards?"

Oliver paused for such a long time, Victoria wasn't sure he was going to give in. But he turned abruptly, went to an olive green file cabinet between the two windows overlooking Music Street, opened the top drawer, scrabbled through the files, and finally produced several stacks of four-by-seven-inch cards.

"As I said, the assessors are working with some of the cards. They're not all here. You can't take these out of the building, you know."

"Thank you, Oliver."

"Use that empty desk. I'll have someone show you how to operate the copier."

"I know how to operate the copier."

Victoria found the card for her own property and the one for Delilah's, several of Delilah's neighbors' properties, and several of Victoria's own neighbors.

"Find what you were looking for?" Oliver asked.

At that point the phone rang. Oliver answered. After a long silence, during which he glanced from Victoria to the copier to the bottom drawer of the filing cabinet and back to Victoria, he said to the caller, "I can't talk now, Ellen. Let me get to another phone." He punched the hold button and set down the phone.

"I'll be right back," he said. "Don't disturb anything while I'm gone."

He headed downstairs to the one private phone in the building. Victoria immediately went to the filing cabinet and found, in the unlocked bottom drawer that Oliver had been eyeing, two thick folders marked "DS." She hurriedly copied everything in both folders, and, without looking at them, tucked the copies into her cloth bag and replaced the folders in the bottom drawer. She was about to sit down again when she noticed the white pasteboard candy box. She peeked inside. Fruit jellies. They called the candy Turkish delight when she was a child. She hadn't had a fruit jelly for a long time. She was just about to help herself to a piece when she heard footsteps coming up the stairs. She closed the box quickly and returned to her seat. By the time Oliver returned, she was sitting in her chair, rosy-cheeked but calm.

Oliver, himself, was pink-cheeked and perspiring.

"I've made copies of a nice selection of cards and will examine them when I get home," said Victoria. She separated out a dozen pages. "Now, will you please show me the bills you sent out for these properties?"

Oliver looked at his watch. "I don't have the time."

"I can imagine," said Victoria. "The bills, please." She settled back in the chair and thumbed through her photocopies. When she got to Delilah's property she sat up straight. Oliver was shuffling through manila folders in the top file drawer.

"Oliver!" she called out.

"What now?" He shoved some papers from his desk into a folder and went over to the filing cabinet.

"Would you please explain this?" Victoria held up the copy of Delilah's card. "Do the assessors know about it?"

"Mrs. Trumbull," Oliver said with exaggerated patience. "Do you want me to find the bills or do you want me to explain the property cards . . ." he looked over at the copy Victoria was holding up and stopped in mid-sentence.

"Both. Bills first. Is this a mistake on Miss Sampson's assessment?" She waved her copy at him. "This says her property is assessed at fifteen million dollars. Yet I understand she was billed based on a twenty-million-dollar assessment. And there's a third bill based on eighteen million. Which is correct?"

Oliver sighed. "The assessment procedure is complicated, Mrs. Trumbull. Assessors need years of training. Experience."

"Oh? To reach three different figures?"

"Our assessments are based on complex formulas and neighborhood designations. A layman can't understand."

"Surely you agree that something is wrong here," Victoria insisted.

Oliver twitched a stack of jammed paper out of the copier and threw it on the floor. "You've gummed up this goddamned machine."

Victoria gathered up her copies of the bills, placed them in the cloth bag along with the copies of the property cards and files marked DS, thanked Oliver, proceeded carefully down the stairs, and marched out to the waiting limousine. Darcy was standing by the passenger door.

Oliver pounded down the stairs behind her. "The check!" he shouted, tripping on the bottom step. "You didn't give me the check!"

But Victoria was smiling up at the chauffeur and didn't hear the assessors' clerk.

CHAPTER 6

Victoria set down her heavy cloth bag next to the limousine. She hadn't realized how many copies she'd made.

"I'll put that on the front seat for you, madam," the chauffeur said.

Victoria hesitated, then passed her bag to him. The only irreplaceable item in the bag was her notebook, with the start of a sonnet she was working on. While the chauffeur was stowing her bag, she studied what she could see of his face. She could make out only his bright eyes, high cheekbones, and cleft chin. And his mouth, of course, set in that twisted half smile. The chauffeur, Darcy, was taller than she was, well over six feet. He might have been playing the part of a chauffeur in a movie. Except for that smile, he had absolutely no expression.

Why was he so familiar?

She took a deep breath and climbed into the backseat. Darcy slammed the door with an expensive thunk. Before they turned onto South Road, Victoria saw his eyes in the rearview mirror, watching her.

The glass partition that separated the driver from passengers slid down silently. "Madam," he said.

"Yes?"

"Miss Sampson has asked that I invite you to tea."

His voice was familiar, too, an actor's deep, resonant voice. Victoria's uneasiness grew. Then she thought of the unappetizing cold tea she'd left on her table. And the police station where Casey was working without her. Did she want to ride alone with this strangely familiar man? Adrenaline kicked in. Of course she did. "Thank you, Darcy, I'd enjoy that."

"Shall I take you directly there, madam?"

"By all means."

He said nothing more. The direction they were going seemed right for the old Hammond place. They turned off North Road between two granite posts onto a dirt track and continued for perhaps a half mile. The limousine came to a fork in the road and paused before turning onto a smaller track. Darcy was watching her in the rearview mirror.

Victoria sat forward. It had all come back to her.

She rapped on the partially open glass. "Darcy?"

He glanced in the mirror. "Yes, Mrs. Trumbull?"

"Back there, 'Two roads diverged . . .' "

"Yes, Mrs. Trumbull. 'I took the one less traveled. . . .' " He smiled.

"It's you, Emery Meyer! Why on earth are you working for Delilah Sampson?" Victoria leaned forward. "Jewels?"

"Please, Mrs. Trumbull. My name is Darcy."

The town clock struck five. Joe Hanover and Lincoln Sibert, two of the regulars on Alley's porch, checked their watches.

"Clock's been running slow for a couple days," said Joe. He leaned against the porch railing. "What in hell do you suppose is going on with the assessors now?"

"What do you mean?" Sarah Germaine had stopped at Alley's on her way home from tribal headquarters in Aquinnah. Today she wore a dressy black sweatshirt with bright feathers painted around the neck and shoulders.

Joe switched whatever he was chewing from one side of his mouth to the other.

"You seen that white limo?"

"You can hardly miss it," said Sarah.

"Belongs to that woman who bought the old Hammond place," said Lincoln, who was leaning against the door frame. "North Shore. Born-again Christian or something."

"Hubby's the born-again, not her," said Joe, chewing.

Lincoln shrugged. "The car's hers, anyway."

Joe spat something off to one side. "Before you got here, the driver waves me over, rolls down the window, and asks the way to Mrs. Trumbull's."

"So?"

"I seen the guy before. Him and Mrs. Trumbull was pret-ty cozy a while back. Why's he need to ask how to get to her place?"

"The same person?"

"I never forget a face. The guy was even cozier with our dear sweet little selectman, Noodles."

"Select-*person*," said Sarah. "Her name is Lucretia."

"Select-*man*," said Joe. "Legal title."

"What about the assessors?" asked Lincoln.

"I'm getting to it. So the limo makes a U-turn and heads for Mrs. T.'s. Twenty,

twenty-five minutes later, limo comes back again this way and lets Mrs. T. off at Town Hall. Mrs. T.'s in there almost an hour, the limo comes back, she gets in, and off they go."

Lincoln made a beckoning sign. "The assessors?"

"Hold your horses," said Joe. "Ashpine comes out shouting, 'You didn't give me the check!' . . ."

"Mrs. Trumbull stiffed him?" asked Sarah, appalled.

"Seems so. Then Ashpine runs across to Ellen Meadows's place. The assessors been confabbing all afternoon."

Lincoln crossed his ankles. "Transacting town business?"

Joe lifted his faded red cap that read "Drains R Us," and scratched his head. "Think they care if it's illegal? Ellen, Selena, and what's her name. All three together."

"Ocypete," said Sarah. " 'Oh-SIP-i-tee,' " she repeated.

Lincoln detached himself from the door frame, went to the edge of the porch, and peered at Ellen's house across the road. "I'd give two cents to know what they're talking about."

"That much?" said Joe.

■ ■ ■ ■

While the Alley's regulars tried to figure out what the assessors were scheming, the three women had seated their clerk on the dining room chair that had one leg shorter than the others, then returned to their places on either side of him.

"Sorry to hear about your neighbor," said Oliver in an attempt at normal conversation.

Ellen stared at him without a word and moved the Tiffany reproduction lampshade so the lightbulb shone on his face. "You are a very stupid man," she said. "Very."

"You're killin' the goose that laid . . ."

"Selena!" Ellen slapped the table and both Oliver and Selena jumped.

"I only meant that . . ."

"Enough!" snapped Ellen.

Oliver's chair rocked onto the shorter leg as he sat forward. "Perhaps you ladies can tell me what the problem seems to be."

"Seems to be!" Ocypete stretched her arms out dramatically, and the gauzy fabric of her sleeves rippled like the wings of a moth.

"A small problem of triple-dipping," said Ellen.

"Avaricious bastard," muttered Ocypete.

Oliver sat back again. "I have no idea what you ladies are talking about."

Ellen interrupted him. "We'd agreed on a four-way split of Delilah Sampson's fifteen thousand dollars you'd allegedly deposited in the setting-aside account, right?"

Selena referred to the notes in front of her. "Three thousand to Oliver, four thousand to each of us."

"Three thousand wasn't enough for you?" snarled Ocypete.

Oliver held both hands in the air. "I haven't the least idea where all this is leading."

"You wearing a wire?" Ocypete asked suddenly.

He turned on her. "What?"

"A wire. You taping this conversation?"

"Don't be ridiculous." A drop of sweat appeared from beneath Oliver's hairline and trickled down his temple.

"You underestimate Miss Sampson, and you underestimate us," said Ellen. "Now Victoria Trumbull seems to have become involved. Are you underestimating her, too?"

Oliver let out his breath. "Mrs. Trumbull? What about Mrs. Trumbull?"

"Everyone in the village saw Victoria Trumbull drive up in Delilah Sampson's limousine," Ellen said. "I suppose she marched up to your office simply to give you a check for her taxes?"

"She didn't give me the check . . ."

"What do you intend to do about this hornet's nest you've stirred up?" Ellen tapped her pencil to demonstrate the stirring up of a hornet's nest.

Ocypete lined up the stack of property cards in front of her. "Victoria Trumbull is not someone you want to diddle with, Oliver."

Oliver shuddered.

Selena read off some figures. "The amount we had agreed to divide was fifteen thousand, three hundred, and some odd dollars . . ."

Ellen interrupted with her own figures. "You planned to skim off an additional ten thousand. Did you intend to share that, Oliver?"

"Unscrupulous!" exclaimed Selena.

"What do you plan to do about this, Oliver?"

"About what?"

Ellen stood, looming over him. "You're even more stupid than Tillie. We were fools to trust you."

A second and third drop of sweat trickled down Oliver's forehead. Selena handed him her hanky. He wiped his face with it and continued to hold it, picking absently at the tatted lace edging.

"Well?" said Ellen.

"There's been a mistake, ladies."

"Goddamned right there's been a mistake," said Ocypete.

"I mean, I'll tell Miss Sampson I made a mistake."

Ellen rested both hands on the table and moved so her face was inches from his. He backed up and the chair rocked. "A three-million-dollar mistake, Oliver? Or a five-million-dollar mistake? Which one, Oliver?"

The clock in the church tolled six.

Oliver stood and his chair fell over. "I'll talk to you first thing in the morning. I've got to leave now."

Ellen stood up straight. "I think not, Mr. Ashpine."

CHAPTER 7

The Alley's porch regulars continued to watch the Meadows house across the road. Lincoln, at the far end of the porch, moved his head one way then the other to get a better angle on what was happening inside.

"Can you see anything?" asked Sarah.

"They got a lamp turned so it shines on his face, like cops giving him the third degree. Looks like he's sweating."

"Those harpies would make anybody sweat," said Joe.

Sarah shivered and pulled the sleeves of her black sweatshirt over her hands so just her fingers showed. "You wouldn't think they'd want to meet at Ellen's so soon after that murder. I mean, it was only just last night."

Lincoln said, without turning his head away from the Meadows house, "Wonder why anyone would kill Lucy Pease. Nice lady. Used to do yard work for her. Looks like Oliver's trying to back away." He laughed. "Doesn't seem to know what to make of those three. He'll learn."

"Hard to believe he's been here for almost five months," said Sarah. "Whatever did happen to Tillie?"

"Walked off the job. Can't blame her, working for them." Joe jabbed his thumb toward the Meadows house.

Lincoln laughed again and pointed his own thumb toward the house. "Ashpine just knocked over his chair."

Joe cut off another chunk of Red Man and popped it into his mouth. "Tillie ran off with someone, for sure."

"You know her?" asked Sarah.

"Year behind mè at the high school."

"Who'd she run off with, her boyfriend?" Sarah asked.

"Edgartown guy. Someone else's husband."

"They turned the light out," said Lincoln. "Heading for the door."

Sarah, Lincoln, and Joe looked toward the Meadows house. An ashen-faced Oliver exited, followed by Selena in her pink sweater and pleated gray skirt. Ocypete came next, floating along in pastel draperies, and then came Ellen in her navy pants suit. Ellen pulled the door shut behind her and the four marched across the road to Town Hall and disappeared from view around the building.

"Ain't that something," said Lincoln.

Sarah turned back to Joe. "Whose husband did Tillie run off with?"

"I didn't say that."

"She seemed like a nice person."

Joe jammed both hands in his pockets and rocked from heel to toe and back again. "Think so, eh?"

Darcy turned left onto the less traveled road and brought the long white limo to a stop.

Victoria spoke up. "What are you doing at Delilah Sampson's, Emery?"

"My name is Darcy now, Mrs. Trumbull. Darcy Remey."

Victoria leaned forward. "The last time I saw you, someone's jewels were involved."

"Uncut stones. With no discernible provenance."

"What happened to them?"

Darcy grinned. "That's for me to know, isn't it?"

"Miss Sampson's jewels this time?"

"Miss Sampson's jewelry?" Darcy laughed. "No, Mrs. Trumbull. No self-respecting thief would touch her stuff." He leaned over the seat. "Mrs. Trumbull, please don't address me as anything but Darcy, from now on."

"What's going on?" asked Victoria. "Who are you working for this time?"

Darcy's grin formed an attractive crease down one side of his face, but he said nothing.

Victoria regarded secrecy as one of the world's great evils, the antithesis of democracy. Should she ask Emery — or Darcy — to take her home on principle, or should she wait and see what happened next?

Curiosity won. "All right, *Darcy.* Take me away."

"Yes, madam," said Darcy. He slid shut the glass divider and the limousine moved on sedately. A short distance from the fork in the road, they passed through an opening in a high stone wall, and the road from there to the house was paved with Belgian block — square-cut stone set in a semicircular pattern. The paved road led toward what was once the old Hammond place and was now Delilah Sampson's trophy house.

Darcy pulled up in front of the grand entrance stairway, and helped Victoria out. She gazed up at the vast new house that stood where the old Hammond place had been. The house was at least three stories high with four chimneys that she could see, and seemed to be a combination of antebellum South and New England as some newly graduated architect imagined New England. The house was shingled, as Island houses should be according to Victoria, but the shingles were still a raw unweathered yellow. Salt air and wind would silver them in time. Glossy black woodwork around the windows reflected the sunlight, and she wondered for a moment if the shutters were plastic. A wide marble staircase led up to a broad porch. On either side of the stairway, pineapple-shaped stone balusters held up the curving marble balustrade. Victoria could see rocking chairs set artistically on the terra-cotta tiles of the porch floor.

"Oiled teak," said Darcy.

"Oh?"

"The rocking chairs."

"Well," said Victoria, taking a breath.

"If you'd like, you can leave your papers in the car, Mrs. Trumbull. I'll make sure they're safe."

"Thank you," said Victoria, taking his arm.

He escorted her up the marble stairs, through a heavy oak door that an attractive young woman in black trousers and a white blouse held open for them. Victoria stepped carefully on thick oriental rugs that carpeted the long hall, not wanting to disturb the pile. They passed imposing rooms, windows embellished with heavy rose-colored draperies. Oil paintings that lined the wall were equally divided between ships at sea and stern portraits of someone's ancestors. When they finally ended up at the glass door to Delilah Sampson's slate-floored conservatory, Victoria was ready to sit down and rest.

Delilah had been seated in a wrought-iron chair. She stood when Victoria approached, and held out her hands. "Thanks for coming on such short notice, Mrs. Trumbull. I'm embarrassed about how I acted at your place." She still wore her gold sweater, but had changed from shorts into cream-colored linen slacks.

"I'm delighted to be invited." Victoria plopped into a white couch that was lower than she expected. She looked around. Along the left side of the conservatory was a well-stocked bar. The right side of the glass-enclosed room was banked with dozens of blossoming plants. "I've never seen so many orchids in one place."

"Those?" Delilah glanced over at the banks of potted plants. "They're Henry's hobby."

Darcy was still standing by the door with his hands behind his back, feet apart.

"Thank you, Darcy. That will be all," Delilah said.

"Very well, madam." He bowed himself out of the room, but before he did, he winked at Victoria, who turned away toward the view of Vineyard Sound and the Elizabeth Islands spread out in front of her. The islands stood out so clearly, she could almost make out individual trees. Below them, a wide sloping lawn led to a small pond that was separated from the sound by a narrow barrier beach. Two swans with four half-grown cygnets trailing behind were mirrored on the still surface.

Victoria sighed with pleasure. "How peaceful." But as she watched, one of the cygnets suddenly lifted its wings, threw its head back, and sank out of sight. "Good heavens!" Victoria struggled to her feet.

"If that was another baby swan, Mrs. Trumbull, we can't do anything. There were eight babies originally."

"Snapping turtles?"

Delilah nodded. "I don't know how many there are. The other day I saw one that was two feet across."

Victoria sank back into the low couch. "I hope you don't swim there."

"Hardly."

After a brief flurry, the swans and the

three remaining cygnets continued to search for food among the reeds at the edge, and the surface once again calmed.

Delilah broke into Victoria's silence. "Would you like something stronger than tea? I've got sherry."

Before Victoria could switch her thoughts from cygnets to sherry, Delilah rang a silver bell on the table, and summoned the young woman who'd opened the front door. Her black trousers, white silk shirt, and shoes with blocky two-inch heels were not quite a uniform, but almost.

"Yes, ma'am?"

She was probably in her late twenties, with pale, translucent skin. Victoria wondered if Darcy had noticed her. Of course he had, she told herself.

"What can Lee get for you, Victoria?" asked Delilah.

"Sherry would be nice."

"Sherry for Mrs. Trumbull, Lee, and the usual for me."

"Yes, ma'am." Lee bowed and disappeared.

Once she'd left, Delilah looked down at her nails and rubbed the bright polish with her thumb. "Did you have a chance to speak with that man?"

"A most uncivil person," said Victoria.

"Completely uncooperative. When he stepped out of the room to take a personal phone call, I made copies of some of his files."

Delilah sat forward. "My files?"

"Files marked 'DS' at any rate. I didn't take time to examine them. I'll wait until I get home."

"Why don't we look at them now?"

Victoria intended to study the files before she showed them to anyone else. "I don't have the copies with me."

"Are they in the limo?"

"Yes, but . . ."

"Then I'll ask Darcy to get them." Delilah reached for the silver bell.

Victoria changed the subject abruptly. She felt possessive about the files she'd purloined. "It's unusually clear this afternoon. You can make out houses on the mainland. The old-timers called this kind of day a 'weather breeder.' Heavy weather is moving in, they'd say."

"Every day is different," said Delilah. "I used to love to look at the view. I'll ask Lee to get Darcy . . ."

"You say, 'used to,' " Victoria said, raising her voice slightly. "Not anymore?"

"With that pond full of reptiles eating baby swans, the view seems sinister." Delilah reached her hand out again, and again, Victoria stopped her.

"Tell me more about your plan to become a farmer."

Delilah clasped her hands under her chin. "I've never been so serious about anything, Mrs. Trumbull. I told you I've put in an order for baby chicks, right in time for Easter. They're dyed Easter egg colors, isn't that sweet? When they grow up they'll lay eggs and I'll sell the eggs. And if I can get a rooster I can grow my own baby chicks."

Victoria refrained from remarking that, considering the law of averages, half of Delilah's baby chicks were likely to become roosters.

"And the goats, Mrs. Trumbull. Lambert Willoughby, who works for the town, has built the most beautiful goat pen. There are only about two thousand fainting goats in the whole wide world. I'm going to join the fainting goat association."

"Don't the goats hurt themselves when they faint?"

Delilah looked shocked. "Of course not. I'd never allow that. When you say 'Boo!' they just keel over, and after about twenty seconds they get up and walk away."

Before Delilah could reach for the bell again, Victoria said, "I was working in my garden this morning. Not as interesting as your farm, but I planted lunaria seedlings that my friend Jordan gave me." She brushed at her dirt-stained knees.

"Lunaria? I don't know what that is."

"Honesty."

"Maybe I can take some honesty to the assessors," said Delilah with a pleased smile.

"I'm not sure they'd get the joke."

Victoria continued to divert Delilah's attention away from the files on the front seat of the limousine. "You have such accommodating people working for you. Both Lee and Darcy are so professional."

"My servants are my friends. I don't like to call them servants, though. That seems demeaning, don't you think, Mrs. Trumbull?"

"Darcy seems a superior person," said Victoria. "Has he been with you long?"

"A little over two weeks, actually. He's amazing. He knows the Island's roads like a native."

"In such a short time. How did you happen to find him?"

"Pure luck. I was taping one of my shows in West Virginia, where Henry's church is. Zebulon is where they produce my television show."

"I interrupted. You were telling about finding Darcy."

"Well after the show, this nice man came up to me with a bouquet and told me how much he loves my show. We got to talking, and it turned out he's been a chauffeur to Saudi Arabian royalty. Can you imagine that!"

"Remarkable," said Victoria. "Why did he leave his former employer?"

"The emir or rajah or something he was working for was shot in a palace rebellion. Isn't that exciting?"

"Very," said Victoria. "Did you have a chauffeur before Darcy?"

"He was nothing like Darcy. I gave him a handsome separation bonus and he was quite happy."

Victoria shifted position on the soft couch. She was cushioned too well. She longed for her firm old-fashioned sofa with its unyielding horsehair stuffing.

"I told Henry my old chauffeur had a family emergency. He'd been with me for five years."

"I suppose you checked Darcy's references?" Victoria asked.

"Absolutely stellar. He showed me a folder full of nice letters from all over the world."

Victoria nodded. Darcy, in his previous incarnation as Emery or Meyer — she never could remember which name he preferred — had made frequent trips to Amsterdam, she knew. He'd popped up in Paris, Moscow, Mexico City, Cairo, London, and Singapore, according to people who thought they knew him. Now, Saudi Arabia. She still wasn't sure what he was. A freelance CIA agent or an opportunistic jewel thief. Someone once hinted that he was a hired killer. Perhaps he was all three.

Victoria was inclined to trust him, within limits. He knew the poetry of Robert Frost, after all. And he owned copies of all her own poetry books. She'd autographed them for him.

CHAPTER 8

Victoria was engrossed in thoughts about roosters, dyed chickens, fainting goats, and jewel thieves, and missed what Delilah said next. When she looked up, puzzled, Delilah repeated it with a throaty laugh. "Just imagine, Darcy drove for royalty and now he drives for me."

"Ah," murmured Victoria, nodding.

Lee entered the conservatory quietly. She held a tray with a glass of pale sherry, a martini, and a plate of dainty sandwiches.

Victoria sat up as straight as she could on the soft couch and helped herself to a watercress sandwich.

Once Lee had gone, Delilah said, "Getting back to that *clerk,* Victoria. Did he correct the mistake?"

"I don't believe there was a mistake. Someone altered the paperwork. Intentionally."

"What do you mean?"

"Who pays your bills for you?"

Delilah pouted. "I'm a ninny about numbers. My lawyer and my financial adviser take care of everything."

"The assessors apparently counted on that." Victoria set her glass on the coffee table in front of her. "How did the latest bill come to your attention?"

"My adviser questioned it, and even I was shocked at how the taxes had gone up. Almost double. In one year." Delilah set down her own glass next to the bell. "Actually, the bill came from the tax collector, not the assessors."

"Mr. Ashpine is tax collector as well as assessors' clerk. The selectmen appointed him to fill out Tillie Willoughby's term."

"The woman who ran off with someone else's husband?"

Victoria frowned. "That's purely a rumor. I'm not much for rumors." She patted her mouth with the dainty linen napkin Lee had provided with the sandwiches. "Mr. Ashpine is up for election this month at Town Meeting."

"We don't want him to win, do we?"

"If no one else runs, he'll win by default."

At that point, the phone rang. Lee slipped back into the conservatory and answered.

"One moment, sir." She handed the phone

to Delilah. "Reverend True would like to speak with you, Mrs. True."

"Lee, it's *Miss Sampson.* How often must I remind you?"

"Yes, ma'am."

Delilah rolled her eyes, sighed, and took the cordless phone. "Henry, darling. Where are you?"

Victoria tried not to listen, but did anyway.

"Darcy will pick you up." Delilah paused. "You want the pilot to stay here?" She leaned forward. "I'm not running a boardinghouse." Long pause. "Listen, Henry . . ." She ran a hand through her hair. "I'm trying to get in a word . . . Henry!" She sighed. "Oh, have it your way. But he stays in the guesthouse. On the couch . . . No, Darcy's in the garage apartment . . ." She slammed down the phone.

Delilah turned to Victoria, her face flushed, her hair awry. "Henry had to go off Island today. One of the church pilots flew him here from Boston, and now the pilot claims he's too tired to fly back. A half-hour flight?"

"You handled that very well," said Victoria.

"My husband can be aggravating. You won't let him know what I told you, will you, Mrs. Trumbull?"

81

"Certainly not."

Delilah stood up and put the phone back in its cradle.

"I'm not sure I understand," Victoria said. "If Henry's not staying in the same house with you, doesn't he suspect that you plan to end the marriage?"

"He thinks I'm punishing him because I found out about his new friend, the alto. A high school sophomore."

"High school student?" Victoria sat up straight.

"She's almost twenty."

Victoria was silent.

"He likes altos," Delilah explained, brushing a crumb from her bosom. "That's how *we* met."

Victoria took a deep breath. "How do you hope to establish your farm without Henry knowing about it? This plan of yours has some impracticable elements."

"It's going to work, Mrs. Trumbull. I know it will."

"How will you explain all the animals?"

"They're my pets." She clasped her hands under her chin. "After talking to you I feel much better. I won't challenge the assessment. Then Oliver won't talk to Henry and I'll have a year to establish my farm."

"You may be too late. While I was in the

assessors' office, Oliver got a call from Ellen Meadows. I got the impression the call involved your assessment. As I was leaving, I saw him hurry across the road to her house."

Delilah dropped her hands into her lap. "Oliver will be furious. Ellen showed me a tax bill that was sent to landowners, and it wasn't at all like the one I received."

"Ellen may have uncovered a scheme that Oliver set up," said Victoria. "Oliver won't gain anything by talking to Henry. He certainly can't blame you now."

"I don't know what to do." Almost absently, Delilah picked up the silver bell and rang it before Victoria could think of a way to distract her.

Lee slipped into the conservatory. "Yes, ma'am?"

"Darling, would you please ask Darcy to come here?" Victoria held her breath. She wanted to examine the copies of property cards she'd made at Town Hall before Delilah saw them. But Delilah told Lee, "Darcy needs to pick up Reverend True at the airport."

"Yes, ma'am." Lee gathered up the sandwich plate.

"Mrs. Trumbull," Delilah hesitated. "I shouldn't have said anything to you. About the farm?"

"I shan't tell him." Victoria finished her sherry and set down the glass. "My house is on the way to the airport. Your chauffeur can drop me off."

Darcy appeared and Delilah gave him his instructions. Victoria levered herself out of the deep sofa.

Delilah stood. "Thank you so much, Mrs. Trumbull."

Victoria smiled. "I look forward to meeting your fainting goats."

Darcy escorted her to the waiting limousine. "Fainting goats, Mrs. Trumbull?"

"Yes." Victoria didn't elaborate as he handed her inside. Once on the main road she rapped on the glass.

The partition slid aside. "Yes, madam?"

"Exactly what are you doing here?"

"I am serving as Miss Sampson's chauffeur, madam."

Victoria sighed. "You're overdoing the Jeeves bit."

Darcy grinned into the rearview mirror.

"What does your being here have to do with Delilah? Besides this bogus chauffeur job, that is."

"Please," said Darcy.

"Probably not Delilah," murmured Victoria. "What about Henry, the husband?"

Darcy's grin was broader. "We have our little secrets, don't we, Mrs. Trumbull. Fainting goats?"

"What's Henry like? The husband."

"He arrived two days ago and took off again this morning for a meeting in Boston. I haven't met him yet."

"Delilah claims he's the spiritual leader of a church called The Eye of God. It sounds like a cult."

"It's an enormous church. He's only one of their clergymen," said Darcy. "Not the head."

"She's a star on one of his television programs. I understand that's how you met her?"

At that, Darcy laughed.

"You're not going to tell me anything, are you?"

"No, madam," said Darcy.

"But you're not after her jewelry?"

"Hardly, madam."

And with that, Darcy slid the glass panel shut.

The limo pulled up to Victoria's west door and Darcy escorted her to the steps, where Elizabeth waited. He handed Victoria her bag of papers and she winked at him, as he had earlier at her. "Thank you," she paused.

"Darcy."

"What was that all about?" asked Elizabeth.

"A friend's chauffeur brought me home," said Victoria, and waved airily at Darcy.

Elizabeth looked quizzically from the chauffeur standing by the sleek limousine to her smiling grandmother. "What have you stirred up now, Gram?"

"I had tea at the old Hammond place," said Victoria.

"Tea?" Elizabeth said. "It's suppertime now."

Darcy slipped behind the wheel and continued on to the airport three miles away. He pulled up in front of the terminal where two men stood with their suitcases. One was a short, round, jolly-looking man with thinning white hair, great wings of eyebrows, and a narrow mustache. The other, presumably the pilot, was about Darcy's height and age, early forties. Darcy controlled a start of recognition. The pilot glanced at him, raised his eyebrows, and looked away.

"Reverend Sampson, sir?" Darcy asked the white-haired man, and touched his cap.

"Reverend *True.* Sampson is my wife's stage name." Without waiting for a response, he went on. "Understand you're the new chauffeur." He nodded with a cherubic smile. Darcy loaded the two suitcases into the limousine and held the door for Reverend True, who started to get into the backseat, then stopped. "Didn't introduce you two, did I. Darcy . . . what's your last name?"

"Remey, sir."

"Right. Cappy . . . ?" he paused.

"Jessup. Cappy Jessup." The pilot smiled. "Pleased to meet you, *Darcy.*" Neither offered to shake hands. The pilot waited for Reverend True to settle himself with his laptop, then went around the limo and sat beside him.

"Do you wish to go directly to Miss Sampson's, sir?" Darcy asked, looking into the rearview mirror.

"Fine." The reverend busied himself with his laptop.

Darcy headed away from the airport. The pilot had not said a word. In the rearview mirror Darcy saw him prop his elbow on the door frame and stare at the scenery, acre upon acre of scrub oak and dead red pine. They dipped smoothly into one of the glacial swales and up the other side.

When Darcy had first met Victoria Trumbull, she'd described the dips in thc road as "thank-you-ma'ams." A swaying horse-drawn wagon would toss a couple together, if they positioned themselves just right, she'd said. He thought of the way she savored the limousine's luxury, stretching out her still fine long legs and leaning back into the soft leather. Darcy speculated, for the briefest of moments, on what might have happened if he'd been born fifty years earlier and then had met Victoria Trumbull.

They came to the outskirts of the village and passed the huge maple trees that surrounded Victoria's house. No one had said anything. Reverend True was still working on his computer. Darcy checked the mirror and saw his face bathed in a bluish light from the screen. He could see the pilot, too, watching him with a slight smile.

On that last job the pilot's name had been Frank Morris. What was Morris doing here on Martha's Vineyard? Clearly, he wasn't about to acknowledge that he knew Darcy. For that matter, Darcy didn't care to acknowledge that he knew Frank Morris, either. Or Cappy Jessup, since that seemed to be his name now.

They passed the police station on the right and Darcy braked at the hand-lettered sign by the mill pond that read "Slow! Turtle Crossing." Two swans sailed on the black surface of the pond.

Darcy knew a few things about the man called Frank Morris. Or Cappy Jessup. He had a helicopter license, he could speak Russian, German, and Italian fluently, and he had been trained to kill.

They turned right at Brandy Brow toward the cemetery, and Darcy tried to puzzle out why Frank Morris was here. To protect someone? Or to kill someone? Who?

Henry or Delilah? Perhaps he, Darcy, was Frank Morris's target. Kill or protect? For that matter, he had his own assignment. Perhaps he and Frank Morris had been hired by the same person. Was Frank Morris there to clean up after removing him from the action?

They skirted the cemetery at Deadman's Curve and passed Whiting's fields, where a murder of crows scavenged for carrion. After the arboretum they crossed the brook. Skunk cabbage was unfurling its bright green leaves. At the split oak, they turned left.

Reverend True tapped on the glass partition. Darcy lowered it. "Take me to Up Island Cronig's, Darcy. I'd better pick up some flowers for the little woman."

Darcy slowed at a wide entrance on the right where there was a large green mailbox, and made a U-turn.

Now that Reverend True had broken the silence, he became garrulous. "I'd take her orchids, but there are plenty of those at the house. My hobby, you know."

"Yes, sir," said Darcy.

"I suppose I should look for something just the opposite, like daisies."

"Very appropriate, sir."

"Quite a gal, Delilah."

Darcy said nothing.

Reverend True settled back into the seat. "Hasn't spoken to me for three weeks. Mad at me, you know?"

"I didn't know that, sir."

"Hysterical over that alto. Cute little piece. Perfectly innocent. Can't say I blame the little woman. Redhead, you know?"

"Yes, sir." They'd reached the Up Island Cronig's turnoff. Darcy parked. "Would you like me to get the flowers for you, sir?"

"Good man." Reverend True shifted onto one hip, reached for his wallet, and extracted two hundred-dollar bills. "Daisies, roses, something like that. Two, three dozen of each. Whatever that'll get you."

"Yes, sir."

As Darcy went through the automatic door into the store, he turned quickly. Frank Morris was watching him.

CHAPTER 9

Delilah tossed the flowers onto the couch. "I suppose you think buying up the entire flower store is going to buy me off? Well, think again."

"Yes, Mother," said Henry.

"Oh, cut it out." Delilah stretched up to her full height plus the three inches her high-heeled sandals provided, and put her hands on her hips. She wore a ring with a gigantic yellow stone surrounded by quantities of small diamonds. "You're staying in the guesthouse. Even though that man is here."

"The pilot?"

"Who else? The alto? Maybe a tenor for a change?" Delilah jangled the silver bell on the end table. "You and he can work out your own sleeping arrangements."

Lee slipped into the room. "Yes, ma'am."

"Do something with those." Delilah gestured at the flowers.

"Yes, ma'am." Lee gathered up the bundles of paper-wrapped flowers and vanished.

Henry checked his watch. "It's about time for a nightcap."

"I've had mine. You may go, Darcy," said Delilah.

"Perhaps he can show me to the guesthouse," suggested the pilot, who'd stood next to Darcy, silent until now.

Delilah waved a dismissal at Darcy. "Take him away."

After the two had gone, Delilah paced to the end of the conservatory. Henry followed.

"I keep telling you, it was nothing, nothing at all."

Delilah spun around and sneered. "Nothing?"

"Just a little fling. Feeling my oats."

"Feeling your oats, you . . . you . . . horse's ass."

"Now, Mother . . ."

"Stop calling me that!"

Henry shook the bell and Lee appeared again. "My dear, get Miss Sampson her usual, and I'll have a Jack Daniel's on the rocks. Make it a double."

■ ■ ■ ■

"Whose side are you on this time?" growled Darcy as the two swaggered toward the guesthouse in the growing darkness.

"Expect me to answer?"

"Watch your step . . . Morris," said Darcy.

"Same to you . . . Meyer," said Frank Morris, or whatever his name was.

Victoria got up early the next morning to water her newly planted honesty. She had plans for the day. Elizabeth had the morning off and had baked muffins with blueberries they had picked and frozen last July.

"Any news about Lucy's murder, Gram?"

"It's early still," said Victoria.

"I saw Lucy's sons at Alley's yesterday. I didn't know what to say to them. I finally just said I was sorry."

Victoria nodded. "That's really all you can say."

Around seven, she gathered up her cloth bag and lilac wood walking stick.

"Can I give you a ride someplace, Gram?"

"No, thank you. It's a beautiful morning for a walk, and I'm going only as far as the police station."

She headed down the drive, swinging her

stick as though a marching band followed. She'd tell the chief about yesterday's visit from Delilah, but without mentioning the reappearance of Emery Meyer as Darcy the chauffeur. Casey had never trusted him, whatever name he used.

The sun was up. Another warm day, and the old-fashioned double daffodils along the side of the road would be in bright bloom. She strode along, flicking last fall's leaves with her stick, uncovering new growth. Redwing blackbirds caroled in the reeds by the pond. Spring, spring! Victoria's heart lifted with the newness of it all.

As she got closer to the police station, the pond and its swans came into view. She thought of Delilah's snapping turtles. The mill pond, too, had its share of turtles.

This morning, Lucy's murder seemed remote, even though she and Howland had discovered the body only the night before last. Thirty-six hours ago. Delilah's problems seemed even more remote. How tiresome to have officials hungering for your money. She'd never have that to worry about.

She crossed the small shell-paved parking space in front of the police station, nudged a duck out of the way with her stick, and climbed the steps into the tiny building.

Behind her, a chorus of ducks and geese clamored to be fed.

Casey was standing behind her desk. Sunlight glinted on her coppery hair. The usually quiet police radio blasted out intense voices and static.

"Good morning." Victoria shucked off her coat and settled into her wooden armchair with a sigh. She'd walked too briskly. "Any developments in the Lucy Pease murder case?"

"The forensic team came, did their thing, and left," said Casey. "The state police are questioning neighbors."

"They got my statement."

"I know." Casey reached for her gun belt and buckled it around her waist. "Your timing is uncanny, Victoria."

Junior Norton adjusted the squelch on the radio. "Morning, Miz Trumbull."

"What's going on?"

"Ten minutes ago, Miss Sampson's chauffeur called the communications center," said Junior. "He found a body in her pond."

"Good heavens. Another death. Who?"

"Male. That's all we know at this point."

Victoria felt a twinge of alarm. She found her baseball cap in her bag and set it on her head. Gold stitching read, "West Tisbury Police, Deputy."

Junior pushed his chair back, stood up with a grin, and saluted her.

"Let's go, Victoria." Casey turned to Junior, who'd seated himself again. He wrote something as he listened to the radio. "Don't forget to shut the door when you leave. Keep the critters out."

Junior lifted a hand in acknowledgment.

Victoria climbed into her seat in the police Bronco and they headed for Delilah Sampson's.

"I'll be retired before the selectmen approve a lock for the door," Casey remarked. "Fasten your seat belt, Victoria."

Victoria found the buckle and complied. "Our police station is a public building."

"I have confidential stuff in there."

Victoria's chin jutted out. "The public has a right to know. You're paid with the public's tax money."

Casey quickly changed the subject. "I understand you've signed up for the Vineyard Haven Police Academy."

"How did you learn that?"

"As you keep telling me, 'You can't keep secrets on the Island.' "

"You'd promised to send me to the police academy. The Vineyard Haven chief signed me up first." Victoria looked straight ahead, her eagle's beak nose lifted.

She was silent until Casey passed the mill pond. "I was at Delilah Sampson's yesterday," she said suddenly.

Casey glanced at her. "How come you didn't tell me before?"

"I walked to the police station to tell you."

They didn't speak again until Casey steered around Dead Man's Curve. "What were you doing at Miss Sampson's?"

"She invited me." Victoria continued to look ahead.

"I had no idea you knew the woman."

"She came by my house yesterday, upset with the assessment on her property. She wanted my help."

"Sheesh! What did she think *you* could do?"

"Evidently, she thought I could do quite a bit." Victoria lifted her chin.

"Sorry. I didn't mean that the way it sounded."

"Her chauffeur drove me to Town Hall, and I discussed the assessment with the clerk."

"Who gave you a lot of grief, I suppose."

"It looks as though Oliver Ashpine and the assessors have concocted a scheme."

"Yeah?"

"There are three different tax bills for Miss Sampson's property based on three

97

different assessments."

"The same property?"

"Yes. I made copies of all three."

"How'd you get them?"

"The Freedom of Information Act. I searched through a file drawer when Mr. Ashpine stepped away from his desk."

"Victoria . . ."

"Last night I went over all the bills for her property. One bill clearly was prepared for the town's records and showed the money the town would receive in taxes. The second bill was much higher, and the third was even higher. That was the bill that upset Miss Sampson."

Casey bore left onto North Road at the great split oak. Tiny pink buds covered the branches of the old tree, saved by volunteer arborists after an autumn gale tore the tree in half.

They drove between the granite posts that marked the way to Delilah Sampson's, and Victoria thought about Darcy finding the body in the pond. Just what was Darcy doing here? He certainly didn't need the chauffeur's job. The Bronco bounced along the track to the fork in the road, where she'd remembered that he was actually Emery Meyer, fellow lover of Robert Frost's poetry. Or was he? Would his next alias be as Mr.

Eye? That would be appropriate, since Henry's ministry was with The Eye of God.

They jounced over a tree root, and Victoria braced herself. "The road is much smoother when one is in a limousine."

"Maybe the selectmen will order one for me, along with a new door key."

"Left, here," said Victoria.

"Anything else you can tell me before we get there?"

"The Reverend True had to go off Island yesterday morning to a meeting. He returned the same day. The chauffeur met him and his pilot at the airport."

"Who's Reverend True?"

"Delilah Sampson's husband."

"Where'd he fly in from?"

"Boston. I gather the plane is owned by his church."

They drove between another set of granite posts that bounded a stone wall onto the Belgian block drive, circled in front of Delilah's house with its grand entrance stairway, passed the guest cottage, and parked in front of the four-car garage. Casey helped Victoria out of the passenger seat, and together they walked down the long grassy slope. Darcy was squatting on the ground well away from a body that lay facedown near the pond.

As they approached, Victoria could see that Darcy's trousers and shirt were wet. Strands of pondweed clung to him. The body, clad in a dark windbreaker and dark slacks, lay on the grassy edge of the pond with his feet still in the water. Occasional wavelets shifted the untied shoelaces of one shoe. The loose ends writhed like young eels. The man's head was turned away from her, and Victoria couldn't see his face.

Casey glanced at the body, then at Darcy, who stood up. "You're the chauffeur, sir?"

"Yes, ma'am."

"I'm Casey O'Neill, West Tisbury's police chief." She took out her notebook and pen. "Your name, sir?"

Darcy glanced at Victoria before he answered, and she nodded. "Remey," he said. "Darcy Remey."

"You shouldn't have moved the body."

"There was a chance he might still be alive, ma'am."

"Any idea who he is?"

"Reverend True's pilot, I believe."

"You sound doubtful."

"I met him yesterday afternoon."

"You know his name?"

"Miss Sampson's husband, Reverend True, introduced him as Cappy Jessup."

Victoria leaned on her stick to examine

the body more closely, then straightened up. "Could he have fallen into the pond by accident?" The man was Darcy's size, slim, with short hair, so muddy she couldn't tell its color.

Darcy said nothing.

Victoria looked around at the overgrown edges of the pond. "He may have banged his head on an overhanging branch."

"How'd you happen to find him, Mr. Remey?" asked Casey.

"Walking Mrs. Sampson's poodles, ma'am. One of the dogs found him."

"Where was the body?"

"Far side of the pond." Darcy pointed. "Facedown among the reeds."

"You carried him from there to here?"

Darcy looked down at his wet clothes. "Towed him by the collar."

"When you realized he was dead, you should have left him where you found him instead of dragging him all the way to this side."

"A large snapping turtle was feeding . . ."

"Okay, okay," said Casey.

"Not much left of his face."

Casey shook her head. "Where are the dogs now?"

"Back at the house."

"Does Miss Sampson know about this?"

Victoria asked.

"I returned to the house with the dogs, shut them in their room, and called the communications center. It was a little before seven. Miss Sampson doesn't usually come down for breakfast that early. I then returned here and stayed with the body."

"And Mr. Sampson?"

"Reverend True," said Darcy. "Reverend True had been quartered in the guesthouse with the pilot."

"Wake them up, all of them," Casey ordered. "Tell them to wait in the house until I get there."

"The conservatory, ma'am?"

"Fine. The state police are on the way."

Darcy started back up the slope to the house, wet trousers slapping against his legs, shoes squelching.

Victoria watched him stride up the lawn. Ahead of him she could see the flashing blue lights of police vehicles and the line of tiny blinking blue lights with which Doc Jeffers had crowned his motorcycle helmet.

"Darcy seems familiar," said Casey, "but I can't place him. Do you know anything about the pilot, Victoria?"

"No," said Victoria. "Nothing at all."

CHAPTER 10

While the state police marked off an area around Delilah Sampson's pond and strung yellow tape around the scene of an unattended death, Oliver Ashpine was wondering how he could deal with the three assessors. He filled Bertie's bowl with Alpo and set it out in the fenced yard, and then began to fix his own breakfast. What could he do?

He poured himself a third cup of coffee. Almost eight o'clock. He slapped a rasher of bacon into the cast-iron pan and broke two eggs on top.

Those harpies. Humiliating him like that. With the Alley's porch loafers watching. What kind of warped constitutions did those women have, meeting in that house of death? You'd think they'd show respect for the dead.

Next door the rooster crowed, and that started Bertie barking. The rooster crowed day and night. The racket had kept him awake most of the night. He could sympathize with Jordan Rivers, who lived across the lane from the Willoughbys. Rivers had complained to the police about the rooster, and, of course, the police did nothing. All Rivers accomplished was to make an enemy out of Willoughby. In no way did Oliver intend to antagonize Willoughby, who had some kind of pull with the assessors.

How was he going to defuse this goddamned situation? He'd lain awake listening to that rooster, trying to decide what to do. Three against one, and together they had decades of so-called service to their goddamned beloved town, and here he was, a newcomer. Not a newcomer to the Island, but a newcomer to this snobby town that called itself "the Athens of Martha's Vineyard." Pfaugh!

He added cream and no-cal sweetener to his coffee and stirred it, then flipped the bacon and eggs. What could he do? He peered out of the kitchen window at the scrub oaks that showed a faint haze of pink. Bertie had finished his dog food and was digging a hole near the fence.

Oliver's house was at the end of Simon Look Road, one of the new developments off Old County Road. Desolate goddamned place. Only three houses along the road were year-round, his and the Willoughby's next door and Rivers's across from the Willoughby's. Complaints about the rooster weren't going to get Rivers anywhere. Willoughby had worked for the town for years. So had his sister, Tillie, whose job Oliver now had.

The rest of the houses on Simon Look Road were summer rentals. Come July, party, party, party. He wouldn't have a moment's peace. Someday, when he had money, he'd move out of this slum. Money, money, money. Always money.

A car went by on Old County Road. The rooster crowed.

He knew what would happen if he tried to unmask those three assessors. Suppose he reported to the selectmen, or stood up in Town Meeting and said the assessors were removing property cards from Town Hall in defiance of state law? And suppose he said they were altering property cards, punishable by a jail term? He smiled at the thought. And suppose he said they were overbilling selective property owners, embezzling funds, and squirreling away townspeople's money in a private account? What would happen? The town would laugh it off, a simple mistake made by three dear old ladies.

He paced to the coffeepot, then realized he still had a full mug. He turned off the heat under the frying pan, slid the bacon and eggs onto a plate, and returned to his seat.

Townspeople would say the assessors had served the town for long and dedicated years. At worst, the confused accounting would be chalked up to approaching senility. The old biddies could always fall back on that.

He picked up his pencil, then tossed it down again.

Who'd get in trouble? He would. That militaristic bitch Ellen would get all self-righteous, and show that he, Oliver Ashpine, was the one skimming money from the town's taxes, and he'd end up his days rotting in a dingy state prison.

Ellen Meadows was the problem. Too bad the neighbor was killed instead of her. He could deal with the other two. Selena, the lightweight, and Ocypete, drifting off on some cloudy remembrance of protest marches past.

A preemptive strike, that was what he would have to do. He moved his chair closer to the kitchen table with his full plate and coffee mug near at hand and a pencil and paper to plan his preemptive strike, then the phone rang. Early for anyone to call. Not yet eight.

"Ashpine here."

He grinned when he heard the voice on the other end.

"I've been thinking about you," he said. "Yes, of course. It occurred to me . . .

"Yes, yes . . ." he said.

"Certainly, but . . ." the caller wasn't letting him get a word in.

"Well . . ." Oliver tapped his pencil on his preemptive strike notes, making small dots.

"Just let me . . ." He listened for a long time, then slammed the phone into the cradle. "Goddamn!" he said out loud. "Hung up on me."

Somewhat rattled, he stood up, stared out of the window at Bertie, who'd given up his digging and was chasing his stubby tail, and sat down again. He was trying to rekindle enthusiasm for his preemptive strike when Bertie started yapping. There was a knock on the back door.

"Come in," he called out, surprised. No one ever visited him, certainly not before eight on a weekday morning. Not UPS or FedEx. Not this time of day.

The door opened and he turned to face his caller.

The rooster crowed. Bertie continued to bark.

Oliver stood and his napkin dropped on the floor. "Oh, for Christ's sake!" said Oliver.

On the North Shore, police cruisers from four Island towns, the state police vehicle, the Tri-Town Ambulance, and Doc Jeffers's Harley were parked by Delilah Sampson's garage, and a group of law enforcement officers gathered around the pond and the defaced victim.

At the last house on Simon Look Lane, Oliver Ashpine's unexpected caller seated himself across from Oliver.

Ellen Meadows had spent a sleepless night wondering what the police had learned about Lucy's killer, and thought how stupid she'd been to insist on sleeping in her own house. It must have seemed strange to townspeople.

At Town Hall, Mrs. Danvers, the town's executive secretary, was opening yesterday's mail. She was tall and lean, almost cadaverous. Her slim tan jeans and shirt with vertical yellow stripes made her look taller and slimmer.

Dale Fender, the selectman who'd ousted Lucretia "Noodles" Woods in the last election, had come into Town Hall early to clear up some paperwork, and was sitting at the big oak table. He and his wife had celebrated their fortieth anniversary day before yesterday, and his wife had assured him that he was mature, responsible, conscientious, and in charge, and that was the way he felt this morning.

"Another one," said Mrs. Danvers, slapping a letter with the back of her hand. "This is the fifth complaint we've gotten this week about the tax bills." She got up from her desk with the letter and slid it across the table.

"Where's Oliver?" Dale asked. "This is his job."

"Oliver is late again. He's worse than Tillie."

"Who's the complaint from this time?"

"Mrs. Summerville, as usual. She hasn't received her tax bill." Mrs. Danvers's glasses had slipped down her nose, and she pushed them back.

Dale sighed.

"Oliver's got to go," said Mrs. Danvers. "I can't spend all my days fielding complaints about his job."

"We can't get rid of him," said Dale. "He's Denny's wife's cousin. Did he call in sick?"

"Not a word from him." Mrs. Danvers

peered over the top of her glasses. "And as you rightly know, this isn't the first time he's pulled this."

"Did you call his house?"

"Got the answering machine." Mrs. Danvers tugged a pencil from behind her ear where she'd stashed it, and dropped into her chair. "He's probably gone fishing. Everyone on the Island seems to think that's a legitimate excuse. Fishing."

Dale shook his head and the strand of hair he'd combed over the balding spot unstuck itself. He smoothed it back into place. "Not Oliver. He hates the out-of-doors." Dale picked up the letter, read it, and held out his hand. "Give me the rest of those complaints, and I'll get my wife to answer them."

CHAPTER 11

"What's the idea of hanging up on me?" Oliver stood, fists clenched on his hips, and looked up. "What do you want now, Willoughby?"

Standing, Lambert Willoughby loomed over Oliver. He strode over to a chair, turned it around, and sat with his arms crossed over the back. Seated, he was almost at eye level, even with Oliver standing. Despite the chill morning, he wore a thin T-shirt tucked into soiled jeans. His bulky arms were covered with tattoos, faded with age to a bleary red and pale blue.

Willoughby was chewing gum. "How much you skimming off our taxes, Ashpine?" He wiped a wrist across his mouth.

Oliver looked for something to lean on and finally sat down. "I don't know what you're talking about."

"You don't, eh?" Willoughby smiled, lips together.

Oliver shook his head.

"You got my sister's job, right?"

"Tillie? Tillie is your sister?"

"Don't play stupid. You know whose sister she is. You got Tillie's job after she run off with that guy."

"Her job's not exactly a big deal," Oliver said bravely. "Not much more than minimum wage."

Willoughby laughed. "I got my sister that job as assessors' clerk. You knew that, right?"

Oliver studied the faded tattoos. Entwined snakes, he thought.

"You think I don't know about the paperwork? About the assessors' setting-aside account?"

Oliver didn't look up. The more he studied the tattoos, the more they looked like snakes. Big, fat snakes.

"Cat got your tongue, Ashpine?"

Oliver looked up.

"You don't think the assessors leveled with me?"

Oliver looked down.

Willoughby went on. "I know about their scam and they know I know. Fact is, they told me. Those three ladies need someone they can trust. Besides me, that is. I told them Tillie was their gal. And she was. Never blabbed a word to anyone. Put aside a nice little nest egg, right?"

Oliver looked away.

"Right?"

Oliver stammered, "I don't know."

Willoughby mimicked him. "You don't know? I'll just bet you don't know. Those three ladies made goddamned sure you knew exactly what you was gettin' into." Willoughby thumped his chest with a fist, then folded his arms again and chewed his gum.

"What do you want?" Oliver watched Willoughby's jaw.

"Same deal Tillie and me had." Willoughby unfolded his arms from the back of the chair and stood up.

Oliver leaned back as far as he could. "What deal?" The smell of his untouched bacon and eggs, so appetizing only a few minutes ago, now made him queasy.

"Fifty-fifty cut." Willoughby smiled.

"Fifty . . ." murmured Oliver.

Willoughby shrugged. "I'm not greedy. Leaves you with a nice piece of change."

"This is the first I've heard . . ."

"Been five months, right?"

"Right," agreed Oliver.

"Tax bills went out this week, right?"

Oliver nodded.

Willoughby laughed, exposing stained

brown teeth and a small wad of pink chewing gum. "I don't suppose we need to put anything in writing, do you?"

Bubble gum. Oliver's legs had begun to tremble.

"Gentleman's agreement, right?" Willoughby thrust out a meaty hand.

Oliver heard the rooster crow. Bertie, who'd stopped barking, started up again.

Willoughby frowned and shoved his hand closer. "Right?" he said louder.

Oliver nodded and stuck out his own damp, limp hand.

Willoughby squeezed, not hard, but firmly. "That's my man." He let go and Oliver's chair wobbled. "Got to feed Chickee. Nice talkin' to you. See you around."

With that, Willoughby strode to the door, opened it, and slammed it shut behind him.

The rooster crowed again.

Oliver scraped his bacon and eggs into the trash. His stomach churned. He staggered into the bathroom, lifted the toilet seat, knelt on the floor, and threw up the three cups of coffee he'd drunk a lifetime ago.

That same morning, Delilah's closed bedroom curtains blocked out the view of the Elizabeth Islands, Vineyard Sound, the beach, and the activity around her pond.

She pushed the curtains aside to let in the morning light, and gave a startled cry.

"Henry, wake up. It's almost ten. Something horrible has happened! I should never have let you stay in my room."

"Hmmm?" The pink comforter on Delilah's heart-shaped bed muffled Henry's voice. "Did you sleep all right?"

"I shouldn't have taken those sleeping pills. I overslept and now look what's happened."

"What has?"

"Get up, Henry. Dozens of people are at the pond."

"Dozens of people?" Henry swung his stocky legs over the side of the bed, stretched his arms over his head, yawned hugely, and reached for the terry-cloth robe he'd dropped over the bedpost in his haste last night.

"Did you hear me? Henry!"

"Coming, Mother."

"Mrs. Trumbull and a lot of uniformed policemen."

"Police," mumbled Henry, tying the belt of the robe. He padded over to the window and stood next to Delilah. He tilted his head and briefly rested his chin on her breast. She had clothed herself in a filmy peignoir that was printed with lavender cabbage roses.

He peered distractedly at the activity around the pond far below them.

"Where are your glasses, Henry?"

"Would help, wouldn't it?" murmured Henry, feeling around on the top of the dresser until he found them.

"You'd better get back to the guesthouse before someone sees you here."

"Right. I'd better." Henry stopped suddenly. "There's no reason I should leave."

"I'm angry with you, remember?" She glared at him. "I should never have let you in last night. Never."

"Ah!" Henry said with a smirk. "Yes. I remember."

Delilah turned to the window. "Mrs. Trumbull and some woman in uniform are walking up from the pond. Get away from the window."

Henry smiled. "I suppose I'd better get dressed. You still make a fine choir girl." He stood on tiptoe and kissed Delilah on her chin.

"Use the door off the deck so you don't wake up the pilot," said Delilah, brushing his kiss away.

Henry bundled up the trousers, shirt, jacket, and underclothes he'd shed last night and tucked them under one arm. He slipped his feet, sockless, into his wingtips and cinched the belt on the terry robe. "I'll be quiet as a mouse," he said. "Ta, ta, Mother."

"Stop that mother crap, and tie your shoelaces."

Henry smiled again. He tiptoed out of the bedroom, shoelaces trailing, and closed the door gently behind him.

Darcy was waiting at the back entrance when Victoria and Casey reached the house. "I haven't informed either Miss Sampson or Reverend True of the drowning, Chief."

"What's the trouble?" Casey asked.

"It would have been awkward, ma'am." Darcy didn't explain. "I'll see if one of them is available now."

Victoria indicated Darcy's slime-covered trousers that were no longer dripping, but were still slapping wetly against his legs. "You'd better change first."

Darcy bowed. "Thank you, Mrs. Trumbull." He escorted Victoria and Casey into the conservatory and left.

Victoria avoided the low couch and sat in a wrought-iron garden chair where she could see the pond. The police had circled the area with yellow tape, as if it were a crime scene, not an accident. The body had been zipped into a plastic bag and lifted onto a stretcher. As she watched, four men carried the stretcher up the sloping lawn toward the garage and out of view.

High heels clicked on the slate floor and Delilah entered the conservatory. "Mrs. Trumbull! What's going on? What are the police doing here?"

Casey stood up. "Miss Sampson, I'm Chief O'Neill, West Tisbury Police."

Delilah's hand went to her throat. "What's happened?"

"A man's body was found in your pond, ma'am."

"A body?" Delilah flung herself onto the couch.

"Your chauffeur believes it's your husband's pilot."

"That can't be!" Delilah shook her head, and her bright hair swirled.

"In the case of an unattended death," said Casey in her official voice, "the police are called. At this time, we have no reason to believe his death is anything other than an unfortunate accident."

"Why the pilot?" asked Delilah.

"I beg your pardon?" said Casey.

"Nobody knew him." Delilah closed her eyes.

118

"Where is your husband now, Miss Sampson?"

"In the guesthouse. The pilot was staying in the guesthouse, too."

"Have you talked to Reverend True this morning?"

"Talked to . . . ?" Delilah glanced from the pond to Casey to Victoria to the orchids, and then to the door.

Casey started to repeat her question. "Miss Sampson, have you spoken . . ." when Henry entered the conservatory.

"Good morning, Mother." He went to Delilah and pecked her on the cheek. "Sleep well?"

"Henry," said Delilah faintly. "The police . . ."

Casey stood and introduced herself.

Henry ignored her extended hand. "What's going on?"

Casey went through the account of a man found dead in the pond.

"My *pilot,* you say, Officer?" Henry dropped into the couch next to Delilah, picked up her beringed hand with his chunky one, and patted it absently.

"Miss Sampson's chauffeur claimed he met your pilot yesterday for the first time. I understand he was staying in the guesthouse with you, sir."

Henry nodded.

"Did you hear him leave at any time during the night?"

Henry smiled. "I'm a heavy sleeper."

"You didn't hear him leave the guesthouse, sir?"

"I'm afraid not." He squirmed into a better position. "I don't know the pilot well. Didn't know him, that is."

As Casey questioned Henry, Victoria glanced from Delilah to her husband.

"He seemed a nice enough fellow," said Henry.

"Would you give me his name, sir." Casey took out her notebook. "I'll need to notify next of kin."

"Of course. Cappy something." Henry paused. "I think it's Jessup. Cappy Jessup."

Casey looked up. "Your plane and pilot?"

"The ministry's plane. The Eye of God ministry."

"How did you happen to engage this particular pilot?"

"My personal assistant did the scheduling." Henry got up from the couch and jingled the bell on the table. "Coffee for everyone, my dear," he said when Lee appeared. "And something to go with it. Rolls or coffee cake."

"Yes, sir. Will that be all?"

He lifted his great white eyebrows at Casey. "Care to ask Lee anything?"

"Later."

"That will be all," said Henry, and Lee left.

"I'll need to talk to Darcy," Casey said, writing something in her notebook.

"Darcy?" asked Henry. "You mean the chauffeur?"

"He found the body this morning. Walking the dogs."

"Yes, of course."

"We won't know until after we get the medical examiner's report how long the pilot was in the pond."

"Several hours, I suppose?"

"I don't know, sir."

Victoria gazed out of the window down the grassy slope to the pond, scarcely registering Casey's interrogation of Henry. Victoria thought of the snapping turtles that lived in the pond. One, at least, was two feet long. And Henry and Delilah were covering up something.

CHAPTER 12

Mrs. Danvers was about to take her salad out of the Town Hall refrigerator when the glass in the door rattled, announcing that someone had entered. She looked up.

"Well!" She straightened up when she saw who it was and looked significantly at the clock between the tall windows. "Nice of you to come to work today, *Mr.* Ashpine." She peered at the assessors' clerk, prepared to tell him exactly what she thought of his late hours. And then she looked again. "What happened to you?"

Oliver was pale. His usually sleek hair was tousled. Behind his thick glasses, his magnified eyes were watery. His natty clothes were awry.

"What's the matter with you?" Mrs. Danvers repeated.

Oliver ignored her and headed toward the boxes that held staff mail.

"Are you deaf?" Mrs. Danvers turned to

face him. "We've already gone through your mail. Someone has to answer the complaints. I certainly can't."

Oliver turned away from the mailboxes and headed toward the stairs that led up to his office.

"If you're sick, the least you could have done was call." When he still didn't answer she added, "I don't suppose you ever heard of a telephone."

Without a word, Oliver stumped up the stairs.

Mrs. Danvers looked at the clock again, lifted the phone receiver to call one of the selectmen, changed her mind and put the receiver down, picked it up again to call one of the assessors, decided against that, and shoved her chair away from her desk.

If Oliver was sick, and he certainly looked sick, why did he bother to come in at all? He wasn't going to accomplish anything, the way he looked. Giving everyone his germs. If he wanted sympathy, he certainly wasn't going to get it from her.

Mrs. Danvers removed her salad from the refrigerator, doused it with more dressing than she had intended, and took it back to her desk, where she chewed steadily, grinding the lettuce and celery and carrots into smaller and smaller indigestible particles.

■ ■ ■ ■

While Mrs. Danvers was working on her salad, Ocypete and Selena were seated on the porch of the Black Dog Tavern overlooking the harbor. Ocypete checked her watch. "This is the second time she's been late. Last time . . ." she didn't finish.

"Last time, Lucy was murdered," Selena said. "Shall we go ahead and order?"

"We'd better. I have a doctor's appointment this afternoon at two."

"I hope it's not serious? One worries so . . ."

"Just a tummy ache," said Ocypete. "Nothing to be concerned about."

"Speaking of doctors, I hope Ellen is all right. Last time it was an emergency medical appointment off Island."

"Dental," Ocypete corrected. "Broke her upper plate."

"I'll have the green salad, darlin'," Selena said to the waitress who'd appeared with two glasses of water. "With just a bit of house dressing. On the side, please?"

"Hamburger," said Ocypete. "Rare. Not pink, red."

"Anything to drink?" asked the waitress.

"Iced tea for me," said Ocypete.

"I'll have the same."

They watched the *Islander* round the jetty and pull into its slip. The waitress brought their orders. Cars and trucks from the ferry drove past. Heavy clouds moved in from the northeast. Ocypete checked her watch. They nattered on about weather, gardens, and summer visitors.

"What could possibly be keeping her?" Selena asked as they nibbled and chewed. "I don't understand how she could sleep in that house under the circumstances."

"This is just like last time."

"In a way, you can't blame her. I mean, Lucy's death. But you'd think she'd call."

A half-hour passed. The *Islander,* loaded for the return trip to the mainland, backed out of its slip, rounded the jetty, and disappeared from view.

Selena forked up the last of her salad and crumpled her paper napkin on the table. "You'd think she'd call."

Ocypete checked her cell phone and put it back in her purse. "Perhaps she left messages on our answering machines."

"Twice in a row. This isn't like her at all."

"Want to stop by her house?" asked Ocypete.

"Maybe the killer struck again. The police seem to think he mistook Lucy for Ellen.

Why did she insist on sleeping in her house after that?"

Ocypete dipped the last hunk of hamburger roll into the pool of blood remaining on her plate. "I'll pick you up after my doctor's appointment. Let's say, four o'clock."

Long after the police left with the body bag, Delilah remained seated on the couch. By now it was almost two o'clock, and she was still dressed in her peignoir and high-heeled mules.

"Henry, I simply can't understand why the police took Darcy away. Clearly the drowning was an accident."

Henry clasped his hands behind his back and paced. His shoes squeaked on the slate floor.

"Your pacing is driving me crazy," said Delilah.

Henry halted abruptly in front of her. His usually cherubic face was dark with anger. "Who's Darcy?"

"My chauffeur, of course." Delilah stood up so she could look down on Henry and flicked her filmy dressing gown around her in a swirl.

"Where'd he come from?"

"The agency in Boston."

"What agency?"

"For heaven's sake, Henry. What's your problem?"

Henry turned his back to her and mumbled something.

"I didn't hear you." She thrust her hands into the pockets of her gown.

He turned again and they stared at each other until he broke eye contact.

She pranced over to the orchids and fingered the bark soil. "Dry. You'd better remind Lee to water them."

"What agency?" he repeated.

Delilah brushed the soil off her hands. "The same one that sent Barry to me five years ago. I've dealt with them dozens of times." She walked back to the couch and sank into it with a flutter of purple and green silk. "Barry quit."

"What reason did he give?"

"A family problem. I don't pry into my staff's personal business."

"Did you call Darcy's references?"

"Of course not. The agency takes care of that." She laid her arm along the back of the couch and looked up at him. "What *is* the matter with you, Henry?"

"The matter with me is that your chauffeur killed my pilot, that's what's the matter." Henry turned and squeaked across the floor toward the windows. "Why? And who the hell is Darcy?"

"What on earth are you talking about?" Delilah flung herself out of the couch again, brushed past the orchids, and stood beside him, hands on her hips. "Who I hire as my chauffeur is my business. And my chauffeur is no killer."

Henry stared up at her. His thick glasses reflected her face. His trim white mustache was slightly askew. "This Darcy person has been here for, what, a week? Two weeks?"

"You're being overly dramatic, as usual. Your pilot fell into the pond by accident." She spoke each word distinctly.

"At the airport, your Darcy and my pilot recognized each other. Why? How did they know each other?"

"What makes you say that?"

"I could tell. Where had they known each other?"

"How am I supposed to know?" Below them the yellow police tape fluttered in the light midday breeze. "I don't know about you, but I'm ready for lunch. Ring Lee, will you, darling?"

"Even if you'd done the sensible thing, checked references, I suppose everything would have been in order. Who is he? Who does he work for?"

"He's an excellent driver. Ring Lee. Or shall I?"

"Of course he would be an excellent driver. And he probably speaks four or five languages and has a degree in killing people." Henry pounded his fist into the palm of his hand. "FBI? CIA? Mafia? Independent? Who, who, who?"

"You left out Homeland Security. Henry, darling, *why* would he want to kill your pilot?" She bent over, picked up the bell, and rang it vigorously.

"Damned if I know."

"He wasn't your usual pilot, was he?"

"I've flown with him a few times."

"What happened to your usual pilot?"

"Yes, ma'am?" Lee had appeared without a sound.

"Sandwiches, please, Lee. And something to drink. White wine."

Lee bowed her head and left.

Henry waited until she was out of hearing. "My usual pilot had a family emergency."

"A family emergency? Naturally." She set her hands on her hips and laughed, then strode the length of the orchids and back. Her peignoir brushed a spray of small brown and yellow blossoms and set it in motion. "According to your fantasy, Darcy and the pilot are probably hired killers. Who are they after? Tell me that. You? Or me?" Delilah stopped her own pacing abruptly. "That pilot could have killed you at any time. Why wait until you got back to the Island?" She resumed her pacing. "On the other hand, if he was here to kill me . . . !" She pointed at her ample bosom.

"Your luncheon, ma'am."

Delilah whirled around. "You startled me, Lee. Knock before you enter, will you?"

"Yes, ma'am. I'm sorry." Lee set down a tray with a plate of sandwiches and glasses of wine. "Will there be anything else, ma'am?"

"Leave Mr. Sampson and me alone and shut the door."

"My name is True. The Reverend True."

Lee bowed and shut the door firmly behind her.

"You were saying, as we were interrupted, 'he was here to kill me.' " Henry's parted lips were moist beneath his mustache. "Your girl now has that nice tidbit to spread around the Island."

Victoria had finished her lunch and was working on her column when the phone rang. "Mrs. Trumbull? This is Darcy."

Victoria held the phone close to her ear.

130

"Where are you?"

"In jail."

"What!?"

"The Dukes County House of Correction. I need help."

Victoria looked at her watch. "I'll be there within a half hour."

She gathered up her cloth bag, checked to make sure her blue hat with gold stitching was inside, shrugged into her padded blue coat, fetched her stick from beside the entry door, and strode around to the front of her house. The elegant front door with its Sandwich Glass panes was used only for grand occasions. It was the only door that was locked, and that because whenever the wind was northeast, the door blew open.

The sky was overcast and she could smell rain, probably arriving by this evening. She stood far enough back from the road so she wouldn't be run down by a speeding construction vehicle. To her left, almost as far away as the police station, she could see a blue dump truck approaching. Sunlight glinted on its polished hood. She stepped forward and stuck out her thumb. The cobalt blue truck slowed and stopped. The driver, a tall young man with a shock of unruly dark hair, got out, reached into the back of his cab, brought out a box for Victoria to use as a step, and helped her up into the high passenger seat.

"Thank you," said Victoria. "You're Bill O'Malley, aren't you?"

"Yes, ma'am. Where are you headed, Mrs. Trumbull?"

"To the jail," said Victoria.

"Visiting a friend?"

"I'm not sure who I'm visiting," said Victoria, avoiding his eyes.

"I have to make a quick stop at the airport first, if you don't mind."

Victoria looked around as the truck started up again. "Are you taking the stumps to the airport?"

"No, ma'am. Just need to stop long enough to get someone's name, and then we'll be on our way."

CHAPTER 13

After her doctor's appointment, Ocypete drove directly to Selena's, a small overly cozy house with most of the furniture slip-covered in chintz. China figurines cluttered the shelves of dark, glass-fronted bookcases.

Selena met her at the door. "Let me take your coat, Petey, darlin'." She glanced at the sky. "Looks like we might have a bit more rain. What did the doctor say?"

"He thought I might have a virus or a touch of food poisoning."

"That raw hamburger you ate . . ." said Selena.

"I've had this since the day before yesterday. I'm supposed to go back in a couple of days if I don't feel better. He's put me on a bland diet."

Selena glanced toward the kitchen. "I hear my phone. Please, make yourself comfortable." She wiggled her fingers. "Be right back!"

A few minutes later she returned, looking puzzled. "That was strange."

Ocypete was seated in one of the easy chairs. The shiny crimson peonies of the slipcover clashed with her tie-dyed layers of magenta and orange gauze. "Who was it?" she asked.

"Ellen. Apologizing. She claims she doesn't feel well and forgot our luncheon date."

Ocypete sighed. "I called her before I left the house to confirm."

"So you said." Selena looked troubled. "You can't blame Ellen for being disoriented, with all that's going on, Lucy killed in her house, but . . ." Selena perched on the sofa. "She did say she was ill."

"That came on suddenly," Ocypete said. "She was entirely herself yesterday. In full control, as usual."

"The way she handled Oliver!" Selena drawled.

They both laughed.

"I almost felt sorry for Oliver," said Ocypete.

"Maybe Ellen's having a delayed reaction. Do you have time for a cup of tea?" Selena stood up again.

"That might help settle my stomach. I'm glad we don't think we need to check on

Ellen after all."

At Town Hall, Oliver switched on his computer. The session with Willoughby this morning had drained him. He felt just as bad as he looked, but before he left for the day, he had to encrypt a large number of files. Either that or copy and destroy them. Those files were valuable and dangerous. No one, absolutely no one, could be allowed access to those files. He *must* get them copied today.

Several times during the afternoon he left what he considered his office on the second floor of Town Hall and walked to Alley's store. He'd bought a *Boston Globe* one time, a package of peanut butter crackers the next, a Diet Coke, a copy of the *Island Enquirer.* He needed to calm down after this morning's encounter and at the same time see what was happening at the Meadows house across the road.

"You should make a list, Mr. Ashpine, save yourself a few trips," said the lanky boy who waited on him. "Going to have more rain. You can smell it in the air."

"We've had enough rain," growled Oliver, as though the weather was the boy's fault.

From Alley's porch, everything at the Meadows house looked the same as it had all day. No one seemed to be around. Ellen's car was not in its usual place under the linden tree. The front window was still open, held up by a wooden stick he could see from here. The breeze that presaged rain billowed the sheer curtains into the room, then an errant current swept them out again, and he could hear the fluttering sound they made in the growing wind. Someone ought to shut that window before the rain came. Although, actually, why should he care?

The sheriff met Victoria at the jail in Edgartown, in what was once the front hall of an elegant captain's house. Victoria knew the sheriff only by sight. But he looked like one of the Nortons, and was probably a cousin of hers.

"Mrs. Trumbull, I'm Tom Look, a great admirer of your poetry."

"Julia Norton's eldest son?"

"The youngest. Walter, John, then me." Sheriff Look's beaklike nose was almost as fine as Victoria's own. They shook hands.

He produced a clipboard with a sheaf of paperwork for her to fill out. "Sorry about the formalities, Mrs. Trumbull," he said. "Times have changed."

"That's quite all right. I understand."

"Mr. Remey is waiting for you upstairs in the conference room. You need help on those stairs?"

Victoria adjusted her baseball cap. "No, thank you." She stood up, looked toward the top of the steep wooden stairs, and started up. Halfway up, she stopped to catch her breath.

"You okay, Mrs. Trumbull?" Cousin Sheriff Look, right behind her, sounded concerned.

"Certainly." Victoria pointed at some ornate carving. "This looks like the original stairway."

"Somewhat the worse for wear. The building dates from around the 1870s and I guess the stairway does, too."

Once she'd caught her breath, Victoria continued up the stairs to the top, where a uniformed guard, a teenager with cropped red hair and freckles, stood by an open door. The door led into a dreary room almost completely taken up by a scarred wooden table, where Darcy sat facing her, his back to the barred window. He stood when she entered.

"I'd like to speak to Mr. Remey alone," Victoria said.

The sheriff checked his watch. "Fifteen minutes enough for you, Mrs. Trumbull?

Richie will stay outside where he can see you, but he won't be close enough to hear you."

Victoria looked at Darcy, who nodded.

She seated herself at the narrow end of the table close to Darcy and with her back to the guard, and unbuttoned her blue coat. "How can I help?"

Darcy's eyes had dark shadows under them. He was still wearing the clothing he'd changed into this morning, not his chauffeur's uniform, but jeans and a plaid shirt. He tapped his fingers nervously on the table and glanced at the writing on Victoria's hat. The corners of his mouth twitched and he stopped tapping.

"I had nothing to do with the pilot's death, Mrs. Trumbull."

"I didn't think for a moment that you did."

"I'm in one hell of an awkward situation. Someone's framing me."

Victoria waited, hands clasped on the table. Darcy began to tap his fingers again. He looked up at the ceiling, where a large fly bumbled against the caged bare lightbulb, then down at the dirty, scarred table. He reached into the pocket of his plaid shirt and brought out a torn sheet of lined yellow paper with a phone number. "There's no one else I can trust, Mrs. Trumbull."

Victoria smiled.

He handed the paper to her. "Please call this number. Identify yourself to whoever answers and say you're calling for me."

"Who shall I say you are?"

"Emery Meyer. They'll know who you mean."

"And then what?"

"Tell them Frank Morris is dead."

Victoria sat forward. "Who?"

"You don't want to know. Tell them I'm in jail, suspected of killing him."

"The pilot." Victoria sat back again. "Do I need to know what this is all about?"

"You're better off not knowing. But you'll be saving my neck by calling. Don't lose that." He indicated the slip of paper. "And don't let anyone else see it."

"I'll memorize it, tear up the paper, and swallow the pieces."

"That's my girl!"

"May I ask who you're working for?"

"You certainly may ask, Mrs. Trumbull. But I won't answer."

Victoria got up with a sigh. "Do you know how long you'll be here?" Her gesture included the entire building.

"That depends somewhat on your phone call." Darcy, too, stood up.

"Is the jail very uncomfortable?"

He shrugged. "I'm in a cell they cleaned up and painted an ugly shade of pink for a lady lawyer they incarcerated a few years back. Aside from the color, it's not too bad."

"And the food?"

"You know that French chef who was convicted of drug trafficking?"

"Howland Atherton is responsible for his being here."

"Thank Mr. Atherton for me, will you?" Darcy patted his stomach and looked at his watch. "Two hours to dinner. By the way, don't, under any circumstances, tell Atherton about the call I asked you to make."

Victoria buttoned her coat again. "Call me if you need anything else. *Darcy,*" she added with a wicked smile.

He looked down and with his finger traced a section of the graffiti that covered the tabletop. "You know that poem of Robert Frost's that begins, 'She is as in a field a silken tent . . .'?" He looked up, and she nodded. "Well, you're my silken tent, Mrs. Trumbull. Thank you."

Victoria took off her baseball cap and turned away so he couldn't see her eyes.

CHAPTER 14

Each time Oliver came downstairs from his office, Mrs. Danvers lowered her glasses and glared at him, then looked significantly at the clock between the windows. He'd tried to ignore her, but each time he felt his face flush.

He scheduled his forays to avoid the Alley's porch sitters, who'd be there shortly after noon, waiting for the mail to be sorted, then reconvene after work to gossip. Oliver was sure they'd seen the way the three assessors had humiliated him. Those porch bums didn't miss much.

He returned to his desk and removed the disk from his computer that he'd dumped all but his last few files onto, gathered up some papers he hoped would look important, and went downstairs in as businesslike a manner as he could muster, holding his hand against his stomach, which had begun to ache. He'd have to go home and lie down for a few minutes before he finished dealing with his computer files.

"Leaving early?" Mrs. Danvers said. "I don't know why you bothered."

"Have to run some errands. I'll be back." Oliver lifted the papers he was carrying so she'd notice.

When he got outside, the rain had started. He dashed for his car, sheltering his head with his papers, slammed the door shut, locked it, and drove slowly past the Meadows house. The window was closed now. He could see a light on in the kitchen. But her car wasn't in its usual place in the driveway. Who'd been in her house?

He shuddered when he thought about that grilling by those three women. He didn't intend to go through that ever again. Treating him like a criminal.

How could he deal with this, apologize? If so, to whom? Say he'd made a dreadful mistake. He was new at the job, after all. He'd promise to correct the bills he'd sent out. Did he dare add that in correcting his terrible mistake, he'd discovered that someone in the assessors' office had been skimming off tax money for years? He might come out on top, after all. He smiled at the thought.

His stomach growled. He'd had no appetite for breakfast. The only food he'd eaten since last night was the peanut butter cheese crackers washed down with Diet Coke and a couple of pieces of Turkish delight someone had left on his desk. The box had been there for a couple of days, but he'd assumed it belonged to someone else and hadn't opened it. Now that he thought of it, why would anyone leave candy on his desk? He didn't care much for sweets, but he'd eaten several pieces without thinking. When he got home, he'd have to put something in his stomach. Chicken soup might settle him.

The rain was heavy now, driven slantwise by the northeast wind. Too much rain this month. He drove slowly past Brandy Brow, where the road was already flooded, past the mill pond and the mill, and turned left onto Old County Road. He'd be home soon, get a bite to eat. Maybe take a quick nap until it was almost time for Mrs. Danvers to leave, then return to Town Hall with a couple of new computer disks. Those last few files were the most important ones, and he wanted to look at them before he downloaded them onto one of his disks or deleted them.

The blue dump truck was waiting in front

of the jail, engine running, when Victoria came out. By now it was raining steadily. Bill O'Malley set down the milk carton step and helped her aboard.

"I didn't intend for you to wait for me."

"My pleasure, Mrs. T. How's your friend?"

"As well as can be expected. I can't bear to think of anyone shut up like that."

"Home again?"

"Yes. It's been a long day." Victoria tucked her cap into her cloth bag.

"Would you like some music?" He reached for the knob but waited for Victoria to answer.

"I'd enjoy that." Victoria settled back in her seat, only to sit forward again when banjo music poured out of the speakers. "I love banjos." She tapped her foot to the music. "I've always loved banjos."

"Monroe, Scruggs, and Flatt," said Bill with a grin.

She had no idea who he was talking about. She listened to the swish of windshield wipers, the steady rumble of the engine, and the music of the Blue Grass Boys, and continued to tap her foot.

The music was so captivating, she didn't notice that O'Malley had pulled up by her stone steps.

"Any time you need a ride, give me a call."

He stowed the milk crate she'd used for a step behind his seat and drove off.

Victoria's phone call on Darcy's behalf didn't solve the mystery. She told the woman who answered who she was and that Emery Meyer had asked her to call. The woman said, "Just a moment, please." Victoria waited, and in a short time a woman's pleasant low voice came on the line. "Mrs. Trumbull, how may I help?" She repeated what Darcy had told her, Emery Meyer jailed for murder. The woman thanked her for calling, didn't ask for additional information, not even her phone number, and hung up.

Victoria felt let down. She examined the slip of paper with the 800 phone number. It gave no clue as to its location. She called the information operator, but got a series of robotic voices telling her to press numbers. Since she had a dial phone, she gave up. She slipped the paper into her phone book, then thought better of it and took the paper to the sink, lit a match to it, and watched the dark ash curl. She crushed the ash with a paper napkin and deposited ash and napkin in the compost bucket.

As she was putting the lid back on the bucket, someone knocked tentatively and opened the door a crack.

"Mrs. Trumbull?"

Victoria looked up. "Come in, Delilah."

Delilah lifted her nose and sniffed. "That's not your supper burning, is it?"

"No, it was nothing important. Tea?"

"If it's not too much trouble." Delilah was wearing jeans with a sharp crease that appeared to be stitched in, and a foul-weather jacket that matched her hair. "I think we've had enough rain." She sat in the gray-painted kitchen chair and talked while Victoria filled the kettle.

"I can't believe the police arrested Darcy for killing that pilot. They'd only met yesterday afternoon. It's obvious his death was an accident. Darcy wouldn't push him into the pond, then pull him out again, would he?"

Victoria didn't answer.

"Now I have no one to drive me."

"How did you get here?" Victoria asked.

"I drove myself."

Victoria, who'd lost her license after her minor accident with the Meals on Wheels van, had little sympathy. She glanced out the window and saw a low yellow sports car parked in the drive. Raindrops pattered on the fabric roof.

"Henry's as bad as the police. He's sure my chauffeur killed the man. He's been grilling me about him."

"Did you tell Henry how you happened to meet Darcy? That he came to your television studio with flowers?"

Delilah extended her fingers and studied the orange-brown polish on her nails. "I told him Darcy came from the employment agency."

"Oh?" Victoria tried to make eye contact, but Delilah rattled on.

"Henry wanted to know about his references. I told him to ask the agency, not me." She stopped for breath.

"There's something you're not telling me," Victoria said. "Darcy is more than your chauffeur, isn't he?"

"Not yet. But I'm working on it." Delilah continued to avert her eyes. "Don't tell Henry, Mrs. Trumbull?"

"I have no reason to tell him anything, do I?"

"The police won't even let me talk to him."

Victoria poured the now boiling water into the teapot, set it on the table along with two mugs, and sat down again.

"He's an excellent driver. I told the agency about him in case Henry checks with them. He gave me a copy of his references, all nicely mounted in plastic sleeves. He's completely trustworthy, Mrs. Trumbull."

Victoria busied herself pouring tea. What was Darcy up to? She wasn't sure she wanted to know.

"I called my lawyers when the police took him away," Delilah continued. "They said they'd get him out on bail."

"Did they give you any idea when that might be?"

"I'm waiting to hear from them. I've been so upset, I can't think straight, which is why I'm coming to you, Mrs. Trumbull."

Victoria held her tea mug up to her lips and watched Delilah, her eyes narrowed against the steam.

"I decided to work on my farm plan to take my mind off . . . you know. But when I went to Town Hall, Mrs. Danvers said I need to produce some deed from nineteen-ten."

"I believe the Hammond family owned the place long before then."

"I guess so," said Delilah. "Mrs. Danvers suggested I ask you."

"Why me?"

"You'd gone to Town Hall in the olden days when it was a school."

Victoria winced at "olden days," but agreed that she'd gone to the academy, first through eighth grades.

"Mrs. Danvers said they stored papers in the attic of the school before it was Town Hall."

"Quite likely," said Victoria.

"She didn't have time to look, but said you knew the building and could probably find them."

"Heavens!" said Victoria, who hated the idea of searching for misplaced papers of any kind. "Exactly what is it we're looking for?"

"Mrs. Danvers said she'd seen something about a deed restriction on the property." Delilah shrugged. "Files from a hundred years ago can't be too big."

Victoria said nothing, hoping the answer to who would do the search wouldn't end up in her lap.

But Delilah said, "Would you consider looking for that paper for me, Mrs. Trumbull? I'll pay you a search fee."

Victoria scowled.

Delilah said hurriedly, "Same rate I pay my lawyers."

"Well . . ." Victoria hesitated. Her budget didn't always allow for luxuries, such as chocolate.

"If you need to hire an assistant, I'll pay him, too. Or her, of course."

"Let me think about it. You'll have to give

me more details about this paper I'm
searching for."

CHAPTER 15

"Oh, for God's sake," said Howland, when Victoria called him that same day about the Hammond deed restriction and his role as assistant deed hunter. The rain was now coming down in torrents. "You didn't say yes, did you?"

Victoria held the phone away from her ear. "You don't need to shout."

"Did you?"

"Not exactly. I've been thinking about it. The job may not be as difficult as we think. I used to scamper around the top floor of the academy with my pal Grace when we were schoolgirls. We weren't supposed to go up there, of course, because it was a boys' dormitory. I remember an area off to one side was for storage of town files."

"Mrs. Danvers can look for the paper."

"She's too busy. And since today's Friday, we won't be able to get into Town Hall until Monday."

"I am also too busy." Howland paused for such a long time, Victoria was afraid he'd hung up. She coughed politely.

He said, "So I'm you're assistant. Is that it?"

"I'll divide the money with you, half and half."

Howland groaned. "I'll pick you up within an hour. I expect it's filthy up there?"

"Probably."

"I'll bring dust masks then."

"We might as well get it over with. It's almost the end of the day."

"Yeah, and it's pouring. See you shortly."

Spring temperatures and rain had greened Victoria's yard. In the border, early daffodils were in bloom, rows of yellow and white blossoms contrasting with the gray sky. While she waited for Howland, she put on her raincoat and scarf and went out to check the honesty she'd planted among the daffodils. She had never grown it before and looked forward to drying the silvery coin-like seedpods. Jordan, who'd given her the seeds, had warned her that honesty was invasive, but she thought she wouldn't mind. A dozen or more seedlings had sent up heart-shaped leaves with scalloped edges.

By the time Howland drove up, she was back in the house, the shoulders of her raincoat dark wet.

"I don't have time for this, Victoria. It's late and I hate hunting for stuff even more than you do."

"Delilah's paying us well."

"Not worth it. Where's that umbrella?"

"I have no idea." Victoria splashed through the puddles in the driveway and climbed into Howland's station wagon.

When they got to Town Hall, Mrs. Danvers indicated an old-fashioned coatrack. "You might want to hang up your wet coat." She opened her desk drawer and gave Victoria the attic key. "I'm sure you know how to get up there. In all the time I've worked here, I've never been in the attic." She shuddered. "Cobwebs. Spiders, mice. Have fun, kids."

When they reached the second floor, Oliver Ashpine turned abruptly from his computer and snapped, "What are you doing here?"

Victoria caught a glimpse of his computer screen before Oliver swiveled around and hit a key that made the screen go black.

"We're going up to the attic."

"What for?"

She said airily, "We don't need to disturb you."

Oliver pushed his chair away from his desk

and stood up. His screen now showed cartoon rabbits that frolicked from one side to the other, occasionally piping up, "What's up, Doc?"

"You have an objection?" asked Howland.

"No." Oliver sat down again.

"Thank you," said Howland.

A locked door next to an open closet led to a steep, narrow staircase. Victoria went up the stairs first, bracing her hands against the walls. At the top she stepped out onto wide floorboards that squealed under her weight. Underlying the smell of mice and old musty papers was the familiar smell of a forbidden place. The bare wood ceiling had the sun-baked fragrance of pine resin. As she walked across the wood floor she smelled remembered scents of camphor, lavender, cedar, mothballs, chalk, and old books. Dust rose in spirals. She sneezed, and when she took a breath to sneeze again, there was an underlying odor of spiders' feasts, dead mice, and decay.

Howland unwrapped the plastic from a dust mask and handed it to her. "If we don't find that paper within the next half hour, let's get out of here." He slipped the elastic over his head and peered over the mask at the cloud of dust that spiraled into the gloomy space beyond.

"Watch where you step, Victoria." His voice was muffled. "Put your mask on, too." The floor creaked as he set one foot after the other carefully on the wide boards. "Something doesn't feel right."

"Don't be an alarmist," Victoria said. "The attic hasn't changed much over the past eighty years. As I recall, it used to smell of unbathed boys. It smells much the same now." She walked around the creaking floor, holding the dust mask in her hand, and noting storage boxes, bookcases, wooden crates, and cardboard file boxes.

"Start with the sectional bookcase, Howland. The files are probably organized in some way. I'll check the boxes on top of the window seat."

"Odd place to store files," Howland's muffled voice said. "Out in the open like that?"

"Someone probably forgot to put them back after they looked at them." Victoria examined the label on the first box. "Whoever looked at them must have done so fairly recently," she said, wiping her hands on a napkin she took out of her pocket. "They're not as dusty as I expected." The file boxes were a mottled black and white with leather tabs on the back. "This one is dated nineteen fifty-four. If all the files are dated, the job won't be too difficult." She picked up a second box. "Unfortunately, they're not in order, but at least we won't have to go through each one." She set the boxes on the floor after she'd looked at the dates.

"Is anything stored inside the window seat?" asked Howland. "The lid has a hinge."

The seat was sturdy enough to have withstood the activities of the small boys who were domiciled up there years ago. Victoria looked for a latch or handhold to lift the top, but, except for the hinge, the lid was flush all around.

Howland placed a marker in the stack of papers he was going through. "Here, I'll help." They both worked to pry up the lid. "Tight fit," Howland said with a grunt. "Forget it. Probably nothing in it anyway."

"I'm curious now," said Victoria. "There's a metal bar next to the window. Perhaps that will work."

Together they pried first on one side of the window seat top, then the other, until it finally loosened.

"There's something in here," said Victoria. "Clothing, or . . ." she stepped back, her hands at her throat.

"What's the matter, Victoria?" Howland

had looked up at her before he, too, noticed what was curled up in the window seat. "Good Lord." He let the lid fall down.

"I'll wait here," Victoria said. "Go downstairs and call Casey."

At Selena's, the cup of tea hadn't helped Ocypete, whose upset stomach was acting up again. The gloomy afternoon had passed into a rainy evening. Her doctor had told her to come back in a couple of days if she didn't feel better, and right now she felt worse than ever.

"I think I'd better go home and get to bed, Selena." Ocypete winced as she arose from the chintz-covered chair.

"Would you like me to drive you home?"

"I can manage." Ocypete gathered up her coat from the bench near the door. "I think the doctor's wrong about food poisoning. I'm sure it's the flu."

"I hope I don't catch it."

"I hope so, too."

"Take care of yourself, Petey. We have a lot of work ahead of us."

"Oliver, you mean?"

"Yes. Oliver, for one."

In the course of searching the Internet some time before, Oliver Ashpine had gone to one of his favorite Web sites and seen something that made him stop the video clip and repeat one section over and over again. The hand of one of the actors seemed familiar — the motions her hand made during the action, her fingers, the vibrant color of her fingernails. The clincher was the distinctive ring she wore that appeared only for an instant. He knew that gaudy ring and the woman who wore it.

Once he'd identified the hand, he recognized the rest of her, although he, himself, had never seen her in person in the buff. The guy she was cavorting with was definitely not her husband. Henry was short and stubby; this guy was lean and probably tall, although that was difficult to determine.

Oliver realized the video would be of some future value. In fact, when Delilah Sampson had shown up at Town Hall yesterday complaining about her taxes, he'd alluded to the video and gotten a totally satisfactory response.

This afternoon, he was viewing the clip again when Mrs. Trumbull and Atherton showed up, and he'd switched quickly to his screen saver. He'd felt queasy all afternoon and had gone home briefly to pick up a new computer disk. But now he felt worse than ever. Probably a combination of Willoughby's call on him this morning, not eating, and then that damned Turkish delight. Normally, he didn't eat much sugar, which might account for why he felt lousy. He didn't think candy spoiled, but maybe it did. Someone had left it on his desk a couple of days ago. Who could have left it? Certainly not Mrs. Danvers, who liked him even less than he liked her. Unless . . .

Ellen stopped at Conroy's Apothecary and waited for the pharmacist to fill the prescription for something to settle her stomach. The rain, heavy at times, had let up, and the air smelled of growing things.

"Pretty strong stuff, Mrs. Meadows," Stanley said. "I don't need to tell you to follow the directions closely."

"Thank you." Ellen left the apothecary, clutching the prescription in its white envelope close to her stomach. She couldn't think of anything she'd eaten recently that might not have agreed with her. Must be some type of flu, although she didn't know of anyone who'd been complaining about the flu from whom she might have caught it.

She drove home slowly, her windshield wipers on slow intermittent, parked her car in its usual place to the left of her house, away from the puddles, and went up the steps, brushing the rain-wet lilacs. In a few weeks they'd be in bloom by her doorstep. She'd come home earlier, before the rain started, to shut the window and had turned on a light. The light was welcome, now. She stumbled into the kitchen, poured a glass of water, swallowed two pills as directed, dragged herself up the stairs, and collapsed onto her bed. She tugged the down comforter over her and turned on her side.

Victoria waited uneasily in the darkening attic of Town Hall, trying not to think about the bundle folded up in a fetal position in the window seat. Rain beat on the roof. Where was Howland? To distract herself she wandered around the vast open room. Boys who'd boarded here had penciled names and dates on the bare wood walls. "Mark Pease, 1898," "Welcome Davies, 1870."

Time passed. Daylight faded. A dangling gutter she could see through the window shifted in the wind and spilled a torrent of rainwater against the glass. The attic was growing dark rapidly, and Howland still had not returned. Victoria searched for light switches on the wall, but electricity apparently had never reached the attic.

When she heard footsteps on the stairs

she let out a breath she didn't realize she'd been holding. She felt her way to the top of the dark stairs.

"Howland, I'm relieved that you're back. We need a light . . ." She didn't finish her sentence.

"It's not Howland, Mrs. Trumbull. Oliver Ashpine. What's going on?"

Victoria could barely see him. "I thought you'd left for the day. Is there a light up here?"

He'd reached the top of the stairs. "It's almost five and Mrs. Danvers has gone home. Where's Atherton?"

Victoria backed up. "He went to make a phone call. He must have gone right past you."

"I didn't notice him."

"Let's go down to the second floor and wait."

"What are you doing?" Oliver said.

"We're looking for an old deed." She brushed past him heading for the staircase. "We haven't found it yet. I'll return Monday." She started down the stairs. "Are you coming?"

"In a minute."

She stopped on the top step. "I'll wait for you right here, then."

He sighed. "Can't see anything anyway."

The second floor was dark except for the lamp on Oliver's desk and a dim glow from his computer screen, where the rabbits continued to frolic. Victoria felt chilled and uneasy. She could smell Oliver's nervous sweat. Or was it her own? She heard his breathing. In the faint light she found her way to the stairs that led down to the first floor.

Where was Howland?

CHAPTER 16

Victoria was at the top of the stairs when she heard Howland's voice on the first floor. She called down, "I'm up here on the second floor. The attic has no light."

"Sorry I was gone so long," Howland called back. "Took me a while to locate the chief."

"Oliver is still here," Victoria warned.

At that, Howland took the stairs two at a time and confronted Oliver. "What're you doing here, Ashpine?"

"Chief? Police chief?" asked Oliver.

Howland spoke to Victoria. "Casey's parking the Bronco. She called the barracks."

"Barracks?" asked Ashpine. "The state police?"

"She'll need a flashlight," said Victoria.

Casey, followed by Sergeant Smalley and Trooper Tim Eldredge of the state police, came up the stairs to the second floor.

Oliver started to get up, then turned back

to his computer and shut it off. "Good night, everyone. Lock the door when you leave."

"Just a moment, Mr. Ashpine," said Casey. "Wait here."

"Who, me?"

"Sit." Casey pointed to his chair, and Oliver sat. "And don't move."

"How long will you be?" asked Oliver.

"Can't tell, sir. We may be all night," said Casey.

"I'm sick!" said Oliver, turning back to his computer.

The police, Victoria, and Howland trooped up the attic stairs by the light of two five-cell Maglites, lifted the lid of the window seat, and shone the light in.

Victoria had not looked closely at the body before. She did now. A woman, shriveled, almost mummified. Her face was turned sideways, and Victoria saw her profile.

Casey shone her light around the body. "Doc Jeffers is on his way."

Sergeant Smalley turned to Tim Eldredge. "Get some extension cords and a light up here. You'll need to stay until forensics gets over to the Island."

"Yes, sir."

"I know who she is," said Victoria.

"Yeah? Who?" asked Casey.

"Tillie Willoughby, former clerk to the assessors."

Oliver turned his computer back on and studied the video clip again. He didn't want to chance someone's seeing it, but he was really pressed for time, and, in truth, he did feel sick. He had to get the video off the town computer, now, before the weekend. He looked up as the sound of jangling chains announced Doc Jeffers. Oliver quickly switched to the screen saver. Doc Jeffers was wearing his black motorcycle leathers. A V-necked green scrub shirt showed in the half-zipped front.

"What's up, Doc?" said the cartoon rabbit.

"Very clever." Doc Jeffers gave him an icy glance and headed up the attic stairs.

"That wasn't me," Oliver called out, but the sound of Doc Jeffers's chains had already faded out of hearing.

Oliver left his computer on and turned his back to the animated screen saver, hugging his aching gut.

An hour later, Doc Jeffers had finished his preliminary examination of Tillie Willoughby's remains and he and Sergeant

Smalley headed downstairs again. Trooper Eldredge called down from the attic to Smalley, "Boss, we're about out of crime scene tape."

"Right. I'll have another roll sent over."

Victoria, Howland, and Doc Jeffers gathered around Oliver's desk. Victoria sat in the visitor's chair, while Howland half-sat on the desk.

"I can't get anything done with all of you hanging around," Oliver whined.

The others ignored him.

"I saw Tillie as recently as last November," Victoria said. "Can a body mummify that quickly? Only five months?"

Doc Jeffers stood on the other side of Oliver's desk, filling out forms. "Dry up there," he said. "Even in winter, it gets hot. Wouldn't take long to desiccate a body. As I recall, she was skinny, almost anemic. Not much body fat. That could account for her condition."

Victoria leaned forward, hands together on the top of her lilac wood stick. "How did she die?"

Doc Jeffers shrugged. "I won't know until they do an autopsy." He finished filling out forms, snapped his black bag shut, and saluted Victoria. "I'd say, at a guess, she was strangled." With that, he disappeared down the stairs, boot chains jangling.

At the word "strangled," Oliver gasped and breathed in when he should have breathed out. That set off a coughing fit. Howland was still perched on the edge of the desk. Oliver's face was red and he pounded his chest.

"You okay?" asked Howland.

Oliver nodded and coughed.

Victoria studied Oliver's computer screen with its bouncing rabbits.

"Put your arms straight up over your head," commanded Howland. "Straightens your esophagus. Here, I'll help." He reached over to Oliver and in doing so hit the keyboard. The rabbits disappeared and in their place were two animated pink bodies, complete with sound effects.

"Good God!" said Howland.

Oliver turned and jerked the computer plug out of the wall socket and coughed some more.

"Is that what you watch on town time?" Howland asked.

Oliver shook his head, unable to speak.

Victoria, who'd seen the few seconds of writhing bodies before Oliver killed the action, looked thoughtful.

Oliver's cough had become a steady throat clearing.

"Let's get out of here, Victoria," said Howland. "Leave this creep to his porn movies."

They were halfway down the stairs when Victoria said, "I believe I know what he's watching."

"What in hell are you talking about, Victoria?"

"Let's go to my house and sort this out."

"Damn," said Oliver once Victoria and Howland had left. "Damn, damn, damn." He thumped the "Caps Lock" key on his keyboard repeatedly with his left index finger, causing a small square of green light in the upper right corner of the board to flash on and off. He'd been careless about that video clip. Now, because of that buffoon Doc Jeffers, Mrs. Trumbull and Howland Atherton had seen what he'd been viewing. He'd have to copy the clip onto a disk and get it off the Town Hall computer immediately. Now. Instantly. He looked through his desk drawers for the blank disks he'd brought from home. They were the wrong disks. "Damn!" said Oliver again, putting his head down on the keyboard.

People were moving around upstairs, probably Junior Norton, the chief, and the remaining state cop.

He couldn't concentrate. He had to get

home and crawl into bed. But he had to do something about the video. He wasn't sure how to encrypt it with a code word, and didn't feel well enough to read up on how to do it. He decided he could safely save the video in some innocent-sounding file, and after thinking a bit, came up with "Honeybee." No one would look there.

He closed down his computer, called up the stairs, "I'm sick. I've got to go home," and left.

"I'm pooped." Doc Jeffers dropped his motorcycle helmet behind the desk in the Emergency Room at the hospital and shucked off his leather jacket, exposing his green scrub shirt. "This had better be a quiet night."

"Pee-yew!" exclaimed Hope, who was on duty. "What have you been rolling in?"

"Don't ask," growled Doc Jeffers. "I need a shower and clean clothes."

"I'll hold the fort, Doc, until you get back."

He hesitated.

"Go ahead. I'm fine." Hope settled herself behind the admissions desk.

Shortly after Ocypete got home and into bed, she was violently ill. She crawled out of bed and collapsed on the floor, her stomach a ball of fire. She managed to knock the phone off the cradle and dial 911.

Ellen felt wretched. She took a couple of aspirins and crept into bed. An hour later she felt worse, and realized she'd better call 911.

Oliver toughed it out for a couple of hours once he got home. Around seven, he dialed 911.

No sooner had Doc Jeffers trudged down the hall to the shower when the Tri-Town Ambulance pulled in, lights flashing. Two EMTs, a slender blond man with slightly tilted eyes and an even slimmer young woman with a buzz cut, wheeled in a stretcher. On the stretcher was a woman in her seventies, a large woman clad in layers of pastel-colored veils. She was holding an arm to her head and her fingers were tangled in her mane of white hair.

Hope stood up.

"Ocypete Rotch. West Tisbury. Abdominal distress," said Jim, the male EMT. His partner stood off to one side.

Ocypete groaned.

There was a faint beeping sound and Jim

checked his pager. "Gotta go, Hope. Another call from West Tisbury."

"Right," said Hope. "I'll worry about the paperwork."

"Where do you want Ms. Rotch?"

"Take her to room two. Thanks, you guys."

Erica, the other EMT, smiled. "Any time."

Ocypete was strapped into a cool bed and kind people worked purposefully around her. They gave her a shot of something, and within seconds she no longer felt pain, and no longer cared.

A half hour later, the Tri-Town Ambulance pulled in again, lights flashing. The same two EMTs wheeled in a stretcher with a second woman in her seventies.

"Hi, again," said Hope. "Who do we have this time?"

The woman on the stretcher had intense black hair and was dressed in a severe navy blue pants suit. Her hands were folded over her stomach.

Doc Jeffers still had not returned from his shower.

"Ellen Meadows from West Tisbury," said Jim.

"Abdominal distress?" asked Hope.

"The same. Where would you like Ms. Meadows?"

Hope checked the chart. "Room three.

Thanks, guys."

"No problem," said Jim.

Within a few minutes, Ellen was on a cool hospital bed with people working on her. And within seconds, she, too, was no longer in pain.

Doc Jeffers returned, scrubbed pink and wearing a blue scrub suit. He lifted his head to peer through his glasses at the admissions slips. "What have we got here?"

"Two cases of abdominal distress, both West Tisbury."

"Stomach cramps, vomiting, diarrhea," Doc Jeffers noted. "Flu."

"Sounds more like food poisoning to me," said Hope.

Doc Jeffers looked over the top of his glasses. "Think so? One of them's been complaining about stomachache for a couple of days."

"Maybe they ate the same thing at different times. Shellfish or mushrooms. Chicken salad."

"Flu's around this time of year. But check it out."

"Certainly," said Hope.

An hour later, while Doc Jeffers was still conferring with his patients, the Tri-Town Ambulance pulled up again at the ER and Erica and Jim wheeled in the stretcher a third time.

Hope was filling out paperwork at the desk. "Another stomachache?"

"You guessed it," said Jim.

This time the patient was a man, a fairly short, plump man with a pasty white face and slicked down hair.

"Oliver Ashpine of West Tisbury," said Erica.

"Room one," said Hope. "Don't bring in any more. That's all the room we've got in the ER."

"Bedtime," said Jim, and yawned. "Good night, all."

"Fruit jellies?" Doc Jeffers asked Oliver. "You sure?"

Oliver moaned.

Hope said, "I'll find out if the other two have eaten any fruit jellies lately." She hurried to the adjoining cubicles in the ER and was back shortly. "They're both out. I'll ask them when they wake up."

Doc Jeffers poised his pen above the form on his clipboard. "Where was the candy?"

"Someone left it on my desk."

"How much did you eat?"

Oliver moaned. "Three pieces. Four."

"When?"

"This morning. This afternoon. Maybe

five pieces."

Doc Jeffers continued to take notes.

"Am I dying, Doc?" whispered Oliver.

"No such luck," answered Doc Jeffers, and scribbled something.

"Wasn't on my desk three days ago," murmured Oliver. "Mrs. Danvers." His voice rose above a whisper. "It's Mrs. Danvers. She's trying to kill me!"

Doc Jeffers turned to Hope. "Take Ashpine to the lab. See what they can make of his stomach contents. Looks as though he ate the stuff most recently."

"You're pumping out my stomach?" Oliver half rose from the gurney in room one.

Doc Jeffers smiled. "Damn right we are," and moved on to the next cubicle to check his sleeping patients.

CHAPTER 17

Early the next morning, Howland, still agitated about Oliver's viewing habits, dropped in at Victoria's. He paced from the cookroom to the kitchen to the dining room and back.

Victoria was working at the cookroom table. "Sit down, Howland. I can't think with you all over the place."

He picked up a copy of the *Island Enquirer* from the kitchen table, rolled it up, and slapped it on the tiled countertop, his leg, the door frame.

"Stop that. There's something I want to say to you. Help yourself to coffee."

Slap! on the cookroom table. "He's a creep, Victoria. Porn flicks! In Town Hall, for God's sake. Right where everyone sees them."

"Please, sit down."

Howland tossed the rolled-up newspaper on the table and sat. "If he's going to watch that stuff, at least he could do it in the privacy of his own home." Howland pulled on his nose, then ran his fingers through his hair.

"I know what that movie was," Victoria said.

He stopped fidgeting. "What are you talking about?"

She traced the lines of the red-checked tablecloth with her ridged thumbnail. "The other day, Delilah confided in me. Before she met Henry, she was a call girl, and she doesn't want Henry to know."

Howland started to say something, but Victoria held up her hand. "Delilah complained to Oliver about her taxes. He threatened to blackmail her. Told her if she made a fuss about the taxes, he'd tell Henry about her past life."

"The video?"

"I believe it shows Delilah."

"In action?"

"Something like that."

Howland picked up the paper again. "Don't dirty your hands with this, Victoria. It's between Delilah and Oliver. Possibly Henry."

"And, quite possibly, Darcy," said Victoria.

"What in hell does her chauffeur have to do with it?"

"I intend to find out."

While Howland was pacing Victoria's house, Henry was pacing the conservatory of Delilah's. His and Delilah's house, he told himself. Where the hell was she? She wasn't in her room and she never got up this early. He pinched off a dead blossom from an orchid plant as he passed, and jammed his hands into his pockets.

Who was Darcy, he wondered for the hundredth time? Darcy even smelled phony. Henry had called the agency and the woman who answered said that Miss Sampson had hired Darcy through them. But he could tell she was lying.

He picked up the silver bell on the table next to the sofa and shook it vigorously.

Almost immediately, Lee appeared. "Yes, sir?"

Henry swung around abruptly. "Where's Miss Sampson?"

"She left about an hour ago, sir."

"At eight in the morning?"

"Yes, sir." Lee waited uncertainly.

"She say where she was going?"

"No, sir." Lee started to leave, then turned. "Is there anything I can do for you, Reverend True?"

At that, Henry stopped pacing and looked

at her closely, which he'd never really done before. Pretty. A nice figure. Pleasant smile. Good hair, good cut. Not too tall. "Lee, right?"

"Yes, sir."

"How long have you been with Miss Sampson?"

"Almost five months, sir." Lee stood straight with her hands behind her back, her feet slightly apart. Henry turned to the orchids and felt the bark soil. "Miss Sampson noticed these are dry. You might water them."

"Certainly, sir." Again, she started to leave.

"You were here when Miss Sampson hired the new chauffeur, right?"

She turned to face him. "Yes, sir."

"What do you think of him?"

She blushed. "He seems quite capable, sir."

Henry smiled. "You like him, eh?"

"No, sir." The flush deepened and Lee looked down. "I mean, yes, sir. He's very pleasant. Dedicated to his job."

Henry changed the subject. "Ever done any acting?"

"No, sir." The blush faded. "Will that be all, sir?"

"Ever wanted to?"

"Act, sir?" She paused. "Not really."

"That means 'yes,' right?"

She smiled. "I guess most little girls dream of acting when they grow up."

"I have a television show, did you know that?"

"Yes, sir. With Miss Sampson. My mother watches it all the time. Very inspirational, she says."

Henry assumed his most sincere expression. "We're always looking for new talent."

"That leaves me out," said Lee, with a laugh. "Zero talent. Besides, I'm not exactly what you'd call religious."

"Not a problem. I have several shows. Would you like to audition for one of them?"

Lee clasped her hands in front of her. "Audition, sir?"

"Yes, ma'am."

"Hollywood?"

"No, no." Henry smiled. "West Virginia. Town called Zebulon."

She shook her head. "I can't leave Miss Sampson, sir. And I take care of my mother. I couldn't afford the time off. Or the travel expense."

Henry raised his great white eyebrows and assumed his cherubic expression. "There's a studio here on the Island. We can arrange to audition you here." He pointed down at the slate floor. "You wouldn't even have to take time off."

"I just don't know." Lee twisted her hands, still clasped protectively in front of her.

"If your test is successful, the pay is good. Help with your expenses. Your mother's support." Henry's smile broadened. "Nice clothes. Dining out. Travel. In fact, travel is part of the job."

"Well," said Lee. "I don't know."

"Think it over. Talk to your mother. See what she thinks about her little girl acting on television. Maybe on a program she watches."

"I'm sure she'd be thrilled, sir."

Henry's smile broadened to a grin that showed his teeth. "I see a great future for you in television." He reached into his back pocket, drew out his wallet, slipped out a card, and handed it to her. "I'll tell my office to set you up with an audition. You've got nothing to lose."

At the jail, Darcy, too, was pacing, but in the claustrophobic cell where he'd spent a sleepless night. The vibrating color of the cement block walls, an unfortunate shade of bright pink, made him edgy.

His reverie on color schemes was interrupted by footsteps along the corridor and the cheery voice of the sheriff.

"Got a call to release you, Mr. Meyer." He unlocked the barred cell door and slid it open.

Darcy turned. "Thanks. Am I free to go?"

The sheriff checked the papers he was holding. "If you're Emery Meyer, like it says here. Thought we listed you as Darcy Remey?"

Darcy smiled.

The sheriff led the way out of the cell block. "Yes, sir. You seem to have some influence in the right places. By the way, there's a redhead out front insisting that she see you."

"She at the reception desk?"

"Want to leave by the back door?"

"No, that's okay."

As they came down the stairs, Darcy could see Delilah, standing in front of the desk gesticulating to the jailer. She turned when she heard them, and her angry expression faded. She stepped toward him and took his hand.

"Darcy, darling, good news. I talked to one of my lawyers, and he says he can have you released into my custody within the next forty-eight hours."

The sheriff laughed. "Ma'am, someone else got to him first."

■ ■ ■ ■

Delilah swept her hair out from the collar of her puffy orange jacket as they left the jail, and tossed the car keys to Darcy. "You drive. It's turned out to be a nice day. Put the top down."

Darcy held the door of the convertible for her and then went around to the driver's side. He started up the car and lowered the convertible's top.

"Much nicer," Delilah said. "How did you ever manage to work that out?" Her voice was full of admiration.

"My release, you mean?"

"My lawyer didn't think he could get you out for at least forty-eight hours."

Darcy shrugged. "They had no reason to hold me."

"But my lawyer said . . ."

"Lawyers!" said Darcy, and his tone stopped Delilah from further lawyer comment.

Instead, she said, "I missed you."

"What's Henry up to?" asked Darcy.

Delilah smiled. "He keeps asking about you. I think he's jealous."

"What's he asking?"

"Where you came from, had I checked

your references, that sort of thing."

"What did you tell him?" Darcy cut around a slow-moving red Volvo.

"I certainly didn't tell him I hired you because you loved my show." Delilah put her hand on Darcy's thigh. "I told him I got you through the same agency I've always used, of course."

"What if he contacts the agency?"

"I called them right away and said I'd give them the credit for finding you and pay double the usual fee."

Darcy nodded.

"Henry said something awfully funny, though."

"Yeah?"

"He said he could have sworn you knew the pilot from before."

Darcy glanced away from the road at Delilah, but she didn't seem to have meant anything sinister. She stroked her hand on his thigh and smiled up at him.

They'd reached the firehouse on the Edgartown-West Tisbury Road when Darcy's cell phone emitted a blast of martial music. He tugged it out of his shirt pocket and turned off the insistent music. He checked the number and returned the phone to his pocket.

"Who was that?" asked Delilah.

"I don't like to use the cell phone when I'm driving," Darcy replied.

"Who was calling you?"

"A business contact."

"A woman?"

Darcy nodded.

They passed Victoria Trumbull's house, the police station, the mill pond.

"Who is she?" Delilah asked. "The woman who called?"

"As I said, business."

"Business?"

Darcy didn't answer.

"I employ you," snapped Delilah, moving away from him. "Everything you do is my business."

"During business hours," said Darcy, and smiled.

They passed the cemetery, Whiting's fields, the new Ag Hall. They crossed Mill Brook on the narrow bridge. In Victoria Trumbull's childhood, there was no bridge, and she still called the crossing "the ford." Bright green leaves glistened in the dappled sunlight.

"Skunk cabbage is up," said Darcy. "A sure sign of spring."

"Who is she?"

They turned left onto North Road and Darcy pulled off to one side. He set the emergency brake, left the engine running, and turned to Delilah.

"Delilah, the woman who called is a business associate, that's all I have to say. She has nothing to do with you."

With that, he released the brake and continued along North Road.

When they arrived at the big house, he stopped in front of the entrance and held the car door for her. She got out without looking at him, and skipped fairly lightly up the marble stairs. On the wide porch at the top of the stairs, Henry was standing, hands jammed fiercely into his pockets, jaw thrust out. Before Darcy moved the car to the garage, he saw Delilah give Henry a peck on the cheek. Henry scowled and gestured at the car. Darcy smiled.

He stopped in front of the garage, hosed down the car, wiped it carefully with a chamois cloth, and called Victoria.

"I'm out of jail, Mrs. Trumbull. Thanks to you. A free man. May I come to your place in about fifteen minutes?"

"Howland Atherton is here with me," said Victoria.

"An hour, then."

CHAPTER 18

After Darcy called Victoria on his cell phone, he left the parked and polished convertible in front of the garage, and went up the outside stairs to the apartment above. Windows along the northwest side looked over the pond and Vineyard Sound beyond. A small window on the east looked over the guesthouse.

He sat at the table that served as his desk and dialed the number that had been left on his cell phone.

The phone was answered on the first ring. "Senator Hammermill's office."

"Emery Meyer, here," said Darcy. "She called me."

"Yes, sir. I'm Kathy, her assistant. She asked me to tell you to fly the plane back to Boston on Monday, then return to the Island. Tickets are waiting for you at the Cape Air counter at Logan Airport. I guess you understand what that's all about? I think it's her church business."

"Right," said Darcy.

"Well, that's it," said Kathy, and hung up.

Darcy returned to Delilah's convertible where he could keep an eye on the house, and continued to polish the already spotless car.

Delilah and Henry were still standing close together on the porch. Even though the garage was some distance away, Darcy could hear his name batted back and forth between them. He still had a lot of work to do for the senator, and with Henry's attitude toward him growing increasingly suspicious, he didn't have much time in which to do it.

Henry went inside and slammed the door behind him. Delilah stuck her thumbs in her ears and waggled her fingers at the door, then descended the stairs and headed toward Darcy. He touched his hand to the visor of his hat.

"That man . . . !" said Delilah.

"I seem to be a problem for him. And you."

"Tough. The car looks nice."

"It should. It's a nice car," Darcy responded. "I'll get the oil changed this afternoon."

"He's suspicious of everyone. He thought

the pilot was some kind of spy. Now you. He's sure you killed the pilot." She touched his upper arm and said softly, "He even thinks we've got something going between us."

Darcy nodded, slipped his arm away from her hand, and went into the garage. He hung the chamois cloth on a rack inside the door, and came back out. Delilah was standing by the car.

"I need to take Monday off," said Darcy. "Is that a problem for you?"

"What for?"

"Personal business."

"That woman who called?"

"Don't go there, Delilah."

She turned away from him. "I suppose so."

"Thanks. I'll be back before five."

When Delilah returned to the house, Henry was waiting for her on the porch. "Who let that guy out of jail?"

She plopped down into one of the porch rockers and fluffed her bright hair. "They had no reason to hold him."

"Murder is a damned good reason, I'd say."

"Henry, darling, I do believe you're jealous."

He started to answer, but just then the

FedEx truck pulled up in front of the house and the driver got out with a clipboard. She ascended the marble stairway and held the clipboard out to Delilah. "Express delivery for you, Miss Sampson. Live animals."

"Live animals?" Henry came out from behind the chair. "What kind of live animals?"

"No idea." The driver descended the stairs to her truck and after rummaging around a bit in the back, brought out a cardboard box with holes punched around the upper edge and ascended the stairway again.

"What's this all about?" said Henry.

The driver looked at the box. "Fowl. Live chickens."

"Chickens?"

"Something I ordered last week," murmured Delilah.

The driver set the large light box, which was about the size of a deep-dish pizza box, on the arm of one of the rockers, setting it in motion. She handed Delilah a pen and pointed to the form on the clipboard. "Sign here, ma'am."

From the inside of the box came an insistent cheeping. The FedEx woman steadied the rocker with one hand.

Delilah dashed off her signature. "Thank

you so much. Henry, give the girl ten dollars."

"What for?" said Henry.

"A tip, Henry. She came all the way down
here . . ."

"That's not necessary," said the driver,
with a tight smile. "Have fun with your
chickens," and with that she descended the
stairs, whistling the whole way, got back into
the driver's seat, shifted into gear, and drove
down the long, Belgian block driveway.

"What the hell?" demanded Henry.

Delilah sashayed toward the door, which
Lee opened for her, and called over her
shoulder. "Bring the box into the kitchen,
Henry darling. Be careful!"

Henry had tipped the box on its side, and
the cheeping turned into pitiful squawks.

In the center of the kitchen was a large
island with a granite top, a double sink, and
a ceramic stovetop. Henry set the box down
on the stovetop. The squawking grew louder
and more insistent.

Lee stepped forward. "I believe you turned
the stove on by accident, sir."

"Oh, hell," said Henry, and moved the box
off the burner. "Give me a knife, someone."

Lee handed him a boning knife, a wicked-
looking implement with a slender blade.

Henry held the knife up to the light and

grinned. "Fresh chicken, anyone?"

"That's not funny, Henry." Delilah pouted. "I wanted to surprise you. The chickens are my little pets."

"You're joking." Henry sliced the strapping tape along the sides of the box lid and handed the knife back to Lee. He folded down the four sides of the box top, one after the other, and stood motionless, staring into the box.

"For God's sake," he said.

Delilah, who'd been watching the box-opening from the other side of the island, came around to her husband's side and peered into the carton.

She clasped her hands under her chin. "Aren't they cute?" She reached into the box and drew out three Day-Glo-colored chicks, one pink, one orange, and one blue. She lifted them up, kissed each one, and then cuddled all three against her cheek.

"How the devil many of those damned things do you have in that box?" asked Henry.

Delilah's voice was muffled by chicken down. "Two dozen."

"Two dozen!" Henry repeated. "Twenty-four! What in hell are you planning to do with twenty-four chickens?"

"I'm going to collect nesting material now,

191

darling." She set the three chicks back in their shipping box, then opened the pantry door, brought out a cardboard liquor box, and skipped out the front door with it.

"What about these animals?" Henry called out.

"I'll be right back." Delilah went out to the lawn and collected newly cut grass the mower had tossed aside.

Henry stalked out after her. "Where are you going to keep them?"

Delilah called over her shoulder, "Lambert Willoughby has built a little enclosure for the chickens and goats."

"Goats?!"

"I wanted to surprise you," said Delilah. "I've ordered six goats."

Delilah was giving her chicks water when the phone rang. "Get that, will you please, Lee?"

After a few moments she looked up from where she was kneeling. "Who is it?"

Lee shielded the mouthpiece. "A call for me, ma'am."

"I'd rather you didn't use my phone for personal calls." Delilah got to her feet. "Who is it?"

"This afternoon would be fine," said Lee into the phone.

Delilah strode over to the phone table. "Hang up," she demanded.

"Call me at . . ."

And Delilah pressed the disconnect button.

"Sorry, ma'am."

"And just who was that?"

"I was making an appointment."

"What for?" demanded Delilah.

Lee flushed. "It was personal, ma'am."

"When you call on my phone, it's my business." Delilah, too, flushed. "Why did you give out my number?"

"I didn't give your number, ma'am. I don't know how . . ."

"You have a cell phone, don't you?" Delilah moved closer to her.

"Yes, ma'am." Lee backed up.

"I don't want you taking personal calls on my phone. On my time."

"I understand, ma'am."

Delilah spun around and returned to her chicks. She missed the look the usually impassive Lee gave her.

She finished giving the chicks their water and apparently forgot the exchange of words.

Lee walked out of the kitchen, her back straight.

In the staff office next to the conservatory, she called back on her cell phone. "I'm sorry we were cut off, Mr. Bronsky. Technical difficulties, I'm afraid." She gave him her own number. "Thank you for offering me the opportunity for an audition, but I have to tell you, I don't have any acting experience."

"This is video, Lee, not the movies. No experience needed. We can give you an audition wherever it's convenient."

"Well," said Lee. "I don't know."

"There's no charge, Lee. Your only commitment is the time. An hour at most."

"I can't get off before five."

"No problem. Six o'clock okay with you?"

"I just don't know."

"No big deal. Nothing to lose, Lee. Shall we say six o'clock? Wear your normal working clothes."

"Well . . ."

"The only thing you have to lose, Lee, is an hour of your time. At worst, you get experience in front of the camera. And at best . . . well, who knows how far your looks and ability will take you."

"My mother . . ."

"Invite your mom. I bet dollars to doughnuts she'd love to see her daughter on TV."

Lee shook her head. "My mother never goes out. Where do you do the filming?"

"Your place, or we can meet you at the Harbor Motel in Vineyard Haven."

"Motel?"

Mr. Bronsky laughed. "We film in the lobby. No problem. See you tonight at six?"

"I guess," said Lee, and hung up.

Howland was still at Victoria's when his cell phone rang. He tugged it out of his pocket, flipped it open, and looked at the display.

"Sorry, Victoria. I'd better answer this one." He went out to his parked car where cell phone reception was better, and returned a few minutes later, frowning.

"Is something the matter?" asked Victoria.

"Something is seriously the matter." Howland rubbed his nose. "The call was from one of my contacts at the hospital. Oliver and two of the assessors were taken to the emergency room last night."

Victoria pushed her chair away from the table. "What happened?"

"Suspected poisoning."

"Good heavens!"

"The hospital won't give out any further information." Howland put the phone back in his pocket.

"Which assessors?" asked Victoria.

"Ocypete and Ellen."

"Is Selena all right?"

"I haven't heard."

"Oliver, too. That doesn't fit at all with what I believe happened," said Victoria almost to herself. "It's all wrong."

CHAPTER 19

Darcy dropped the limo off at Tiasquam Repairs for an oil change and walked the half-mile to Victoria's. He turned onto New Lane, and sat with his back against a wild cherry tree that overhung Victoria's meadow where he was sheltered from the wind. From there, he could see her house. Bees hummed around the cherry blossoms that had begun to open. Spring sunlight filtered through the branches and warmed him. After a few minutes he shed his jacket. He could see Howland's station wagon parked under Victoria's Norway maple. He pulled up a blade of bright new grass and chewed on it, listening to the bees and the sound of far-off surf on the south shore. He watched and waited.

After a quarter of an hour, Howland appeared at the top of the steps with Victoria behind him. He turned and said something that made her laugh, then got into his station wagon and drove off.

Darcy shook out his jacket, put it back on, and strolled across the stubbly pasture.

Victoria was standing at the top of the steps, buttoning her sweater. She watched him approach. "Good morning, Darcy. Where's your limousine?"

"At the butcher shop." When she looked puzzled, he added, "Tiasquam Repairs," and then when she looked worried, "Getting an oil change."

"Come in. I'm relieved to see you. How in the world did you escape from jail?"

"Thanks to you, Mrs. Trumbull."

"It's almost lunchtime. Would you like an omelet?"

"Sounds good. I'll help."

Ten minutes later, Victoria slipped the golden brown omelets onto warmed plates. Darcy set out utensils and they seated themselves at the cookroom table.

"What did you need to see me about?" Victoria asked.

"Somebody framed me, Mrs. Trumbull. I suspect it was Henry." Darcy leaned forward, elbows on either side of his plate.

"Why would he?"

"That's what I've got to find out."

Victoria cut into her omelet. "I gather the person I called had some influence in getting you out of jail."

"The number you called was the private number of the woman who hired me. She called the sheriff."

"Who hired you?"

"Senator Hammermill."

Victoria set her fork down and whistled softly. "Geraldine Hammermill? She's on the Homeland Security oversight committee, isn't she?"

"She's also on the board of trustees of Reverend True's church." Darcy paused to finish his own omelet. "She claims he's been embezzling church funds."

"Henry?"

Darcy nodded. "The senator contacted the FBI and they referred her to me." He cleaned up the last morsel on his plate and sat back. "The bureau told her the situation called for a freelance operator, not the FBI. At least, not at that point."

"Was she alerted because Henry suddenly has money?"

"Partly."

"It's Delilah's money he's spending. Two million dollars in the three years they've been married."

"Henry has spent more than Delilah's two million, and he's not spending it on clothes. Something big is going on. The church is missing almost a million dollars."

Victoria set down her napkin. "It must be a wealthy church. I'd never heard of it before I met Delilah."

"The Eye of God is a huge operation. They've built a cathedral in West Virginia and another in Elko, Nevada. Churches all over the States. Television ministries throughout the world. Money pours in. The church is worth more than two billion dollars."

Victoria widened her eyes. "Delilah seems to think Henry is the head of this church."

"Good God, no. He's way down on the pecking order. One of at least two dozen TV evangelists."

"But he had access to church funds, I take it."

"Must have. The senator and her church committee found irregularities in the financial reports and investigated over a six- or seven-month period. They concluded that Henry was the culprit. The church can't file charges against him until they have proof."

"Your role is to find that proof, I gather."

Darcy nodded. "I don't know what he's spending it on. Drugs, gambling, blackmail — something that requires a large sum of money."

"Why are you coming to me?"

"With the murder of the pilot . . ." Darcy paused. "I don't know whether you'd heard, he was strangled, like Tillie and Lucy."

"I hadn't heard." Victoria took a deep breath. "That makes it even more likely that the murders are connected."

"Henry's not sure who or what I am." Darcy gazed out of the window where the steeple of the village church was visible over the trees. "He's uncomfortable around me. Doesn't know whether I'm Delilah's boy toy or whether I've been sent by someone to break his knees."

"Perhaps Henry wants to deflect blame from himself."

"Henry apparently spent the night the pilot was killed with Delilah, although that's open to question."

"I thought Henry was banished to the guesthouse."

Darcy smiled. "Around ten he slipped out of the guesthouse and into the main house and, I assume, Delilah's heart-shaped bed."

"Heart-shaped?"

"Trust me," said Darcy. "Our girl can't resist Henry, even if he and she aren't speaking."

"Have the police notified his family?"

"The pilot's? I don't know. His family may be difficult to track down. He told Henry

201

his name was Cappy Jessup, but I knew him as Frank Morris. He wasn't Henry's regular pilot."

Victoria suddenly recalled the phone call Howland had received before Darcy arrived. "Oliver Ashpine and two of the three assessors, Ocypete Rotch and Ellen Meadows, are in the hospital. They've been poisoned."

"What!"

"Someone called Howland from the hospital while he was here. That's all I know. I didn't mean to interrupt, but I thought you'd want to know."

"Did the hospital give out any details?"

"No."

"Of course not. Privacy laws." Darcy drummed his fingers on the table.

"Someone singled out two of the assessors and their clerk. I wonder if Selena Moon is all right."

"Strange," said Darcy.

"I agree. Perhaps a disgruntled taxpayer has taken matters into his own hands."

"By the way," Darcy grinned suddenly, "I need your help."

"What would you like me to do?"

"Find out what's going on between Henry and Lee."

"Why Lee?"

"Lee's been Delilah's maid for five

months. When I arrived two weeks ago, I got the impression Henry hadn't even noticed her. That's changed over the last day or so. Something's happened between them." He brushed crumbs off his hands onto his napkin and crumpled it.

"She's certainly attractive," said Victoria. "I was under the impression you were interested in her."

Darcy shook his head. "My work doesn't include fraternizing with the staff. Henry treats Lee like a commodity. Doesn't seem to be personal. What's he up to?"

"I can't imagine. His television show?"

"Fundamentalist Christian? Not Lee."

Victoria thought for a long time. "All these strands must be connected — the three deaths, the assessors' scam, Henry's money, Oliver Ashpine." She looked up at the beams in the cookroom ceiling and the collection of baskets hanging from them. "Poisoning doesn't fit, does it?"

Both were quiet.

"Oliver Ashpine," said Victoria again. "Oliver Ashpine. I wonder . . . ?"

"What *I* wonder," Darcy interrupted, "is why two assessors were poisoned and not the third."

"Selena." Victoria sat forward. "I've got to call to make sure she's all right."

■ ■ ■ ■

After Howland left Victoria's, he drove to Town Hall. On the first floor, he nodded to Mrs. Danvers, who peered at him over the top of her glasses without a greeting. He climbed the stairs to the second floor. None of the other Town Hall workers had arrived yet. He checked his watch. Almost ten o'clock.

He ensconced himself in Oliver Ashpine's chair, switched on Oliver's computer, and waited for it to boot up. Where would Oliver have filed the video he'd been watching? Howland opened various folders and files, but nothing seemed to lead to a porn video until he saw a folder labeled "Honeybee."

"I can't believe the man would be that stupid," Howland muttered, as he clicked the mouse on "Honeybee."

But the video opened, in full glowing color with sound. Howland quickly lowered the volume before Mrs. Danvers could hear it.

The segment that pictured Delilah was less than three minutes long, lost in an hour-long episode that showed interminable variations on the theme of writhing, sweaty bodies. How on earth did Oliver wade through all that garbage to identify those few minutes?

No doubt about the identity of Delilah, now that he knew what he was looking for. He'd brought a blank disk with him and copied the three minutes onto it. He wasn't sure what he could, or should, do with his copy, but he slipped the disk into its paper folder and stowed it in his green canvas briefcase.

A small candy box sat on the corner of Oliver's desk. Howland had eyed the white box while he worked. He was moderate in most temptations, but not when it came to sweets. He opened it and looked in. Fruit jellies. Oliver would never miss one piece.

But if he ate that first piece he'd eat the next, and nothing would be left in Oliver's box. With a sigh, he wiped his mouth with the back of his hand, rubbed his nose, closed down Oliver's computer, and went downstairs.

"Find what you wanted?" asked Mrs. Danvers.

"Yes, thanks," said Howland. "Where is everyone? It's after eleven."

Mrs. Danvers turned to her computer. "The selectmen sent the staff to what they call 'Graciousness Training.' "

Howland hid his grin behind a cough and

thought of the fruit jellies he hadn't
touched.

CHAPTER 20

Victoria washed their luncheon dishes, and Darcy dried.

"Connections. You may be right, Mrs. Trumbull. The three murders might be connected, but damned if I can see how." He looked out of the window. "Oh, for God's sake."

West Tisbury's police Bronco pulled into the drive.

Victoria arose.

"I'm getting out of here," said Darcy.

"Wait a bit." Victoria was almost at the door when a second vehicle pulled up behind the Bronco. A shield on the side showed a bunch of grapes surmounted by what looked like a crown with a sail and a harpoon about to strike something, presumably a whale. Above the shield was the announcement in gold letters, "County of Dukes County" and below the shield, also in gold letters, "Sheriff."

"I'm gone," said Darcy, and headed toward the door that led into the woodshed. He shut the door behind him. A moment later, he opened the door, retrieved his mug, and left the door open a crack.

A third vehicle pulled up as Victoria went outside. This one had a circular emblem with an Indian in the center holding a bow and arrows. A star shone over his shoulder. Gold lettering around the circle read "Massachusetts State Police."

Junior Norton was driving the Bronco. Casey lowered the window on the passenger side. "The guys want to talk to you, Victoria." She nodded at the two vehicles behind her.

"Ask them to park so they don't block my driveway."

A few minutes later, five law enforcement officers gathered around the table in Victoria's cookroom, Casey and Junior Norton of the West Tisbury Police, Sergeant Smalley and Trooper Tim Eldredge of the state police, and Sheriff Look of the County of Dukes County.

"Good morning," said Victoria. "Nice day."

"Morning, Mrs. Trumbull." Sergeant Smalley nodded. "Seems as though we've hit a dead end, and we'd like to talk to you."

"Would you like coffee? I'll make fresh."

"That would be fine," said Smalley.

Tim Eldredge got up. "I'll make it, ma'am. Your coffeemaker is like my grandmother's."

Victoria drew up her chair so it faced the door to the woodshed, her back to the meadow.

After some small talk, Smalley cleared his throat. "We'd like to ask you for assistance."

Victoria smoothed her hair. "I'm not sure how I can help, but I'll be glad to do whatever I can."

When the coffee finished dripping, Tim brought in steaming mugs and cream and sugar, passed them around, and seated himself next to Smalley.

Smalley gestured around the table for Victoria's benefit. "As you've undoubtedly gathered, Mrs. Trumbull, the Island's law enforcement agencies are cooperating on the recent deaths in West Tisbury."

"Tillie Willoughby, Lucy Pease, and Cappy Jessup, the pilot," Casey reminded.

"All three were throttled," said Smalley. "I understand, Mrs. Trumbull, that you discovered two of the three bodies. I'm sorry you had to go through that. Terrible."

Sheriff Look leaned toward Victoria, his arms folded on the table. "You've had dealings with Darcy Remey, also known as

Emery Meyer, the man we held for questioning, haven't you?"

When Victoria visited Darcy at the jail, the sheriff had been friendly. Now he was almost hostile. "Yes," Victoria said. "I know who he is."

"What can you tell us about him?"

Casey interrupted. "You should mention, Victoria, that you met him some time ago when he was called Emery Meyer."

"Jewel thief, isn't he?" asked the sheriff.

"That's open to question." Victoria's jaw tightened. "He's well-educated." She thought of Darcy's collection of her poetry. "Widely traveled, and he's taken a position as chauffeur with the television star Delilah Sampson."

"Senator Hammermill of West Virginia demanded that we release him, whatever his name is."

"You had no reason to hold him."

"Only that he found the pilot's body, moved it, took his time about calling the authorities, and, according to Reverend True, knew the deceased." The sheriff smiled. "Not conclusive, but suggestive."

Victoria sat up straight. "Since I found two of the bodies, am I a suspect?"

"No, ma'am. Not at all."

"Is that all you wanted to talk to me

about," Victoria pushed her chair away from the table, "the guilt or innocence of Miss Sampson's chauffeur? I have nothing further to say to you." She started to rise.

Smalley held up a hand. "Hold it, Tom. I think we're off to a wrong start."

"Indeed," said Victoria.

"Please, Mrs. Trumbull," Smalley said. "We were hoping you could shed some light on several things that have all of us . . ." he paused. "Quite frankly, we're stumped."

Victoria sat again, but her mouth was still turned down. "Where would you like to start?"

"It's unheard of to have three unrelated unexplained murders occur within such a short time. We've discussed this among ourselves — the West Tisbury police, state police, and sheriff's office — and can't find any common thread that would connect them. And yet . . ." Smalley shrugged.

"The three murders definitely are connected," said Victoria.

Smalley lifted his shoulders. "We can't see how."

"If I were you, I'd start with the assessors."

"The assessors have nothing to do with the murders," said the sheriff.

"Did you know that they're skimming

money off the town's taxes and have been for years?"

Sheriff Look and Sergeant Smalley glanced at each other and then at Casey. Tim Eldredge wrote in his notebook. Junior Norton watched Casey, who pushed her coffee mug away from her, frowned, and avoided their eyes.

Victoria noticed the uncomfortable expressions of the five gathered around her table. "I found out only recently about the assessors' scam. Tillie was probably involved."

Casey leaned forward, apparently about to say something, but stopped herself.

"You've asked for my thoughts," Victoria said. "If I were you, I'd get an independent auditor to look into town property assessments in recent years. I'd check banks to see if the assessors have a savings account. Tillie, too. Investments. They undoubtedly invested their money in something."

Tim Eldredge turned a page in his notebook and continued to write.

"It might be worthwhile to investigate Oliver Ashpine. He was appointed by the selectmen at the assessors' request to fill out Tillie's term after she disappeared. He may know something about her death. If I'm correct, Tillie's job was worth a considerable amount of money."

"We looked into that," said Smalley. "The job pays a bit over minimum wage. Hardly a motive."

"You might go through Oliver's files. He keeps them in the locked bottom drawer of his file cabinet."

The sheriff looked down.

"Mrs. Trumbull," said Smalley, "you don't seem to understand what we're after. If what you say about the assessors is true, that's one thing. But we're trying to solve three murders, not investigate an alleged scam."

"It's all connected," said Victoria.

Casey unhooked her equipment belt and lowered it to the floor with a thud. Her face was flushed. "Uncomfortable bunch of tools."

"Please continue, Mrs. Trumbull." Smalley turned to the others. All but Trooper Eldredge, who was writing, had their arms folded tightly over their chests. "We invited ourselves to Mrs. Trumbull's house to hear what she has to say, so I suggest we listen to her."

Victoria ran her thumbnail along the checked tablecloth, tracing the crack formed by the table leaf. "I'm convinced that Lucy Pease was killed by mistake."

"Lucy and Ellen don't, or didn't, look at all alike," said Casey.

Victoria smoothed the tablecloth over the crack. "Lucy was killed in Ellen's house. The killer could reasonably assume Ellen would be there."

"That would indicate the killer didn't know either of the two women," said Smalley.

"Maybe not. Lucy was killed in the pantry, where it's quite dark," Victoria continued. "I discovered that Oliver has his own scam in addition to the assessors'. The assessors may not have known about his scam until Delilah Sampson complained about her tax bill. All of them have been stealing tax money." Victoria looked around the table. No one met her gaze. Several shifted uncomfortably. "That's all I can think to tell you."

"I'm afraid we've wasted your time, Mrs. Trumbull," said Smalley. He stood, and the others got up as well. "You've given us a lot to think about. Thank you."

The rest looked everywhere but at Victoria.

"Junior, take the Bronco back to the police station," Casey ordered. "I need to talk to Victoria."

"Want me to come by in a half hour, Chief?"

Casey bent down and picked up her gun belt. "If Victoria can hike to the station, I can."

Junior saluted Casey and Victoria, and left.

As soon as they were gone, Victoria seated herself at the head of the table again where she could see the woodshed door, still ajar. She waited for Casey to say what she had on her mind.

Casey paced the small room, apparently trying to decide how to start. She finally sat down across from Victoria, who held her hands around her empty coffee mug.

"You realize, don't you, you embarrassed me in front of the guys."

"I didn't mean to," said Victoria.

"Why didn't you tell me all that stuff first?"

Casey's face was still flushed. Victoria felt a surge of sympathy. "I didn't expect them to come calling, Casey. This was information I've just put together. When you and they asked me my thoughts, I told you."

"You have to be careful what you say."

"Oh?"

"The assessors have nothing to do with the murders." Casey adjusted her belt and snapped shut the case that held her radio.

"Those three ladies have been working for the town for years."

"A combined total of ninety-seven," said Victoria.

"The town respects them. You know that, better than I do. They've been voted in repeatedly."

"Because of inertia, not respect."

"Nevertheless," Casey went on, "you've got to give them credit for dedication. They're working for the town." Casey emphasized the last four words.

"They're working for themselves," said Victoria. "No one else."

"You can't spread the rumors you're saying about them, Victoria."

"I don't spread rumors," Victoria snapped. "You know I don't."

"A few minutes ago you told my colleagues some pretty strong stuff about the assessors and their clerk. And what about Darcy or Emery? You hadn't told me about him, either. That same guy who was around town some time ago?"

Victoria, offended by the accusation of rumormongering, ignored Casey's question. "What I told you was not rumor."

"As my deputy, you're a representative of the West Tisbury police." Casey's voice shook. "You're held to a higher standard than other citizens. You can't go around libeling people."

Victoria rose from her seat. "My personal standards are every bit as high as the police standards. Probably higher. I'm not libeling the assessors." She slapped her palm on the table. "They and their clerk are stealing tax money. A criminal act. They've got to be stopped."

"You have no proof, Victoria. Until you do, you're opening up the department and yourself as an individual to one hell of a lawsuit."

"I *have* proof."

"Yeah? And you're withholding that from me, too?"

"I obtained my proof as a private citizen. If I give it to you, it will most likely not hold up in court because of the way it was obtained." She glared at Casey. "The police have to go through strict procedures to get the proof I've told you exists. I suggest you get started right away, before that evidence is destroyed."

"Victoria . . ."

"I explained to the group," Victoria swept her arm at the empty chairs, "that you must get access to files in Oliver Ashpine's bottom file drawer. He keeps it locked. Get an outside accountant to go over the files. And do it soon. Oliver is getting wind that something is up."

"I suppose you're not going to share this evidence with me?"

Victoria folded her arms across her chest.

Casey sighed and stood, too. "I recognize that stubborn Yankee streak of yours. I guess I don't want to know how you got hold of it. Breaking and entering?"

"Not at all," said Victoria. "Of course not."

Chapter 21

Casey marched out of the kitchen and shut the door firmly behind her. Victoria heard her footsteps echo across the bricks of the entry floor, clump down the stone steps, and fade away in the new grass.

She waited for the chief to disappear down the driveway, safely out of sight, before she pushed open the woodshed door. Darcy was crouched behind it, and she almost knocked him over.

She held her hand out to steady him. "They've gone."

Darcy got up slowly, rubbing the calves of his legs. "Cramps," he explained when Victoria looked concerned. "Interesting." He stretched his arms over his head and bent from side to side. "Very interesting."

Victoria still smarted over Casey's scolding. "I don't spread rumors."

"No, of course you don't." Darcy sat at the table and continued to rub his legs.

Victoria cleared away the empty coffee cups, took them into the kitchen, and set them on the counter. "Did you learn anything?" she asked when she was seated again.

"I learned that Chief Casey O'Neill is super sensitive about the opinions of 'the guys.' "

Victoria nodded. "I apparently ruffled her feathers by not informing her first."

"I also learned that the cops suspect me of something, but they're not sure what." Darcy smiled. "And they're not one bit comfortable with the idea of confronting three little old ladies. Entrenched, respectable, and fragile little old ladies."

"Those three assessors are no more fragile than I am," said Victoria, her face set in disapproval. "Stereotyping the elderly, as usual." She lifted her beaky nose. "Those little old ladies are fully aware of their power. No one dares challenge them."

"Don't look at me that way, Victoria. I'm on your side." Darcy checked his watch. "They've probably finished with the oil change by now. I've got to get the limo back to Delilah's."

Darcy started to get up, and Victoria suddenly remembered what she'd meant to tell him. "There was an interesting development last evening. We surprised Oliver watching a pornographic movie on his computer."

Darcy sat back with a smirk. "We, Mrs. Trumbull?"

"Howland and I. The actress was Delilah."

"No way!"

"Howland is at Town Hall now, copying the video."

Darcy laughed. "The Reverend True's missus. That explains Oliver's blackmail plan."

"If I were she, I would not care to have that movie publicized."

Darcy looked at his watch again. "I can stay for a few minutes more." He stood up. "I've got to work this cramp out of my leg."

"Dehydration," said Victoria. "Drink some water."

"Can't hurt." Darcy went into the kitchen and returned with two glasses of water. "One for you, Mrs. Trumbull."

"Thank you."

"I'm going to look into why the pilot, Cappy Jessup, the guy I knew as Frank Morris, was the one to fly Henry to the Island," said Darcy, sitting down again. "Henry didn't seem to know him, at least not well. Was he checking up on Henry? Or Delilah? Or me? Who sent him, the church?

If not the church, who? I've got to find answers to those questions." He drank his water. "And there's another unknown. What do you know about Oliver Ashpine?"

"Unsavory, rude, and officious."

Darcy held his hands up as if to ward her off. "Don't hold back on my account."

Victoria frowned, thinking about Oliver with his painted-on hair and arrogance, blatantly stealing tax money. "It seems likely, to me, that Oliver killed Tillie."

"To get her job? It's not as though the scam was paying off hundreds of thousands. At most, we're talking about a few thousand, if that. Hardly motive for murder. How long had Tillie been the assessors' clerk?"

"About eight years," said Victoria. "Not more. She was only in her mid- to late twenties, I would guess."

"Attractive?"

"Quite pretty." Victoria thought for a moment. "Long blond hair, brown eyes, a nice trim figure."

"Would she have known about the assessors' scheme?"

"Someone besides the assessors had to be in on it, and their clerk and tax collector is the most likely one."

Darcy raised his eyebrows. "Why tax collector?"

"The town has a system of checks and balances to prevent this very kind of scheme from happening. Separate jobs held by different people." Victoria sipped her water. "But Tillie held the two critical positions — tax collector and assessors' clerk." She thought a moment. "Her brother Lambert has worked for the town for years. He's likely to know about the scheme, too."

"The tax collector is an elected position, right?"

"Yes. Tillie was up for reelection every three years. She ran unopposed each time. The assessors made sure of that."

"When she didn't show up for work, didn't anyone report her missing? She'd been dead for five months."

"She was an independent young woman." Victoria paused. "Everyone assumed she'd run off with Fred Smith, a man she'd been seeing for several months. His wife reported him missing around the same time."

"Has Smith shown up?"

"I haven't heard," said Victoria.

"I'll check out Fred Smith." Darcy pulled a small notebook out of his shirt pocket and wrote in it. "What about Lambert Willoughby?" Darcy continued to write. "Tillie's brother."

"Lucy Pease, the woman who was killed,

was Lambert Willoughby's mother-in-law," said Victoria.

"Odd, his sister and his mother-in-law both killed. Did Willoughby and his mother-in-law get along?"

"As well as could be expected," said Victoria. "They were civil to one another. Tillie, of course, was no relation to Lucy Pease. The two were what we Vineyarders call 'connections.' "

Darcy stood up again, still rubbing his calf. "Did Tillie have any other family?"

"Only Lambert, his wife, and their three children, as far as I know. Is the water helping with the cramp?"

"Seems to be." He went into the kitchen and returned with another glassful. "Yet no one wondered about not hearing from Tillie for five months? They didn't report her missing?"

"They may have wondered, but apparently did nothing to try to locate her."

Darcy shook his head as though he couldn't understand such a family.

Victoria smiled. "What about you, Darcy-Emery-Meyer? Does your family know where you are now and where you've been for the past five months — or more?"

"Touché, Mrs. Trumbull. So Tillie disappears," he continued. "Oliver shows up and the assessors hire him. Where did he come from?"

"He'd had various jobs here on the Vineyard, mostly in the Oak Bluffs town government. Nothing significant. He seemed qualified enough. No one else applied for the position, and based on the assessors' recommendation, he was hired."

"Sounds as though he took a drop in pay."

"I suspect the assessors let him know he'd be supplementing his pay significantly."

Darcy went back to his notes. "Tillie and her brother Lambert both worked in Town Hall?"

Victoria nodded.

"Tillie disappears, no one makes any inquiries, Oliver applies for her job and is hired. Since tax collector is an elected position, how did Oliver end up with that job, too? Just like Tillie?"

"On the assessors' recommendation the selectmen appointed him to fill Tillie's unexpired term. He's up for election this month."

"Then what?"

"He's likely to win. He's running unopposed."

"A fine kettle of fish," said Darcy, going back to his notes. "What's next in our chronology?"

"Oliver took over Tillie's job as tax collector. The tax bills went out this week. Delilah complained about the high assessment on her property, and Oliver threatened to blackmail her." Victoria paused and smiled faintly. "You might want to see the film he found to blackmail, her with. Howland can make a copy for you, if you'd like."

"No, thanks just the same."

"When Delilah met Henry, she thought he was the head of the church and wealthy beyond her fondest dream, but it turned out he's on a clergyman's salary. He was after her money, not the other way around."

"Nice people," said Darcy. "So she intends to divorce Henry. What does he have to say about that?"

"She hasn't told him, although I'm sure he suspects. According to Massachusetts law, if they divorce, he gets half of all she owns. Establishing her farm will cut the assessed value significantly."

Darcy laughed. "Fainting goats and dyed chicks."

"She's not stupid," said Victoria. "And she has a certain sense of style. She's learned that tractors are available in several colors."

"A pink tractor," Darcy said thoughtfully, and went back to his notes. "Would Delilah have known Tillie?"

"Possibly. Delilah's been here for several years. But I doubt if she ever went into Town Hall before she confronted Oliver a few days ago."

"Delilah may have known Frank Morris. Her show is filmed in West Virginia, and he may have flown her there."

"A number of loose ends to tie up," said Victoria. "We need to get started."

CHAPTER 22

For several months, Jordan Rivers had been awakened long before dawn by Chickee, the Willoughbys' rooster. Chickee was housed in a ramshackle pen on the far edge of the Willoughby property, immediately across the narrow dirt road from Jordan's own property and close to his house. The rooster would burst into sudden loud voice at any time of day or night.

Jordan called on Victoria Trumbull, who was weeding the new plants he'd given her.

"I told you, honesty is invasive," Jordan said. "You may be sorry."

"I hope so," said Victoria, with a smile. "We can use more of it."

"I admired a stand of honesty in the Willoughbys' yard and took a handful of seeds," Jordan continued. "Now I can't get rid of the stuff. If you think it will help, I'll scatter seeds around Town Hall."

He crouched down beside her, pulled a

few weeds and tossed them off to one side.

"Let me show you what a black-eyed Susan seedling looks like," said Victoria diplomatically, retrieving the seedling from Jordan's weed pile.

"Sorry, Victoria. I'm going crazy with that rooster."

"I suppose he wakes you early, greeting the dawn?"

"Dawn!" said Jordan. "I wish it were only at dawn. He kept me up all night last night, crowing. He's not a normal rooster. Everything and anything sets him off. Car lights. A slammed door. An inquisitive skunk. Their kids." Jordan made a wry face. "His crowing starts up Ashpine's mutt, who's part wolf."

"Wolf?"

"A Jack Russell, actually."

"Mr. Willoughby seems like a reasonable man." Victoria pointed with her gardening tool. "That's a tiger lily seedling, not a weed. Why not suggest that he move Chickee's pen to the other side of their property?"

"I did. Want me to replant it?"

"Don't pull them up if you can avoid it, but there are plenty. No great loss. What did Mr. Willoughby say?"

"He demurred. Said there'd always been

a chicken coop there, even before I built my house."

"Would he be willing to get rid of Chickee?"

"I suggested that, too, and the youngest, the three-year-old, started to cry." Jordan stood up and crossed to the other side of the border and began to yank weeds. "Making Sweetie Pie cry has ensured the permanent enmity of the entire family."

"What about talking to the animal control officer?"

"I did. I filed a complaint, but Joanie said this is an agricultural town, and chickens are agricultural."

Victoria was silent, thinking.

Jordan said, "You know that poem of yours, where you were in the city one time and imagined that the sound of traffic was the sound of surf on the south shore?"

Victoria nodded.

"I've tried imagining that Chickee's voice is no different from the sound of the city, sirens in the night, horns honking, brakes screeching, kids screaming, gunshots, that sort of thing. It's not the same. I bought a white noise machine, but it can't compete with Chickee." He held up a plant. "Ragweed?"

"Chrysanthemum. Why not limit yourself

to grass."

He nodded. "I tried earplugs, but they hurt my ears. I tried shutting the windows at night, but that makes it too stuffy to sleep." He looked up at Victoria, who was patting soil around a plant she'd rescued from his weed pile. "Besides, the glass rattles when Chickee crows and amplifies the sound. I'm going mad, Victoria!"

How ironic, Victoria thought. A rooster was all it took to upset Jordan, when in real life, when not on spring vacation, he dealt equably with school life in the city despite knives, guns, chewing gum, and sass.

"I've thought about wringing Chickee's neck, poisoning him, or shooting him," said Jordan. "I'd have to get an air gun, of course."

"I'm surprised that he hasn't been attacked by skunks or hawks before now."

Jordan brightened. "Can they get in the chicken coop?"

"I should think so, depending on how well built the coop is, of course."

"Rickety," said Jordan, thoughtfully.

"Try overfeeding him," said Victoria. "That's humane."

Jordan smiled faintly.

"Perhaps you could convince Mr. Willoughby to sell Chickee to Delilah Sampson. She's planning to start a chicken farm."

"The woman who bought the old Hammond place?"

"She lives at least three miles from you."

Jordan stood up and brushed off his hands. "You've given me a great idea, Mrs. Trumbull. Thanks."

Victoria watched him fasten on his helmet, get on his recumbent bicycle, and peddle off, wondering what it was she'd set in motion.

Jordan planned his rooster-napping with care. If he were to approach the pen, Chickee would crow and continue to crow until silenced. He would have to lure the Willoughbys — husband, wife, and three small children — away for an hour or so.

Jordan had sent the family, anonymously, a movie pass good for this Saturday's matinee.

Saturday was a gorgeous day when Jordan would ordinarily have ridden his recumbent bike into the State Forest on the bicycle trail. Instead, he waited at home. The matinee was at two o'clock. At one-thirty, Mrs. W. and the two older children went out through their front door, the door that always set the rooster off. The door slammed. Chickee crowed. Ashpine's Jack

Russell barked.

Jordan waited for Mr. Willoughby and the youngest. But the wife buckled the two kids into their seats in the SUV, got into the driver's seat, and took off.

What about Mr. W. and Sweetie Pie?

Jordan took a couple of cold bottles of Sam Adams out of his refrigerator, slipped out his side door, and went over to the Willoughbys. He could see Mr. W. through the glass panes in the door, sitting in his Barcalounger watching TV along with the youngest child, who had taken all the clothes off her doll and was marching the naked doll along a line of wooden blocks.

Jordan knocked. Mr. Willoughby looked up, heaved himself out of the Barcalounger, and opened the door.

"Chickee bothering you again?" he asked, lifting up his T-shirt and scratching his exposed belly.

"I thought you might like a cold beer," said Jordan, holding the two bottles out. "Peace offering."

Willoughby examined them. "Don't much like Sam Adams. My beer's Bud."

Jordan looked around. "Where's the wife and kids?"

"The movies." Mr. Willoughby pulled his shirt down and yawned. "Guess I'll try one of the Sam Adams after all." He held out a hand and Jordan passed over a cold bottle.

Jordan shifted from one foot to the other, waiting to be asked to have a seat. "Movies?"

"Someone sent a movie pass."

Jordan held out a bottle opener.

"Don't need it." Mr. Willoughby twisted off the bottle cap and settled back in his Barcalounger.

Jordan seated himself on an overstuffed ottoman and used the opener on his own beer. "Didn't you want to go?"

"Hate the movies," said Mr. Willoughby. "Saturday is nothing but damned kid stuff." He gestured at his daughter, who was staring at Jordan, her thumb in her mouth, the naked doll held by one foot. "Anyhow, Sweetie Pie here's coming down with something. Got the sniffles."

Jordan, careful about his own health, wheeled the ottoman backwards, away from the child.

"What's on your mind?" Mr. Willoughby tipped his bottle up and poured a portion of the contents down his throat. He examined the bottle. "Bud's better."

"Just wanted to be neighborly," said Jordan politely. "Mend fences, so to speak."

"Yeah? Mend fences by siccing a goddamned lawyer on me. Thanks a lot, pal."

"That seemed the way to keep things from getting personal," said Jordan. "Let the lawyers work it out."

"Nothing to work out. My kids have a pet chicken. West Tisbury's agricultural. Chickens are agriculture. What's your beef? Don't like the country? Move back to the goddamned city. We was here first, asshole."

Jordan rose to his feet with dignity, leaving his untouched beer behind. He pushed his glasses, which had slipped partway down his nose, back into place with his third finger, and walked out of the Willoughbys' house.

He heard Mr. Willoughby's laugh and the word "asshole" repeated as he shut the door carefully behind him.

Back in his own house, Jordan pondered over a new strategy. If Chickee simply went missing, Willoughby would assume that he, Jordan, was responsible, which would, in truth, be the case.

An airplane flew overhead. Chickee crowed.

Willoughby would retaliate in some gross way.

But suppose some predator were to break into Chickee's pen and do away with him, the way Victoria Trumbull had suggested, leaving a few feathers and a trace of blood. Jordan smiled for the first time in hours. Skunks, raccoons, and hawks. The Island had plenty of those and they loved fresh chicken. Since Jordan didn't actually wish to have Chickee killed, he would have to extract Chickee from the coop, then wreck it as though a hawk or skunk had broken into it.

The following morning, Sunday, the Willoughbys left for church, carrying snot-nosed Sweetie Pie wrapped up in a pink bunny-printed blanket. The door of their SUV slammed shut. Chickee crowed.

Jordan smiled.

He pulled on his deerskin gardening gloves and retrieved the basket of tools he'd prepared the night before after talking with Victoria. Knowing her sense of honor, he'd neglected to tell her his plans. He had shown interest, subtly, he thought, when she told him about the signs of predation.

He'd bought an oven roaster chicken and taken out of the body cavity the paper packet containing neck, liver, and gizzards.

A car went by on the main road. Chickee sent up a cry.

Jordan watched the driveway he shared with the Willoughbys until he was sure they

236

were gone, then tiptoed through the scrub oak and across the lane that separated their houses. With a claw gardening tool he would make this seem like the work of a hawk's talons.

Chickee's pen was about the size of a coffee table, two feet by three feet and about two feet high. He pried loose the wire over the top of the pen. Chickee strutted back and forth, his comb bright red and standing up straight, his head thrown back, in deafening full cry.

Ashpine's Jack Russell took up the cry, and the dog's frenetic barking seemed to be coming closer.

Jordan scattered a few feathers he'd taken from his pillow, and emptied the packet of liver and gizzards into the pen. Chickee stopped crowing long enough to peck at the bloody mess, and Jordan seized him by his feet. Chickee, himself, dropped a couple of feathers in the skirmish, and Jordan thrust the rooster, head first, into a burlap grain bag he'd brought with him for the purpose. As he retreated to his car, an energy-efficient hybrid, he brushed out his footsteps with a branch he'd snapped off an oak tree.

Before he got into his car, he was aware that Bertie had stopped yapping. The dog was trotting toward the wrecked coop. Ashpine didn't usually let Bertie roam free. There was, after all, a leash law in West Tisbury, and Ashpine seemed obsessive about obeying the law.

Jordan kept an eye on Bertie while he tied the mouth of the grain bag with twine and placed it carefully on the backseat of his car. The dog stopped near the wreckage. His stumpy tail wagged and his tongue hung out in a sort of smile. Jordan wondered briefly if he should take Bertie back to Ashpine's house, but decided he'd better deal with Chickee first.

The bag writhed, swelled, subsided, and emitted muffled squawks. He slammed the car door shut, got into the driver's seat, put the car into gear and drove down Old County Road to State Road, turned left, and made his way to Delilah Sampson's enclave.

CHAPTER 23

At the post-service coffee hour in the parish hall, Victoria approached Mrs. Willoughby, who was holding Sweetie Pie. "Lovely sermon, wasn't it?" Victoria held a slice of banana bread in one hand and a cup of coffee in the other. "I'm so sorry about your mother. When is the funeral?"

"Next week. We can't believe it, Mrs. Trumbull. She was such a kind, gentle person. Who would want to do that to her?"

"If I can help in any way . . ."

"Thank you." Mrs. Willoughby jiggled the little girl in her arms.

"Is this your youngest?"

"Sweetie Pie," said Mrs. Willoughby, jouncing the girl. Sweetie Pie ducked her head. "Her name is really Lucy. She was named after my mother." She held a tissue to her daughter's nose. "Blow! That's a good girl!"

"Your mother must have enjoyed her.

These spring colds can be trying," said Victoria. "How is your rooster?"

"Everybody in town is talking about that rooster. You'd think they'd have better things to talk about. Personally, I'd like to get rid of it. He gives me a big fat headache. But . . ." she looked at Sweetie Pie, who stuck her thumb in her mouth.

"I understand." Victoria nibbled her banana bread.

"Besides, you know the way my husband Lambert is."

"I know he has a reputation for being strong-minded."

"Stubborn, you mean. The guy next door complained about Chickee. Didn't even complain, simply asked if Lambert would move Chickee's pen to the back of our property. Lambert dug in his heels."

"Oh?"

"Now we've got lawyers involved and nobody's speaking to anybody."

At this moment Delilah joined them.

"Have you met Delilah Sampson, Mrs. Willoughby?"

"Annie," said Mrs. Willoughby, offering her hand. "Pleased to meet you. And this is Sweetie Pie."

"What a darling baby!" Delilah extended a scarlet-tipped finger and tickled Sweetie

Pie under her chin.

Sweetie Pie lurched back in her mother's arms and screeched, "I am not a baby!"

"She's not usually like this," Annie apologized. "She's not feeling good."

Delilah forced a polite smile and turned to Victoria, her back to Annie and her contagious, squalling child. "I came over to invite you to lunch, Mrs. Trumbull."

Victoria wiped her sticky hand on the napkin under her coffee cup. Facing Annie Willoughby, she could see her look of distaste as she examined Delilah's back, from her brilliant red hair to her gold sandals and the flame-colored sateen in between.

"Thank you," said Victoria. "I'd enjoy that."

The Willoughbys arrived home from church to a scene of apparent carnage. Bertie, Ashpine's Jack Russell, was lying half-in, half-out of the wreckage of Chickee's cage, gnawing on what looked like the innards of a chicken.

Annie Willoughby, the first to realize what had happened, tried to hustle the children into the house.

"What is it, Mommy? I want to see, too," whined Lambert the Fourth, who was seven.

"Me, too," said Arnold, who was five.

Lambert the Fourth, or Quat, for short, stamped his feet and rooted himself to the ground in such a way his mother couldn't tug him loose.

"Why won't you let me see!"

"You never let us do anything," echoed Arnold.

"Lambert?" called Annie, her voice on the edge of frenzy, "take care of that dog!"

Sweetie Pie, who'd been napping in her mother's arms, woke up. "Chickee! I want my Chickee!"

Mr. Willoughby collared Bertie and dragged him to Oliver Ashpine's house next door, preparing a speech in his mind on controlling his mutt and figuring out how much money he could exact from Ashpine to pay for a new coop and the trauma his kids were suffering. The screen door at the back of the house was locked, but the screen had a flap at the bottom, obviously to let Bertie in and out.

"Ashpine!" Mr. Willoughby bellowed into the kitchen through the locked door. "Where in hell are you?"

No answer.

"Get your ass out here, and pretty god-damned fast!"

No answer.

Mr. W., furious now, wrenched the locked door open and dragged the whimpering Bertie inside. "Ashpine!"

No answer.

He hauled Bertie from room to room searching for his master. "Where in hell is the bastard?"

He found a leash hanging on the back of the screen door and attached it to Bertie's collar and knotted the other end around the table leg. He then returned to the scene of the crime.

Annie was standing in the door of the Willoughbys' house, still holding Sweetie Pie. "Lambert, Oliver left a message on the answering machine. He's in the hospital and wants us to take care of Bertie."

"I'll take care of Bertie, all right." Willoughby's face turned a purplish red. "I'll kill the bastard's goddamned killer mutt."

At Delilah's, Victoria looked around. "Where are the chicks?"

"In their new home. Lambert Willoughby has built the nicest pen for me. It will hold both my goats and my chickens." Delilah fluffed her hair. "And the nicest man called me out of the blue and offered me a rooster. I told him I plan to raise chickens, and he said I would need a rooster."

"You need only one rooster."

"He's bringing me only one."

"But . . ." said Victoria, thinking the odds were against two dozen chicks growing up to become two dozen hens and no roosters. She suddenly had an uneasy thought. "What's the name of the man?"

"I don't recall. Something biblical, I think. Aesop, or something. I wonder where Lee is?" She pushed a buzzer next to the refrigerator, and in a few moments, Darcy appeared.

"Can I help you, madam?"

"Where's Lee?"

"I believe you gave her the morning off."

Delilah checked her watch. "It's quarter to twelve now."

"Yes, madam. Is there something I can do for you?"

Delilah turned away. "I want to see her when she comes in."

"Certainly, madam." Darcy glanced at Victoria, who smiled, and he left.

"Let's go into the conservatory, Mrs. Trumbull. I can't imagine what Lee's doing, taking off this morning."

Victoria followed her down the long hallway into the orchid-filled plant room, and settled into a wrought-iron garden chair. She'd been standing during the coffee hour and was glad to sit.

"I can't imagine what's got into her," Delilah said, sitting on the sofa across from Victoria. "She's usually trustworthy. Yesterday afternoon she took a personal call and was quite mysterious about it."

Victoria waited politely for the rest of the story.

Delilah stretched her arm along the back of the sofa. "I'm very lenient with my staff, but one thing I can't stand is having them make personal calls on my time."

"You have such a lovely view," said Victoria. "I can see the water tower on the mainland."

"I'm sure her taking time off today had something to do with that call yesterday."

"What call?" said Henry, who strode into the conservatory at that moment. "I need a drink. Can I fix one for anybody else?" He ambled over to the wet bar across from the orchids.

"Lee, darling. She got a mysterious personal call yesterday afternoon, and then asked for this morning off."

"Church," said Henry, pouring scotch into a glass. "Tell Darcy to come in here, will you?"

Delilah raised her eyebrows at Victoria and whispered, "Lee's not a churchgoer." She jingled the silver bell.

"Scotch, Mrs. Trumbull?" asked Henry. "Bourbon, sherry, white wine?"

"White wine," said Victoria. "Thank you."

"Madam, you rang." Darcy appeared suddenly. Henry turned abruptly, spilling the drink he was pouring.

Delilah smiled. "Reverend True wants to speak to you."

"Sir," said Darcy, bowing.

"Who the hell are you?" said Henry. "Who sent you? Where did you come from?"

"Mrs. Sampson's agency sent me, sir."

"*Miss* Sampson," said Delilah.

"She's Mrs. True, when she's not acting," Henry snapped.

"Yes, sir," said Darcy.

"You didn't answer me. Who *are* you, anyway?"

"Mrs. Sampson's, that is, Mrs. True's, chauffeur, sir."

"The hell you are. You knew my pilot, didn't you?"

"The pilot looked familiar, sir, but I'd mistaken him for someone else."

"How did you get out of jail so quickly? A murder rap is serious stuff."

"The sheriff had no reason to detain me, sir."

Henry held his drink in his right hand and

pointed his forefinger at Darcy. "I don't like you, whatever your name is. I don't trust you, and if you were working for me, instead of my wife, I'd fire your ass."

"Oh, Henry. Stop it!" said Delilah.

Darcy bowed. "Will that be all, sir?"

"Goddamned right, that's all. Watch your goddamned step. 'Will that be all, sir?' " he mimicked.

Darcy backed out of the room.

"What's the matter with you, Henry, making a scene like that in front of my guest?" Delilah paused. "Jealous, that's what. You're jealous."

Henry handed a glass of wine to Victoria, who thanked him.

"Goddamned banty cock. Nothing to be jealous about."

"By the way," said Delilah, "I'm expecting a Mr. Jericho."

"Jericho?"

"Some name like that. He's bringing me a rooster."

At which point, Lee entered. "A Mr. Rivers to see you, ma'am."

Victoria sat up straight and set her wineglass down.

"Show him in, please, Lee. And I want to talk to you later."

"Yes, ma'am."

Jordan Rivers, usually nattily dressed in pressed chinos and crisp shirt, straggled in, his shirt partly unbuttoned, and his chinos exuding a strong barnyard smell. He dragged a swollen burlap feed bag behind him and the contents of the bag squirmed, squawked, and flapped.

"How do you do?" said Delilah, extending her hand. Jordan apparently didn't see her hand and Delilah returned it to her lap.

Victoria rose to her feet. "Jordan, you didn't . . . ?"

Jordan pushed his glasses back on his nose and smoothed his hair into place. "I didn't expect to see you here, Mrs. Trumbull."

Delilah, too, rose to her feet. "How lovely. You two know each other." She eyed the burlap bag. "Is that my rooster?"

"Who's *this* guy?" demanded Henry.

"Jordan Rivers," said Victoria.

"Would you care to stay for lunch, Mr. Rivers?" Delilah asked. "We're having Lee's special chicken salad. She can set another place."

"Thanks, I would," said Jordan. "Where would you like me to put him?"

"Take him the hell outta here," said Henry, waving an arm.

Jordan looked from Henry to Delilah and back.

"Give Jordan a drink, darling. He looks as though he needs one."

"Just water," said Jordan.

Henry smacked his forehead with the palm of his hand, then poured a glass of wine and handed it to Jordan, who set it aside. "Perhaps someone will tell me what's going on?"

"Is that Chickee?" asked Victoria.

"What?" said Henry.

"Let's see him," said Delilah. "Open the bag, right now."

"Okay," said Jordan. He untied the knot that held Chickee captive and stepped back.

An angry rooster made his way out of the bag, looked around, ruffled his disarranged feathers, scratched himself, lifted his head with its angry red comb, and crowed.

CHAPTER 24

Darcy parked Delilah's red Jeep under Victoria's maple tree early the next morning and strolled through the bright new grass. Cobwebs, sparkling with last night's dew, were miniature sheets spread out to dry.

Victoria greeted him at the kitchen door. "I've never seen that car before. Is it new?"

"I have the use of it while I'm at Delilah's. I'm flying to Boston today and won't be back until later this afternoon. I'm on my way to the airport now."

"Have you had breakfast? What time is your flight?"

Darcy grinned. "The flight's whenever I schedule it. I'm returning the church's plane. Are you offering me breakfast?"

"I am. Come in." Victoria set out bacon and eggs, cereal and milk. "I didn't know you were a pilot."

"Multiple talents," said Darcy. "I stopped by," he said, once they were seated, "because the goats arrive today. Delilah would like your company."

"When are they due?"

"Sometime this afternoon."

"I'll talk to Lee while I'm there, find out what I can about her relationship with Henry."

"I suggested to Delilah that she show you the new goat pen Lambert Willoughby built. She's sending Lee to pick you up. You can tell her you'd like to rest in the conservatory for a few minutes because you're feeling faint or tired . . ." He stopped when he saw Victoria's expression. "You can fake it. Lee will want to make sure you're okay and will probably stay with you. If not, you can ask her to. Something like that."

Victoria lifted her crisp bacon and bit the end off. "I suppose I can do that."

"It's important to know what Lee and Henry are up to," Darcy said. "Also, whatever you can find out about Lee's background, without being too obvious. Where she's from, how come she's working here. Delilah was upset about a call Lee got yesterday. What was that call about?"

"I wonder if she knew Tillie?"

Darcy looked up from his eggs. "What?"

"Lee might have known her. Tillie was Lambert Willoughby's sister."

"He's the guy who built the goat pen."

"He works for the town and owns, or owned, the rooster Jordan Rivers kidnapped."

Darcy had just forked a mouthful of eggs into his mouth, and burst into laughter, sputtering egg onto the tablecloth. "Sorry," he said between guffaws.

Lee picked Victoria up in her own car, the one held together with duct tape, and Victoria sat beside her in the passenger seat.

"Sorry it's such a mess," said Lee, picking up a lone takeout coffee cup.

Victoria, accustomed to her granddaughter's car, dismissed the mess. Lee concentrated on her driving and they were at Brandy Brow before Victoria spoke.

"Quite exciting about the chickens and fainting goats, isn't it?"

"Yes, ma'am."

"Do you have any animals yourself, Lee?"

"My mother has a cat, ma'am."

"I have a cat named McCavity," said Victoria. "Have you had other animals at some time?"

"Yes, ma'am. I had a horse named Marblehead."

It was warm in the car, and Victoria unzipped her sweater. "My husband Jonathan was in the cavalry in the world war and had a horse named Hammerhead. I guess his horse and yours shared common traits."

Lee warmed slightly. "Stubborn. Like a mule," and she turned to Victoria and smiled.

"Did you grow up on the Island?"

"Yes, ma'am. Right here in West Tisbury."

Victoria frowned. "I don't recall seeing you. What's your last name?"

"Miller, ma'am. Lee Kauai Miller."

"From Deep Bottom? The horse farm?"

"Yes, ma'am. My family didn't mix much. My mother came from off Island. Hawaii. And I went to school off Island."

"Deep Bottom is so far from town, it must have been difficult to make friends."

"Not really, ma'am. Kids used to come to our place all the time to ride. I had lots of friends."

"Do you still see them?"

"Not much anymore." Lee looked away. "My best friend was Tillie Willoughby. But we all thought she ran off with that man from Edgartown. Then it turned out . . ." she stopped.

"I can imagine how terrible you must feel. How did you end up working for Miss Sampson?"

"When Tillie disappeared, I was disgusted with her. Now I feel so guilty. At the time, I thought she'd run off with this married man who was about twenty years older. His kids are older than me." Lee shivered. "I figured he was her ticket to get off the Island."

"We Islanders need to see the rest of the world before we settle down," Victoria said, sympathetically.

Lee nodded. "But when I leave, Mrs. Trumbull, I intend to pay my own way. The employment agency sent me to Miss Sampson's on a trial basis and after a couple of weeks, she asked me to stay full-time."

"That's quite a compliment to you. I can imagine that she might be difficult to work for."

Lee shrugged. "She has good days and bad. Mostly she's okay."

They turned into the road that led to Delilah's, and Lee was quiet until they pulled up in front of the house.

"Miss Sampson told me to take the limousine to fetch you, but I'd be scared to scratch it or something. Darcy treats it like a baby."

"Your car is just fine."

"Actually, Mrs. Trumbull, it's Tillie's car. I always feel a little funny driving it, you know? Her brother lets me use it because we were friends." Lee helped Victoria out and went up the stairs with her.

Delilah met her at the front door. "I'm so happy you're here, Mrs. Trumbull. The goats should arrive any time now."

"Would you mind if I rested a bit first, Delilah? May I sit in the conservatory?"

Delilah looked concerned. "Certainly, Mrs. Trumbull. I'll take you there, then when Lee reparks her car, she can stay with you."

Victoria settled herself on the soft couch and waited. She felt much too warm and she felt left out of the action involving the arrival of the goats. She wore her usual gray corduroy trousers and the heavy wool sweater Fiona's parents had given her. In a short time, she heard Lee's quick footsteps and assumed a weary attitude.

"Are you okay, Mrs. Trumbull? Can I help you in any way?"

"I'm fine," said Victoria. "I'd just like someone to sit with me for a few minutes, that's all."

"Certainly, ma'am. Shall I get you a glass of water?"

Victoria was about to say yes, when she thought about the limited time she had to quiz Lee. "I'd rather not have you leave."

"Yes, ma'am."

"When I was here yesterday," Victoria began, "Miss Sampson seemed upset about your taking a half day off."

"She's mostly pretty fair, but she doesn't like the staff getting personal calls on her phone. I never give anyone her number, but someone called me on her phone and she went into orbit."

"One call doesn't seem unreasonable."

Lee smiled. "I had the most amazing experience."

"Oh?"

"Reverend True asked me to audition for a part on one of his television shows. My mom watches Miss Sampson's show all the time. He asked me not to say anything about it to his wife."

"Why not?"

"I guess he thought she'd be jealous."

"Go on."

"The call I got was from a man from the TV station. That was the call that got Miss Sampson all bent out of shape."

"Did she know who was calling and what he was calling about?"

Lee shook her head. "No way. I called him back on my cell phone, and after I got off work, they did a test film of me."

"Here on the Island?"

"In the lobby of the Harbor Motel. People

came in and out and stared at me like I was a celebrity. It was fun, actually. I wasn't nervous at all."

"How exciting. Was it an interview?"

"Sort of. It was really exciting when they asked me to come back yesterday morning for a further audition. That's why I wanted the morning off, and I didn't want to tell Miss Sampson why. They said I was a natural. That the camera liked me."

"What sort of show might you be in?"

"Reverend True has several shows besides the one Miss Sampson stars in. Hers is an inspirational, religious show, and I told him that wasn't my thing."

"Your mother must be pleased."

"He asked me not to tell her, didn't want to get her hopes up, I guess. She's pretty protective of me."

Victoria eased herself out of the sofa, and immediately Lee got up to help.

"Thank you, Lee. I'm rested. Do you suppose the goats have arrived yet?"

Lee walked beside her for a few steps. "I enjoyed talking to you, ma'am."

"Perhaps I'll get to see you on film."

Lee blushed. "You're sure you're okay now, Mrs. Trumbull?" She hurried ahead of Victoria, looking back occasionally, down the long hallway past the portraits and doors that led to rooms on either side. She opened the great front door and Victoria marched briskly out onto the high wraparound porch. From there, she had a panoramic view of the long driveway and Vineyard Sound to her left.

"Can you see the goat van?" asked Lee.

Victoria shaded her eyes. "Not yet."

CHAPTER 25

"Isn't this exciting, Mrs. Trumbull?" Delilah joined Victoria at the top of the steps. She was wearing a bluish green down jacket that matched her eyes. "The driver of the van called from Vineyard Haven to get directions. I'll have the first fainting goats on Martha's Vineyard!"

"I look forward to meeting them," said Victoria. "How many will you have?"

"Six. A buck and five nannies. Would you like to see my goat yard?"

"Yes, indeed."

Victoria zipped up her sweater against the cool air and Delilah led the way down the marble stairs with the ornate pineapple balusters. At the foot of the steps they turned right past the guesthouse and the garage, to a large grassy area enclosed with a green chain-link fence and shaded by still bare oak trees. Delilah opened a gate, and they went through into the fenced-in area.

There was a small barn off to one side.

Delilah swept her arms in an arc that took in the barn and the enclosure. "Lambert Willoughby built all this. Shall we go into the barn?" She added in a whisper, "Henry has no idea this is the start of my farm. I told him the chickens and goats are my pets."

Victoria followed her up a ramp that led into the light airy building. She stopped to breathe in the scent of new wood and hay before looking around. Inside were six stalls, each with a chest-high door and a shiny brass nameplate.

"Do you like it?" asked Delilah.

"Wonderful," Victoria said. "I gather you haven't named the goats yet."

"Not yet. I want to get to know them first." She stopped with a squeal of delight. "Here he is now. You know Lambert, of course?"

"Not well," said Victoria.

A huge man came out of one of the stalls, shoving a pencil behind one ear and holding a clipboard in his free hand. He was taller than Victoria, and not fat, exactly, but what she'd call hefty.

"Do you know Mrs. Trumbull, Lambert?"

"Sure. Everyone does. How you doing?" He offered a meaty hand and Victoria shook it, feeling fragile, although his handshake was gentle.

The front of his cutoff T-shirt depicted an eagle that seemed incongruously to be wearing a helmet. The bird held a pistol in one upraised talon. The other talon stood on what looked like a machine gun. An American flag waved in the background.

"You've built a lovely barn," Victoria said.

"Thanks. You seen the stalls?"

"I showed them to Mrs. Trumbull," said Delilah.

"They seem comfortable," said Victoria.

"Goats are sociable. The chickens pretty much wander around. I'll show you where they'll stay when they're laying. 'Course, that's not for a while."

Victoria and Delilah followed him to the corner of the barn where a dozen boxes were stacked. Each was about twice the size of a shoe box and was filled with sweet-smelling hay. A burlap curtain was pulled to one side.

"How cozy," said Victoria.

"Chickens like to be warm." Willoughby lowered the curtain.

"If you'll excuse me, I'll watch for the goat van," said Delilah, and tripped over to the barn door, leaving Victoria and Willoughby to tour the rest of the goats' accommodations.

"Tillie was your sister, wasn't she?" said Victoria softly. "I'm so sorry about her death."

Willoughby wiped his arm across his mouth. "Five months, and we never knew she was right there all the time."

"And what a terrible shock to lose your mother-in-law, too."

"Yeah, well."

"You work in Town Hall, don't you?"

"Mostly out on the road, but, yeah. Have an office right below where . . ." He paused. "When I get my hands on the bastard who did that to Tillie — excuse me, ma'am . . ."

"Understandable," said Victoria. "Were you close to your sister?"

"She was a wild one, but yeah. She had a room at our place where she stayed at."

"Have the police talked to you?"

He lifted his T-shirt absently and scratched his belly. The muscles in his upper arms writhed and Victoria became aware of the faded tattoos of boa constrictors that covered his arms from shoulder to elbow. "Yeah. Sergeant Smalley was at my place." He looked down at his feet and kicked at a wisp of hay. "What can he do? It's been five months, for God's sake. Thought she'd run off with that guy, and all the time . . ."

"We'll find whoever killed her," Victoria said with assurance.

Willoughby looked up from his dusty boots and actually smiled. "Understand you're a cop yourself."

"A police deputy," said Victoria, smoothing her hair.

"I'll show you where the baby chicks are now," Willoughby said, changing the subject. "She," he jerked his head at Delilah, who stood at the barn door, a hand shading her forehead, "she got these poor little chicks, day-old chicks. They was dyed Easter-egg colors. Illegal. Like it should be."

"The color will grow out, won't it?"

"When they get their feathers. I don't know what goes on in her mind. 'Cute.' 'Darling.' The poor goddamned animals don't want to be cute. I put them in here." He showed Victoria a large pen lined with hay with a heat lamp suspended at a safe height over it. The two dozen colorful chickens, looking much like Easter eggs, huddled under the lamp.

Lambert shook his head. "How would you like to be a day-old chick doused in a vat of dye? A wonder any of 'em survive."

"Do you raise chickens?"

"Did. But it's work. She," another jerk of

his head, "doesn't know what work is." He sighed. "Not my place to tell her. Up until yesterday my kids had a pet rooster. The neighbor's Jack Russell got into the pen and tore him up."

"Who's your neighbor?" asked Victoria, afraid he meant Jordan.

"That slick weasel Oliver Ashpine."

Victoria nodded agreement. "I've had some dealings with Mr. Ashpine. A difficult man." She thought about the rooster Jordan Rivers had delivered to Delilah yesterday. Clearly, he had kidnapped the Willoughbys' rooster.

"Did you see the dog?" she asked.

"The dog had bust the pen open and was lying there, chewing on a gizzard."

"Really?" asked Victoria, appalled. "Feathers?"

He shrugged. "Everywhere."

Delilah called out from the barn door, "Here they come now!"

A horse carrier pulled in through the enclosure's open gate and stopped next to the barn. A boy, who must have been about ten, slid out of the passenger side, ran to the gate, and started to shut it, but at that moment, a full-grown rooster strutted in through the gate, pecking at some morsel that appealed to him. He lifted his magnificent head and crowed.

Willoughby started. "Goddamn!" He left the baby chicks' pen and strode past Delilah, who was watching the driver of the horse carrier, a brawny man with auburn hair and a huge auburn mustache. He was in the driver's seat, filling out paperwork.

Victoria looked around for a place to sit, and found an overturned galvanized bucket. She eased herself onto it.

The rooster spread his wings, lifted his head, and crowed again.

"Goddamn," said Willoughby again. "If that ain't Chickee I'll eat my hat! How'd he get here?"

The horse van had pulled all the way into the yard, and the boy closed the gate. The driver looked down at Delilah with liquid brown eyes. "Where would you like us to leave your goats, ma'am?"

"How'd Chickee get here?" demanded Willoughby.

"Lambert," said Delilah to Willoughby, "where shall we unload the goats?"

The driver got out of the van, adjusted his skintight jeans, and strode toward Delilah, who watched with fascination the movement of the muscles of his thighs. He wore a thick leather belt with a brass buckle that looked like the brand of a significant ranch out west someplace. And cowboy boots, of course, dusty, with high heels worn down from rough riding on the range. He grinned at Delilah, showing large white teeth beneath his mustache.

Delilah gasped and clutched her hands together.

"Where'd you find Chickee, Miz Sampson?" asked Willoughby.

Delilah didn't hear.

Victoria thought quickly and rocked forward on her bucket seat. "I believe Jordan Rivers rescued your rooster."

"Rivers . . . ?" said Willoughby. "Rivers?"

The driver's voice was like velvet and steel and mahogany and silk. "Didn't know if you had the right kind of feed, ma'am, so I brought along some alfalfa hay and a salt block."

"Oh, thank you so much," Delilah chirped.

"From that mutt?" asked Willoughby. "Rivers rescued my Chickee from that mutt?"

"It looks that way, doesn't it?" said Victoria, avoiding his eyes.

"You want me to unload the goats for you, ma'am?"

"Would you! That would be so kind!" Delilah said, oblivious of the other conversation.

"Roy!" called out the driver.

"Sir!" said the boy, coming to attention.

"Sounds like I owe Rivers an apology," said Willoughby.

The driver said, in his soft voice, "Lower the ramp. No noise, you hear? Gentle, now."

"Yes, sir."

Six little black and white goats trotted down the lowered ramp, one after the other. They were about two feet tall with bulging eyes and big floppy ears.

Delilah clapped her hands together and shrieked, "Darling! How darling!"

And the six little goats toppled over, one after another, their legs straight up in the air.

"Oooooh!" cried Delilah, clasping her hands under her chin.

Willoughby scratched his head. "Where'd the dog get that gizzard?"

CHAPTER 26

After several seconds, the goats got to their feet and began to explore their new pen. Victoria, too, started to struggle to her own feet from her low bucket seat. She'd left her lilac wood stick at home and her heavy sweater weighed her down. Willoughby and the driver immediately rushed to her aid and helped her up.

"Thank you." Victoria straightened her sweater.

"A pleasure, ma'am." The driver returned to his van and brought out a clipboard that he presented to Delilah. "Sign here, please, ma'am."

Delilah looked from his boots to the worn places on his jeans where he'd kept something in his pocket, to his plaid shirt, open at the neck, exposing a white T-shirt and gold chain, and finally to that sensitive, cruel mouth with its crooked smile. Delilah swallowed and glanced up. "Do you plan to stay overnight on the Island?" she asked.

"Yes, ma'am. We need to get back to town to book a motel room for tonight."

"I owe that boy an apology, Miz Trumbull," said Willoughby. "Jordan Rivers, hey? I never would've expected Rivers to save my kids' rooster. From a mad dog like that."

"You never can tell about people," said Victoria.

Delilah took a deep breath that expanded her chest. "You're more than welcome to stay here. In my guesthouse, of course." Pause. "Both of you."

"Don't want to trouble you, ma'am." The driver lifted his cap with a knuckle.

"Oh, please!" Delilah clasped her hands under her chin. "You can help my little goats settle in."

The driver looked at the boy, who shrugged.

"Well, thank you, ma'am."

"And what are your names?"

"He's my son, Roy," the driver said, indicating the boy. "I'm Giles. We'll make sure your goats are settled in before we leave here tomorrow morning."

"And I'll make sure your room is made up." Delilah bustled away toward the guesthouse where Henry had been banished for the past few nights.

269

Lambert said, "Miz Trumbull, I want to tell that boy Rivers how sorry I am I misjudged him."

Victoria thought about Jordan's new role as hero. "He would appreciate that, I'm sure." She'd better warn Jordan. "Shall I go with you? I can hold Chickee."

"I'd appreciate that, Miz Trumbull."

Victoria looked around, but Delilah was already at the door of the guesthouse.

In a short time Henry emerged carrying a half-open gym bag with a shirtsleeve waving out of it. Delilah followed. Victoria heard Henry say, "You warned him about the snapping turtles, I trust?"

"I can bring you home, Miz Trumbull," said Lambert.

"Thank you."

Victoria settled herself in the passenger seat of Willoughby's battered red pickup, clearly identified as his because of the mismatched blue right front fender. She waited for him to capture the rooster.

Willoughby finally cornered Chickee in the goat pen. He gathered the rooster up tenderly, holding Chickee's feet with one hand, wings with the other. He elbowed a new-looking towel off a hook just inside the barn door, caught it with his teeth, wrapped it around Chickee somehow, carried the now docile rooster over to his truck, and handed the towel-wrapped rooster to Victoria.

"He won't hurt you, Miz Trumbull."

The rooster lifted his head and tilted it to stare at Victoria with first one beady eye, then the other. Victoria smoothed the ruffled feathers on his head and neck.

"See? He likes you." The truck started up with a rattle.

Delilah and Henry, partway up the marble stairs, deep in conversation, had their backs to Lambert's truck and didn't appear to notice.

Giles and young Roy unloaded bales of hay from the van, and the tiny goats nuzzled the boy and the hay.

When it seemed possible that the truck might get them as far as Simon Look Road, where Oliver Ashpine, Lambert Willoughby, and Jordan Rivers lived, Victoria asked, "Does Chickee have a new coop?"

Lambert slapped the lamb's wool cover of the steering wheel. "That goddamned mutt — excuse me, ma'am. Tore the old one all to pieces."

Victoria nodded. Jordan had asked her about predators breaking into chicken coops.

"Will it take you long to build another?"

"I can get enough of it done in an hour. I reckon I'll put the new one on the other side of my property. Ashpine's side." Willoughby thumped the wheel again. "That'll show him."

"I'll be glad to watch Chickee while you work on the new pen," said Victoria.

"Chicken sit?" Willoughby glanced at Victoria with a sly grin.

"Certainly." Victoria continued to stroke the rooster's head. Chickee extended his neck and made a kind of gurgling sound.

"Well, if you don't mind, Miz Trumbull. He'd like that."

Willoughby turned off Old County Road onto Simon Look. The truck rattled over the washboard surface and finally stopped at one of three houses in a sort of rough cul-de-sac. The yard was cluttered with an assortment of old cars and plastic toys that had weathered from red, yellow, and blue to sickly shades of pink, beige, and gray. Victoria looked beyond the broken cars and toys to the house.

"Good heavens!" she exclaimed.

The house was nowhere near the size of Delilah's, but it was every bit as big as Victoria's huge rambling old farmhouse. Except Willoughby's house was brand new.

"Built it myself," said Willoughby, proudly.

Where had he come up with the money for this three-story edifice with its tall brick chimneys, slate roof, and shiny copper gutters? A greenhouse extended off to one side. Victoria could see an indoor swimming pool beyond with stained-glass windows along one side. It occurred to her that she might look at Willoughby's property card. Had the assessors assessed this grand house? And for how much?

"What d'ya think?" said Willoughby.

"Astonishing." Victoria stopped patting Chickee, who twisted his head around and pecked her hand.

"Wants you to keep doing that," said Willoughby. "Well, I better go on over to Rivers's place. Apologize. Take my medicine."

"May I come along?"

"Glad to have you."

Victoria tucked the bundled-up rooster, who was making cooing noises, under one arm and she and Willoughby dodged between the old cars and broken toys.

Willoughby stopped at the corner of his property. "Scene of the crime. Look at that, will you."

Whatever the coop had been, it was now only a pile of chewed-up sticks and twisted chicken wire. The ground was splotched with what looked like blood. Stray feathers wafted up as they stood there, circled and settled again. Willoughby picked one up.

"Looks like a duck feather," he said. "The kind you find in pillows." He rubbed the feather between his fingers.

"Is that where Jordan Rivers lives?" Victoria asked, pointing across the dirt road to a modest Cape with a solar panel on its roof.

"That's his car, but I don't see his bicycle. Got one of those kinds where you sit down like a Barcalounger." He turned and started down the road to his place. "I'll get going on that coop, long as he's not here and you don't mind holding Chickee."

They'd only gone a few steps when Jordan returned, bicycle helmet sparkling in the patches of sunlight that filtered through the oak trees, his dark glasses reflecting Willoughby, Victoria, and Chickee.

Jordan's face paled as he stared at the rooster. His jaw dropped. His feet slipped off the pedals. The bicycle tilted and he stuck out one foot to keep it from falling over.

"What . . . ? Who . . . ?"

On the way from Delilah's Victoria had practiced what she would say.

She gave Jordan a broad, false smile and

winked her right eye. "Jordan, Mr. Willoughby is thrilled that you saved Chickee from that dog next door, isn't that right, Lambert?"

Jordan stared at Willoughby.

Willoughby held out his hand. "I'm man enough to say I was wrong about you, boy."

Jordan slipped his fingerless doeskin glove off his right hand. "But . . ."

Victoria said quickly, "That was clever of you to take Chickee over to Delilah's where you knew he'd be safe."

"I apologize," said Willoughby. "Come have a beer with me while I build a new pen."

"New pen . . . ?"

Willoughby grunted out what passed for a laugh. "Ashhole's turn." He nudged Jordan with an elbow. "Get it? Ashhole! I owe you this one. I'm putting the new pen next to his house. That mutt's not gonna break down this pen."

Jordan looked from Victoria to Willoughby and back again. He swallowed. "A beer? I don't suppose you have a Sam Adams?"

"Bud Lite," said Willoughby. "Better get used to it. You're coming over more often. I don't usually misjudge people like I did you." He slapped Jordan on the back. "Good man."

"I've got to put my bicycle away."

"I'm starting on that new coop," said Willoughby. "Can't keep Miz Trumbull holding the bag, so to speak." He disappeared around the corner of the house.

"What's going on?" said a dazed Jordan.

"As they say, go with the flow," said Victoria. Chickee made another cooing sound. Victoria patted his head. Willoughby reappeared with three cans of Bud.

He held one out to Victoria. "Miz Trumbull?"

"Later, thanks," she said.

"You can set him down. Done up in the towel like that he can't move." Willoughby headed toward the back of the house again. "C'mon, Rivers, old buddy."

"I'll be with you in a minute," said Jordan.

"While you're building the new pen, I'll pick up the mess the *dog* made." Victoria scowled at Jordan. She'd seen a rake leaning against a scrub oak.

Willoughby stopped. "No, ma'am. Don't you touch that. I wouldn't let a lady clean that mess up. No way. My grandmother, may she rest in peace, she'd be about your age now. I wouldn't let her lift a hand. Us young folk can take care of the heavy work, right, Rivers?" Jordan hadn't made his escape yet. Willoughby slapped him on the back again. "Your job is to take care of Chickee, Miz Trumbull."

Chapter 27

Victoria felt her face flush. Old lady, indeed. Willoughby's voice echoed in her mind: Leave the heavy work for us young folks. She set Chickee, still wrapped in his towel, under the beach plum bush. She waited for Willoughby to disappear around a corner of the house, and immediately started to disentangle the rake from a honeysuckle vine that had grown around it.

Chickee's coop had been small, too small, Victoria thought. No wonder he'd crowed all the time. The coop had been about the size of the coffee table in her parlor and about the same shape. Clearing up the wreckage would be a simple task.

She puzzled over the ends of the broken wood frame, which seemed to have the sort of marks a hammer or a crowbar might make. She thought about that as she worked.

Jordan, still holding the handlebars of his

bicycle, cleared his throat. "Mrs. Trumbull?"

Victoria lifted her head regally and looked down her nose at Jordan. He seemed very young and very slim in his snug-fitting black and green bicycle suit. But he was old enough to know better. No matter how difficult Lambert Willoughby was, and she agreed he was difficult, Jordan had no business leading him to believe his pet had been mauled by a dog.

Victoria pulled a black plastic garbage bag from another beach plum bush where the wind had blown it.

"I didn't want to hurt the rooster, Mrs. Trumbull. I thought I was giving it a good home."

She wrenched off a two-foot section of chicken wire mesh from the chewed up boards it had been stapled to and worked it into the plastic bag, careful not to snag her hands on the rusty ends. "Why don't you put your bicycle away and join Lambert in that beer he's offered you? He believes you saved Chickee."

"If it weren't for you, Mrs. Trumbull . . ." Jordan looked down at the ground. He unsnapped his bicycle helmet. "I don't seem to be able to do anything right."

"Chickee's new coop will be as far away

from you as is possible, so you've won. Accept it graciously."

"I can give you a ride home, Mrs. Trumbull. When you're through, that is."

"Thank you," said Victoria. "This shouldn't take me more than a half hour."

Jordan wheeled his bicycle across the dirt road to his place. From the far side of the Willoughbys' property, Victoria heard sawing and hammering.

She separated out the rest of the chicken wire from the frame, set the plastic bag of chicken wire off to one side, and made a pile of the burnable wood.

Jordan, in pressed jeans and a collared knit shirt with something embroidered on the pocket, hurried past her, waving as he did.

In a half hour Victoria had cleaned up the worst of the mess, and began to rake the ground where Chickee's pen had been.

She had been raking for only a few minutes when she heard a frenzied yapping, and a medium-sized white dog with brown markings over one eye rushed over to her from the direction of Oliver Ashpine's house. Victoria braced herself and held the rake at the ready. The dog was trailing a leash that was attached to his collar. The trailing end was obviously chewed through and was slimy wet. He skidded to a stop in front of Victoria, stumpy tail wagging.

Victoria had expected him to jump up on her. When he held up a paw, she took it, and patted his solid flank. "Hello, pup." The dog wriggled.

From under the beach plum bush, Chickee made a clucking sound. The dog paid no attention.

"Do you see that rooster, pup?"

The dog cocked his head to one side, tongue out.

She studied the dog. "You didn't tear up the chicken coop, did you." A statement, not a question.

The dog barked once.

"I saw tool marks, not tooth marks."

The dog crouched in front of her, rear end in the air, tail wagging.

"Let me untie that leash." Victoria leaned the rake against a tree and the dog stood patiently until he was free, then danced around her in circles.

Chickee clucked. The dog continued to ignore him. Victoria took up the rake again and raked the sandy soil from the edges of the area toward a depression in the middle. The dog raced back and forth in front of her.

"Don't get in my way, pup."

The dog bounded over to the pile of dirt

Victoria had raked to the middle and started to dig.

She decided to let him dig. A good time to rest. The dog pawed at the loose dirt, tossing it behind him in a rooster tail spray. He barked and occasionally looked behind him at Victoria as though he wanted to make sure she was still watching. She leaned on her rake and laughed. "A mouse! Find a mouse!" she called out, and the dog dug faster.

In the background she was vaguely aware of the sound of hammering. Chickee flopped around, unwrapping his towel as he did.

The dog stopped digging, pawed and sniffed at something he'd unearthed, and looked back at Victoria.

She leaned down to look. "What did you find, pup?"

What he'd found was a thin metal box about the size of a paperback book. A Christmas candy tin. Victoria bent over and tugged it away from the dog, who stood expectantly.

Victoria took a folded paper towel out of her pocket and wiped off the tin. The box had only a slight touch of rust. It couldn't have been in the ground more than a few months because no roots had grown around it. The Santa Claus on the lid grinned merrily.

She suddenly realized that the steady hammering, which had gone on for the past hour, had stopped.

She worked at the tight-fitting lid. It was probably rusted on. It took awhile, some prying with a nail she found, but she finally opened the lid. Inside, wrapped in bubble plastic, were a disk and an envelope. She couldn't read the label on the disk.

Willoughby's voice sounded from around the corner. "Another Bud, Rivers old buddy?"

By now, Chickee had worked his feet loose. He hopped toward the voice, trailing his towel behind him.

"Thanks, Lambert old boy, old pal," said Jordan. "Another time. I promised to take Mrs. Trumbull home."

Victoria quickly tucked the disk back into the slim tin and slipped it into the front of her gray corduroy trousers. She pulled her heavy sweater over it and looked down. Her stomach looked flatter than usual, but then Willoughby was not likely to examine a little old lady too closely. She would give the disk to Howland Atherton who could figure out what was on it.

Jordan appeared around the corner accompanied by Willoughby, who was wiping his hands on his jeans.

The dog barked. Victoria quickly raked dirt to the middle to cover the indentation where the tin had been.

Willoughby stopped and stared at the dog. "What the hell . . . ?"

"I believe it's Mr. Ashpine's dog," said Victoria.

"Bertie. Damn right it's Ashpine's. How'd he get loose?" He turned to Victoria. "You didn't clean all that mess up by yourself, did you?"

"It was no trouble," said Victoria.

"I hope you didn't spend too much time on it, I mean, digging?"

"Nothing like that," said Victoria.

Lambert looked around. "Wonder when Ashpine is due back from the hospital?"

Victoria smoothed the front of her sweater where the flat rectangle showed. "The dog was trailing a leash, which he apparently chewed through."

"He attacked . . ." Willoughby was interrupted by Chickee, who, freed of the towel, lifted his wings, threw his head back, and crowed.

At the hospital, a male technician with curly dark hair that surrounded his bald head like a tonsure handed Doc Jeffers the report on the contents of Oliver Ashpine's stomach. Doc Jeffers thumbed through the report while he stood next to Oliver Ashpine's bed. The technician waited.

Oliver groaned.

Doc Jeffers patted Ashpine's arm absently while he read. "Small, globular, nearly black berries." He looked over his glasses at the technician, who shrugged. Doc Jeffers continued. "Berries, along with stems and leaves, were apparently crushed to produce juice used in making the jellied candy. Some berries left intact."

"Fortunately," said the technician. "Only way we could tell what the candy was made from."

"And the berries . . . ?" asked Doc Jeffers.

The technician stood up straight and took a deep breath. "Elderberries, sir."

Doc Jeffers stared at him.

"Elderberries," the technician repeated.

"My grandmother drank elderberry wine. Lived to a hundred and two."

"Mine, too," said the tech, "only she died at eighty-six. Wine, jam, and jelly. Pies. She made elderberry ice cream a few times."

"As kids, we'd strip elderberries off the stems and eat 'em."

"Me, too," said the tech.

"You've ruled out everything else?"

"Yep."

"What was in the candy other than elder-berries?"

"Sugar, pectin, vinegar, butter. That's it. Mostly strained ground-up elderberries, stems, leaves, and bark."

Ashpine moaned again. "I'm going to be sick."

"You are sick," said Doc Jeffers, and turned back to the tech.

"I looked up elderberries on the Internet, Doc. It's a familiar berry, all right, and considered edible, but several years ago eight people in California got sick from drinking elderberry juice."

Doc Jeffers looked at the tech over his glasses.

"The eight were helicoptered to a hospital in Monterey," the tech continued. "Acute gastrointestinal and neurologic symptoms."

Doc Jeffers looked down at Oliver's pale face.

"Nausea and vomiting, abdominal cramps, weakness. Dizziness and numbness," said the tech. "The elderberry juice was served at a church picnic."

"My advice is to avoid those damned church picnics," said Doc Jeffers. "Who the hell made the candy, and did they know what they were doing?"

"Mrs. Danvers," gasped Ashpine. "She's killed me."

"You'll be fit as a fiddle by tomorrow morning," said Doc Jeffers. "Get some sleep."

"I want a guard by my door!"

"You're watching too much television," said Doc Jeffers. "Want me to give you something to help you sleep?"

CHAPTER 28

"I want to make sure Giles and little Roy are comfortable," said Delilah. "Lee, darling, Henry is moving out of the guesthouse to make room for them. Help him get settled in the upstairs guest room," and she breezed back toward the pen where the driver and his son were watering the goats.

Lee went up to the second floor. As she passed Delilah's bedroom she saw Henry folding a shirt. How was the screen test? Had she qualified? The palms of her hands were damp and she wiped them on her black trousers.

Henry finished folding his shirt and emptied the contents of his bag onto Delilah's heart-shaped bed.

"Reverend True, sir?" Lee began.

Henry looked over his shoulder. "Why, hello, Lee."

"Can I help put your things in the guest room, sir?"

Henry smiled. "Thank you. Put them in the right-hand dresser drawers in here. Miss Sampson's room."

"Miss Sampson asked that I help you move into the guest room, sir."

"This is where I'll be, thank you. Put my things in the right side of the dresser."

"Miss Sampson usually keeps her lingerie there . . ."

"If Miss Sampson's clothing is in there, move it out." He waved his arm in the direction of the bed.

"Yes, sir."

Henry seated himself at Delilah's dainty dressing table, white with ornate pink and gold roses. He leaned back in his chair and watched Lee fold the clothing he'd taken out of the guesthouse.

"Been checking out your video," he began.

Lee stopped folding and looked at him.

"Nothing definite to offer you, as yet, but things are looking good."

"Thank you, sir."

"We'll need another screen test. You up for that?"

"Whenever you say, Reverend True."

Henry went to the door. "You're doing a fine job here at the house, Lee. Keep up the good work."

Lee flushed. "Thank you, sir." She picked

up a pair of undershorts and began to fold them.

Henry watched from the door. "I think you've got the makings of a fine actress, Lee," and he went out into the hall and closed the door behind him.

After he left, she walked slowly over to Delilah's closet, opened it, and selected a turquoise silk kimono. She put it on over her white blouse and black trousers and with one foot set carefully in front of the other, strolled over to the full-length mirror on the opposite wall. She turned first one way, then the other, belted the kimono, then unbelted it, lifted up her hair and dropped it again.

She didn't hear the door open.

"Just what do you think you're doing?" Delilah stalked into the room. "Take that off and get out."

Lee slid out of the silky garment and looked for a place to hang it.

"Drop it. Just drop it right there." Delilah pointed at the bed. "Go to your room. I'll see you first thing tomorrow morning. In the kitchen."

Victoria summoned Howland to her house to check out the DVD from the tin Bertie had unearthed under the defunct rooster coop. He was in the upstairs study, arms folded, and he was tapping his foot impatiently.

"It's going to take awhile for this ancient machine to boot up. How old is your computer, anyway?"

"Four years," Elizabeth said.

"No wonder. Let's have the disk."

"Will you be able to play it?" asked Victoria.

Howland shrugged. "If we're lucky." He took the DVD from her and examined the label. "Made by some company I've never heard of. TruArt Productions." He slipped the disk into the player. Elizabeth watched from behind him.

He clicked on various instructions that popped up on the computer screen. "Okay, so far."

While Howland was working with the computer, Victoria examined the envelope that had been in the tin along with the disk. It was addressed simply "Tillie," and had been opened. She unfolded the note that was inside.

"Who's it from, Gram?" asked Elizabeth.

"It's signed 'Lucy'."

"Lucy Pease? How weird, I mean, you guys found both bodies."

Howland looked up. "What's strange is to

find the note and DVD under a chicken coop."

"The note is to Tillie from Lucy. She's returning the DVD, thanks for letting her see it. 'You have a great future in films,' she says, and she compliments Tillie on her art." Victoria turned the note over. "Here's the explanation for the hiding place. She says she'll drop the DVD off at Town Hall, and tells Tillie to hide it when she gets home, where Lambert won't find it." Victoria looked up with a smile. "Her 'nosy son-in-law,' she says."

"I didn't realize Lucy was Lambert's mother-in-law," said Elizabeth.

"He's married to Lucy's daughter, Annie." Victoria continued to scan the note. "Lucy's sorry Tillie's family doesn't appreciate her acting passion. Tillie can always come to her, and so forth."

"Does she mention any names?" asked Howland.

"No names." Victoria put the note back in the envelope. "I had no idea Tillie and Lucy were so close."

Loud music suddenly blared out of the computer. Howland turned down the volume. "We've got something now."

After they'd seen the first two minutes, Victoria said, "That's enough," and Howland ejected the DVD.

Elizabeth muttered, "She calls that acting?"

On screen, Tillie had pranced around what looked like a motel room in bra, panties, and high-heeled opera pumps in time to music that Howland turned down still lower.

"That's embarrassing," said Elizabeth. "How could she possibly want anybody else to see that?"

Victoria sat back after Howland took the disk out of the computer. "I must say, she has a nice trim figure."

"Gram!" said Elizabeth. "Why do we need such stuff?"

"She saw it as art," said Victoria. "Apparently, Lucy did, too." She turned to Howland. "Can you find out anything about the company that produced it?"

"TruArt Films," Howland read from the disk. "I'll do what I can."

Selena dropped by the hospital that evening to visit Ocypete and Ellen. Hope was on duty at the desk in the Acute Care Unit filling out paperwork.

"Hi, Miss Moon," she greeted Selena. "Miss Meadows and Miss Rotch are in the room overlooking the garden. Pretty view. The daffodils are in bloom."

"I've been so worried. How are they?" asked Selena.

"They're fine, all three of them. They can go home tomorrow morning." She smiled reassuringly at Selena. "What do you have there?" She nodded at the white pasteboard box tied with thin purple ribbon that Selena held.

"Fruit candy I made for them. Organic. My own recipe." Selena's drawl was more noticeable than usual.

Hope, who'd known Selena forever, smiled. "Today's the first time any of them have felt like eating. They're fully recovered, so I'm sure they'll enjoy a homemade treat."

"Is it all right to go on in?"

"Sure," said Hope. "They'll be glad to have company."

Selena tiptoed down the short hall. "Knock, knock!" she said. "I've been so worried about you!"

"Can you believe it?" said Ocypete, who was sitting up in the bed nearest the door. "Three of us. It's a wonder you didn't succumb."

"Was it the flu, Petey?"

"Poison," said Ellen, who'd put aside the

book she'd been reading when Selena entered.

"Poison?" Selena's hand went to her throat. "What kind of poison?"

"They didn't say. Just that we'd all three eaten something that didn't agree with us."

"I don't really think it was *poison* poison," said Ocypete. "What do you have there, Selena?"

"I made some candy. Especially for you," said Selena. She held a hand up to her mouth to veil her next words. "I didn't make enough to share with, you know who."

"Quite right," said Ellen.

"My own recipe from berries I froze last summer."

Ocypete said, "A purple ribbon! I just love purple."

"I know you do." Selena slipped off the ribbon and opened the box.

Ocypete peered into it. "How pretty!" Translucent purple squares powdered with sugar nestled in little, white, pleated paper cups. "I adore fruit jellies. Were those your candies in Town Hall?"

"Yes," said Selena, blushing. She looked down at her feet. "I thought Mrs. Danvers and the girls upstairs might enjoy them."

"I ate more than my share," said Ocypete. "A piece from Mrs. Danvers's desk. Then a day or so later I saw the box on Oliver's desk, and I ate at least three more."

"I'm so glad you enjoyed it," said Selena.

Ellen spoke up from her side of the room. "Have a seat, Selena."

"Thank you. I mustn't stay too long. I don't want to tire you out."

"Nonsense," said Ellen. "We're completely recovered, right, Petey?" She reached for the box of fruit jellies and helped herself to a piece. "How about you, Selena?"

Selena giggled. "I'm not much for candy, I'm afraid."

"All the more for the rest of us," said Ellen. "How about you, Petey, candy?"

Ocypete looked over the choices and took one of the larger pieces. "We've recovered fully, but the hospital is keeping us overnight, just to be sure."

"I think that's only right, don't you?" said Selena. "I hear the food is good."

"Outstanding," said Ellen. "Yesterday, neither of us felt like eating, but the doctor said we can eat whatever we feel like today."

"And so today we are," said Ocypete.

"The food is nicely prepared, nicely seasoned, and hot," said Ellen.

"And what's not supposed to be hot is nice and cold," added Ocypete.

Selena stood up. "I really must go. Is there

anything I can get you girls?"

"No, thanks. We'll be home tomorrow."
Ellen looked over the side of her bed.

"Do you need something, Ellen?" asked
Selena.

"I found it. The control button." She
adjusted her bed to sit bolt upright. "I hate
to bring this up, girls. But when we get
home, we have a problem to deal with."

"Oliver," said Selena. "I was afraid of
that."

CHAPTER 29

Late that night, Ellen and Ocypete took turns throwing up in the bathroom that adjoined their room. Hope, still on duty, called Doc Jeffers. The message on his answering machine said he was spending the night on his boat, fishing, and to call the Coast Guard in an emergency — he gave the number — and they'd contact him on Channel 16.

Hope took care of her patients first, then went through the communications procedures to leave a message for Doc Jeffers. What kind of poison caused such a peculiar relapse, she wondered? Just as the three West Tisbury patients were about to be discharged, two of them had become sick again. Blood work was normal. The symptoms didn't seem like mushroom poisoning, which did have a delayed reaction. In that case, acute stomach pains usually went away before the test results were in, and a day or two later, the patient was dead. The hospital — and she, the nurse in charge — had to be careful. Had to be overly cautious.

Ellen and Ocypete must stay at least another twenty-four hours. Hope couldn't predict what Doc Jeffers would decide, but that was how she would handle this. She checked on the third West Tisbury victim, Oliver Ashpine. He seemed fine, no symptoms as yet. But she'd keep an eye on him.

The next morning, early, Delilah confronted Lee in the kitchen. "How dare you! Just what were you doing in my room?"

Lee clearly hadn't slept well. Her face was pale and her eyes were swollen. "I was putting away the Reverend True's clothing, ma'am."

"Which is where I found them last night. Didn't I tell you he was to go in the guest room?"

"Yes, ma'am."

"You didn't listen to me."

"Reverend True . . ." Lee paused. "Reverend True, he insisted his things go in your room, ma'am."

"The Reverend True doesn't pay your salary, *Miss* Lee, I do." Delilah pointed at her bosom. "He slept in the guest room last night. Without his things. And who gave you leave to dress in my clothing, the Reverend True?"

Lee hung her head.

"Did he? Did he tell you to go into my closet and pick out a silk kimono and parade in front of my mirror? Did he?"

Lee looked at the ground.

"Answer me!"

"No, ma'am."

Delilah pulled up a barstool to the granite island, sat, and put her elbows on the counter. Lee continued to stand. "What's come over you in the past few days? Up until then, your work was entirely satisfactory. I intended to give you a raise, and you'd only been with me five months."

Lee clasped her hands behind her back and continued to look at the floor.

"I insist on knowing what's going on, Lee."

Lee shook her head and choked out a sob.

"I can't believe a family problem would lead you to trespass in my closet and parade around in my clothing." Delilah waited. "Well?"

"I'm sorry, ma'am."

"If it weren't for five months of excellent work, I'd fire you on the spot, you understand?"

"Yes, ma'am."

"You give me an explanation now, this minute, or you can pack up your things and leave. Right now." Delilah stabbed a manicured finger at the granite countertop.

"Reverend True asked me not to tell you," Lee blurted.

"Oh, he did, did he? And what are you not supposed to tell me? And why?"

Lee extracted a damp handkerchief from her pocket and wiped her eyes. "He gave me a screen test."

Delilah's eyes opened wide. "Screen test?"

"Yes, ma'am."

"What did he give as a reason for not telling me?"

Lee choked back another sob. "He was afraid to hurt your feelings."

"Hurt my feelings? What are you talking about?"

"He was afraid you'd be . . . you'd be . . ."

"Jealous?" demanded Delilah.

Lee nodded miserably.

"Did he tell you what the screen test was for? Certainly not my show?"

Lee shook her head. "No, ma'am."

"Well," said Delilah. "Well." She thought a moment. "The church has other shows, but Henry has nothing to do with their programming. Nothing at all. What's he doing?" She looked at Lee, usually so cool, now anything but. "Tell me this, Lee. Did that mysterious phone call you got the other day have anything to do with the screen test?"

The young woman nodded.

"What kind of screen test did he give you?"

"He wasn't there, ma'am."

"What kind of screen test was it?" Delilah asked. "Where was it?"

"At the Harborside Motel."

"What?!"

Lee looked up. "In the lobby, ma'am. Guests were coming in and out and watching."

"I see. And what were you supposed to do?"

"Walk back and forth, look over my shoulder like a model, smile, sit down on the easy chair in the lobby, and get up again."

"Oh, for God's sake," said Delilah. "I suppose he agreed to pay you?"

Lee nodded and looked down again.

"Dare I ask how much? Was it to be by the hour?"

"Yes, ma'am. Twenty-five dollars an hour."

Delilah laughed. "You're selling your soul cheap, you know. Porn stars get a lot more than that."

Lee blushed and looked confused.

"Are you that naive? You don't see what you're getting into?" She turned away from the cringing girl. "Sit down, Lee."

Lee pulled up a second barstool to the other side of the granite island, facing Delilah, and sat, winding her damp handkerchief around her hand.

Delilah leaned forward, elbows on the counter. "Listen, kid. I've been through this. Same old, same old. Here, have a tissue. Take two." She pushed a box of tissues toward Lee, who took one. "That bastard is setting you up. The next screen test is in a motel room, and you walk around in a bathing suit or in your bra and underpants. Once you get used to that, it's just your panties. Then in the buff. And then . . ."

"Stop!" said Lee. "It wasn't like that at all. Reverend True is a minister!"

Delilah laughed. "You have a lot to learn." She paused and looked away. "So do I." She put her elbows on the counter again. "I'm giving you another chance, kid. But you stay away from my husband. And when he invites you for the next screen test, tell him absolutely not. Understand?"

"Yes, ma'am."

"Had he paid you anything?"

Lee nodded.

"How much?"

"A hundred dollars."

"A hundred dollars for a few minutes in front of the camera?" Delilah laughed again. "Pretty tempting. You don't get that kind of pay from me, right?"

Lee averted her eyes.

"Do you want to continue to work here, or not?" Delilah waited. "I'll take care of moving Reverend True's things into the guest room. You take the rest of the morning off. And think about it."

Lee shredded the tissue she was holding. "Yes, ma'am."

"Believe me," said Delilah softly. "I understand."

While Ellen and Ocypete were dealing with their latest bout of abdominal distress, Howland paid a call on Victoria. She was at her typewriter, pecking out with two fingers her column for the *Island Enquirer*.

She pushed her typewriter aside when she saw him. "Sit down, Howland. I hope you've got news for me."

"Not sure you can use it in your column, but yes, I've got news." He reached into his green canvas briefcase and brought out a sheaf of paper. "The company that produced Tillie's DVD is called TruArt Films, registered in Delaware. I got a list of the board of directors and major investors."

"Oh?" said Victoria, sitting forward.

"I traced each member of the board. Several of them are directors of another company called TruArt Productions with bank accounts in Virgin Gorda."

"The Virgin Islands?"

"Yeah," said Howland. "Ironic."

"Go on," said Victoria. "Coffee, by the way?"

"I'll pass. I traced TruArt Films and Tru-Art Productions still further through a complex of interlocking directorships, and that led me to West Virginia."

"I think I know what's coming."

"I'm sure you do. Henry True is the principal stockholder in TruArt Productions."

"I'm almost afraid to ask what it is they produce."

"Porn films. Videos. Big, big industry. Sold over the Internet. Headquartered in Zebulon, West Virginia."

"That's where the Eye of God Ministry is located. Is the church a front for TruArt?"

"The two aren't affiliated, as far as I can tell. TruArt is Henry's venture. Young women like Tillie, girls, really, perform in front of the camera for creepy voyeurs."

"Lee," said Victoria, standing up. "We've

got to alert her." An instant later, she recalled something. "Darcy! I wonder if he's back from Boston? I've got to contact him."

CHAPTER 30

Victoria looked for Lee's cell phone number in the Island directory, but it wasn't there. She was wondering how to get in touch with the girl without calling Delilah when a car rattled into her drive, an Island car with ragged ends of duct tape fluttering from patched rust spots. Lee's car. Victoria set down the phone book and went to the door.

"Mrs. Trumbull?"

"Lee, you're just the person I want to talk to. Come in." She looked closely at the young woman. "What's the trouble?"

"I don't know, Mrs. Trumbull," and tears flowed.

Victoria herded her into the kitchen, ripped off a paper towel, and handed it to her. "Sit down," she pointed to one of the gray-painted chairs, "and I'll make tea."

Two cups of tea later, Lee had told Victoria about the career in film Reverend True had promised her, and about Delilah's demand this morning that she stay away from him.

"Reverend True told me not to tell Miss Sampson about the screen test, but I did. He said she'd be jealous, and he was right." Lee blew her nose on the damp paper towel. "This is a chance of a lifetime for me. To be a real actress." She wrung her hands. "It's my dream come true, and Miss Sampson is going to fire me if I don't give it up. I should never, never have told her."

"What exactly did Miss Sampson say to you?"

"I don't even want to tell you, Mrs. Trumbull. It's embarrassing. I didn't realize what kind of mind she has."

"She told you Reverend True is making pornographic films, is that it?"

"Did she tell you the same story?"

"She didn't need to," said Victoria. "I doubt if she knew he was producing films other than his religious ones until she talked to you."

"But . . ."

"Do you know how to make a computer play a DVD?"

"Yes, ma'am."

"Come upstairs with me to the study. I want you to see the first few minutes of a movie of Tillie Willoughby. As you know, I found her body. She'd been strangled."

"She was my best friend," said Lee softly. "I was so angry with her. And all the time . . ."

They were partway up the stairs when Victoria stopped abruptly.

"What is it, Mrs. Trumbull?"

"I have to make a phone call downstairs. The DVD is on the desk next to Elizabeth's computer."

Victoria returned to the cookroom, found Darcy's cell phone number on a slip of paper in her phone book, and dialed. A robotic voice told her she was out of the area of cell phone coverage. She thought about calling Delilah on her regular phone, but decided against that. Instead, she phoned Howland, got his answering machine, and left a message.

She climbed back up the stairs to the study. The music from Tillie's DVD blasted out, full volume. Lee was watching intently. She glanced up from the screen when Victoria came into the room.

"Have you seen enough?" Victoria asked.

Lee nodded. She ejected the disk and turned off the computer. "Tillie never told me about this." She waved at the blank screen.

Victoria sat down in the armchair next to

the desk and waited to hear the rest of what Lee had to say.

"I was pretty stupid, wasn't I, Mrs. Trumbull? I mean, I trusted Reverend True. My mother watches his show all the time, the one with Miss Sampson."

Lee was quiet for several moments. She stared out the window, her hands in her lap. The Norway maples overhanging the drive showed a haze of spring green.

Victoria waited.

Lee gestured at the DVD on the desk. "That's exactly what Miss Sampson said would come next. Walking around a motel room in your underwear. And then . . ."

Victoria nodded.

"Are you sure Reverend True produced that, I mean, Tillie, you know?"

"Yes."

Lee put her elbows on the desk and her head in her hands. "I don't understand."

The phone rang, Howland returning Victoria's call.

"I need to talk to you," Victoria said. "I'm upstairs with Lee."

"Has she seen the DVD?"

"Yes."

"I'll get there as soon as I can, Victoria."

Lee dropped her wadded up paper towel into the wastepaper basket. "Miss Sampson gave me the morning off, but I'd better get back. I need to apologize to her. The last thing she said to me was, she understood."

"Yes," said Victoria. "She would."

Delilah removed Henry's clothes from her bureau drawers and flung them, helter-skelter, into the hall outside her bedroom. She slammed the empty bottom drawer shut and tossed a pair of his shoes onto the pile of clothing. At that point Henry appeared, yawning.

"You have a good night's sleep, Mother?"

"You bastard!" She hurled a boot at him. "You disgusting piece of filth!"

He caught the boot and held it. "Did you miss me last night, Delilah, my sweet?"

"Wipe that smile off your fat face and get out of my house!"

"Did you forget? You threw me out of the guesthouse and turned it over to goat boy and son."

"Out," said Delilah, pointing to the stairs.

"I love it when you're angry." Henry dropped the boot onto the pile of clothing, pushed the pile aside with his foot, and stepped toward her.

"Don't you move another inch this way, or I'll . . ."

"You'll what, Mother dear?" Henry moved

another step forward. His broad grin showed large teeth beneath his narrow mustache. "Show me what you'll do. I love . . ."

A large pottery lamp stood on a table just inside Delilah's bedroom door. She grabbed the cord and wrenched the plug out of the electric outlet, seized the lamp by its neck, and, using both hands, smashed the base over Henry's head. Henry looked surprised. Then his eyes wobbled and rolled up until only the whites showed. He collapsed onto the heap of clothing and shards of rose-colored pottery.

"Bastard!" screamed Delilah, and kicked him with the toe of her high-heeled satin mule. "You bastard!"

"Where to, Victoria?" Howland had returned in response to her call.

"I've got to see if Darcy's back yet. I need to get a message to him."

"About the DVD?"

"About Henry."

Darcy heard a scream coming from the big house, then another.

He dropped the chamois cloth he was using to polish the limo, and ran toward the marble stairway. He took the steps three at

312

a time, burst through the partly open front door, paused to decide where the screams had come from, and dashed up to the second-floor hall, where Delilah stood over the prostrate body of her husband.

"Bastard!" she shouted at the unhearing Henry. "I hope I killed you, you . . . you . . . filth!"

Darcy brushed aside the broken pottery and knelt next to Henry. Blood pulsed from a jagged cut on the top of his head, trickled through his thin white hair and around his right ear in a bright red rivulet. Darcy felt along Henry's slack jaw and found a strongly beating pulse.

"Call nine-one-one," he shouted at Delilah, who stood where she was, silent and scowling.

Darcy shook broken pottery out of the pajama top he'd been kneeling on, made a pad of it, and pressed it against the gushing wound. "Call nine-one-one, Delilah! Now!"

"Miss Sampson?" Lee, returning from Victoria's house, came up the stairs. "Miss Sampson! What happened?" She stopped. And stared.

"Reverend True's had an accident," said Darcy. "Miss Sampson's in shock. Call nine-one-one. Use the phone next to her bed."

Lee dashed off.

"I'm not in shock," said Delilah.

Lee was back shortly. "The ambulance is on its way. Is he going to be okay?"

"Probably," said Darcy. "Someone needs to stitch up his head cut and check for concussion. Make Miss Sampson a cup of strong tea, then wait out front for the ambulance."

"Yes, sir." Lee hustled down the stairs.

Darcy continued to press on the wound and looked up.

"Okay, Delilah, what happened?"

"I should have killed him."

"Care to tell me why?"

"That sanctimonious bastard. The Reverend. Man of God. Producer of inspirational films. Minister to thousands of little old ladies glued to their TV sets. Ha!"

Darcy's leg was cramping, and he shifted position. "What are you talking about?"

"I want him to rot in jail."

"What triggered this?" Darcy nodded at the unconscious clergyman and continued to press on the makeshift bandage.

"Lee's mother watches my show. Therefore the Reverend True, who produces my show, must be a saintly man."

"Yeah?"

"He told Lee she'd make a great actress.

314

Screen tests, clothes, money, travel."

Darcy grunted. "Not a religious show, I gather."

"The religion of Henry True." Delilah rubbed her finger and thumb together. "Money, money, money."

Henry groaned.

Delilah said, "Is he coming around? That lamp was one of a pair."

Darcy released pressure on the wound, stood, and kneaded the cramp out of his calf. "Take over," he said. "Hold this on the cut. I've got to make a call."

Jordan took a six-pack of Sam Adams across the road to the Willoughbys' and went around to the far corner where Lambert Willoughby was stapling chicken wire to the posts of Chickee's new pen.

Willoughby looked up. "Don't go for my Bud Lite, eh? Guess I'll take one of them, then." He stood up, dusted his hands on his jeans, and accepted the Sam Adams Jordan offered him.

Jordan walked around the outside of the fenced-in area. "A lot bigger than Chickee's old pen, I see."

"Give him room," said Willoughby. "Might get a dozen or so hens to keep him company. Sell the eggs." He shook his head at Jordan's offer of a bottle opener and twisted the cap off. "Chickee was Tillie's pet, you know. She won him at the Fair." He wiped the neck of the bottle with the palm of his hand and took a swig before he went on. "I'd like to know what the cops are doing to find her killer. Cold trail, now. Five months. Christ!" He wiped his forearm across his forehead, leaving a smear of grime. "She was a wild one, but not mean, if you get me."

CHAPTER 31

Howland glanced into the rearview mirror. "There's an ambulance behind us, Victoria."

They'd turned left onto North Road at the big split oak. The ambulance, coming from the fire station in North Tisbury, had turned as well. Howland pulled over to let it pass. Well ahead of them, it signaled a right turn.

"That's Delilah's road," said Victoria.

Howland followed the ambulance down the dirt road for a quarter mile to the fork, where the ambulance made a left turn.

"That's her driveway," said Victoria. "Hurry!"

They passed between Delilah's granite posts onto the Belgian block pavement, and pulled up behind the ambulance in front of her great house. By the time Howland parked, the EMTs had already disappeared into the house.

Howland raced after them, leaving Victoria to climb the marble steps more slowly. When she finally reached the inside stairway, she paused and heard the brusk and unfamiliar voice of a man giving directions and a woman answering. The ambulance crew. Someone must be injured.

By the time she reached the second floor, EMTs had lifted the unconscious Henry onto a stretcher and strapped him in. The two, a man and a woman, looked too slender to heft Henry's bulk, but they carried the stretcher gently down the stairs and out the front door.

When Victoria stepped aside to let them by she saw the heap of blood-soaked clothing and broken pottery on the floor where Henry had lain.

"Accident," Darcy explained. He brought out a chair from Delilah's bedroom for Victoria. The others — Delilah, Lee, and Howland — stood silently around the mess on the floor as if it were a campfire that might warm them. Darcy joined them, rubbing his hands together as though he was warming them in front of the blaze.

One of the EMTs returned to the second floor holding a clipboard. No one had spoken during his absence. "I need to get the patient's name, next of kin, that sort of thing."

318

"Next of kin . . . ?" Delilah clutched her throat.

"The patient is stabilized, ma'am." He looked around, clearly trying to puzzle out who was in charge. "The hospital needs a contact, someone they can call." He shifted his clipboard from one hand to the other.

Delilah murmured, "Darcy, take care of this. I can't."

"His name, sir?"

"Henry True. The Reverend Henry True, Miss Sampson's husband."

"What hit him?"

"He fell into a lamp," said Darcy.

"I tried to kill him." Delilah turned away and burst into tears.

Darcy frowned. "An accident. Miss Sampson is upset."

From the open front door, Victoria and Howland watched the ambulance round the bend in the driveway and disappear from sight. Bare branches of the oak trees reflected flashing lights, marking the progress of the ambulance.

Delilah joined them at the doorway, followed by Darcy. "I can't deal with it." She shuddered. "Darcy, tell Lee to bring me some brandy. I'll be in the conservatory." She started down the hall.

"I need to get to the hospital right away," Victoria said. "Will you be all right if we leave you, Delilah?"

Delilah turned. "The hospital?"

"Casey will be responding to this, I'm sure. I need to be with her."

Delilah nodded. "I simply can't face the hospital and all the questions. I can't face Henry."

"I understand." Victoria headed across the porch toward the steps and Howland's station wagon.

Henry came to as the EMTs wheeled the stretcher into the emergency room.

"Where am I?" Henry murmured.

"You're in the hospital," said Hope, who was still on duty. She looked up from the interminable paperwork she was filling out at the admissions desk. "You guys again. Not another West Tisburyite?"

"Afraid so," said Jim. "Reverend Henry True. Head lacerations, possible concussion."

Henry mumbled, "Fucking bitch tried to kill me."

Hope stood up. "Room three. Doc Jeffers will be with him shortly."

The EMTs wheeled Henry into the examining room, and in a short time Jim returned to the admissions desk.

"Someone tried to *kill* him?" asked Hope.

"Broken crockery, a lot of blood, his wife in hysterics saying she tried to kill him, and the chauffeur says the victim hit his head on a lamp. Want me to call the chief?"

"Yes," said Hope. "I think that would be a good idea. Tell her to be sure to bring Victoria Trumbull with her." Hope smiled. "I think this calls for my great aunt's sleuthing ability."

"Mrs. Trumbull's already on her way," said Jim.

Mindy LePere, the nurse on duty in Acute Care, bustled into Oliver Ashpine's room.

"How're we doing, hon?"

Oliver was sitting in a chair beside the window reading a magazine. His stockinged feet were propped up on the radiator under the window, and he was dressed in a hospital gown that left his back exposed. His privacy was protected by a pair of bright blue undershorts printed with red and black cartoon mice.

Oliver said, "Is the doc letting me out today?"

"I'm afraid we have to wait until tomorrow," said Nurse Mindy. "Doc Jeffers is afraid you might have a relapse, and we don't want that, do we?"

"We want out!" Oliver removed his feet from the radiator, sat up straight, and flung his magazine onto the floor. "I've got to get back to work."

Nurse Mindy thrust a thermometer into Oliver's mouth, grasped his wrist, and checked her watch. "We're going to have a roommate," she said brightly. "He'll be nice company."

Oliver looked up and mumbled, "Who?"

"We want to keep our mouth shut for another few seconds."

"Who?" demanded Oliver.

The nurse removed the thermometer and noted something on a chart. "A lovely man. You'll like him."

"Dammit," said Oliver to her retreating back. "Don't tell me who I'm going to like."

He picked up his magazine and started on the crossword puzzle. A few minutes later, he heard the squeal of rubber tires on the linoleum, and an attendant accompanied by Nurse Mindy wheeled in a gurney loaded with a short, chubby man whose head was swathed in a turbanlike bandage. Oliver looked up briefly. The man seemed groggy and Oliver had no desire to talk to either the man or the nurse. He went back to the crossword puzzle.

The attendant drew the curtain that separated the new man's bed from his. Oliver ignored the grunts of the attendants and groans of the patient as they shifted him from gurney to bed.

Nurse Mindy popped her head around the curtain. "How're we doing, hon?"

"Great," said Oliver, getting back to his puzzle.

"We'll be another minute or two."

Oliver was pondering over a six-letter definition for "create effervescence" when the nurse said something to the attendant that Oliver only half heard. The last few words included "the reverend." Oliver lowered his feet back onto the floor and sat up straight.

The reverend? A clergyman? How many clergymen were on the Island? At least a half dozen, he supposed. It couldn't possibly be Reverend True, could it? Delilah Sampson's husband? That would be just his luck.

Oliver was planning to use a bit of persuasion on Delilah. He would threaten to tell her preacher hubby about her shady past if she made even a slight fuss about her taxes. But he'd never met Reverend True or seen him in person.

He was ruminating on the identity of the

patient in the next bed and didn't hear approaching footsteps.

"Oliver!"

He sat up straight. Then stood, tried to cover his back with his hospital gown, and dropped his magazine again. Ellen and Ocypete stormed into the room. They brushed past the closed curtains, Ellen clad in a red-plaid flannel wrapper and Ocypete in a neck-to-floor muumuu.

"What do you want?" said Oliver, forgetting for a moment the man behind the curtain.

Ocypete seated herself on Oliver's bed.

Ellen remained standing. "We need to talk."

Oliver immediately recalled his situation and nodded at thc curtained bed next to his. "This is not a good time."

"*Someone* poisoned us," said Ellen, ignoring Oliver's attempts to shush her. "Tried to kill us. If Ocypete and I hadn't vomited everything up last night, we might have died." She studied Oliver, who said nothing. "How did you escape?"

"I don't know what you're talking about," said Oliver, and sank back into his chair.

"You almost got away with it, didn't you? Pretending you were another poisoning victim."

"Pretending?" Oliver thought of the dis-comfort of having one's stomach pumped out. "What do you mean?"

"You knew we were going to expose your little game, didn't you?" Ellen crossed her arms over her chest.

Oliver, caught off guard, shook his head.

"You figured if you killed Ocypete and me and gave yourself enough poison to seem to be a third victim, you'd get away with it, didn't you?"

"What?!" said Oliver, suddenly remember-ing. "It wasn't me!"

"We've had all we can take from you," said Ellen. "We trusted you, brought you in on our little setting-aside business."

Oliver began, "This isn't the place . . ."

"I can't think of a better place," said El-len. "We gave you a golden opportunity. Partnership in a modest venture, and you betrayed us."

"You got greedy," put in Ocypete from her seat on the bed.

Oliver stammered, "Don't talk about it," and nodded toward the next bed.

"You had to go behind our backs and make your own private deal, didn't you?" said Ellen. "Well, we'll see who winds up in prison, *Mister* Ashpine. With attempted murder on top of embezzlement."

"For God's sake, shut up!" said Oliver.

Ellen unfolded her arms and jabbed a finger at him. "Don't you tell me to shut up."

"Don't even think of returning to Town Hall," said Ocypete, slipping off the high bed, and the two women swept out of the room.

Oliver heard, from behind the curtain, what sounded like a chortle.

He jerked the curtain open. The plump man's eyes under shaggy white eyebrows were open, watching Oliver, and he was smiling. Oliver checked the name on the chart at the foot of the bed. Goddamn his luck. "Henry True, is it? Reverend Henry True."

"Attempted murder, eh?" Henry wheezed. "Strong stuff, there. I take it you're Ashpine, the tax collector, right?"

Oliver said nothing. The consequences of this man knowing about the tax scam were horrendous.

"Those little old ladies got you by the short hairs, I gather." Reverend True let out another chuckle, at which he groaned and put his hand up to his bandaged head. "The wife got me good." He tucked his hand back under the blanket. "Got a temper, she has."

Oliver's throat constricted. His stomach

rumbled. He steadied his shaking hand on the table between the beds.

"Sounds as though we have — ouch! — some business to discuss, once we get out of here," mumbled Reverend True.

Oliver took a deep breath to calm himself and looked around frantically. What could he do? How was he going to get out of this mess? If only Ellen and Ocypete had kept their goddamned mouths shut. He could have apologized to the taxpayers, said he'd made an unfortunate mistake.

Henry moaned. "They didn't give me enough painkiller. Got to keep awake. Possible concussion, you know."

Now that Reverend Henry True, Delilah's husband, had heard about the scam, he, Oliver, was going to prison, for sure. Prison! He'd die in prison. The very idea of being shut in with a bunch of criminals . . . ! Locks, bars, steel doors . . .

He glanced at the heavy water carafe next to his bed and reached out his trembling hand. What was he thinking? He drew his hand back.

"Owwwww!" said Henry. "When I get out of here . . ."

Oliver could feel the sharp acid of bile rising up from his gut. Again, he glanced around. In a panic he snatched up the pillow from his own bed and thrust it down firmly over Henry's face.

"Hey!" said Henry, voice muffled. "Help!" He let out a series of muffled noises, kicked his feet, and tugged at the pillow. Oliver forced it down with all his strength.

He was intent on holding the pillow against Henry's struggles and didn't hear footsteps approaching the room.

"Henry?" said the low, clear voice of Victoria Trumbull. She stopped. "Oliver! What in heaven's name are you doing?" She snatched the pillow off Henry's face and jabbed the button to summon the nurse.

Oliver stumbled away from Henry's bed. "He was trying to . . ." he gasped.

CHAPTER 32

Victoria was bending over Henry's inert body, head close to his face, when Howland stepped into the room.

"Sorry it took me so long, Victoria. Couldn't find a parking — What the hell?"

Victoria glanced up. "I've rung for the nurse."

"Is he dead?" The crisp white bandage that swathed Henry's head contrasted with his flabby gray face. "I didn't realize he was that badly hurt."

Henry's eyes fluttered open and he gasped, lips moving in and out.

Oliver slipped to the side of the room next to the windows. He'd apparently recovered enough from the shock of Victoria's arrival to realize he had to get out of there, and right now. He clutched the sides of his hospital gown together behind him and sidled past Howland. He was almost at the door when Victoria called out.

"Stop him, Howland. Don't let him get away."

Howland seized what he could of the back of Oliver's gown and hauled him into the room.

Oliver stammered, "Reverend True was trying to — I just — He would've —"

"Would've what?" Howland held the gown firmly.

At that moment, Nurse Mindy bustled in. "How are we doing, Reverend . . . Oh my!" Reverend True lay like a beached codfish, occasionally gasping for air. Mindy, too, hit the button on the side of Henry's bed to summon more help. She lifted Henry's eyelids, and held her finger against the side of his neck.

Before anyone answered Mindy's summons, Casey arrived with Junior Norton. "Victoria? What are you doing here? I got a message that Henry's wife attacked him."

Howland twisted the fabric of Oliver's hospital gown even tighter. "Victoria just saved Henry from this creep."

"I can't breathe!" gasped Oliver.

Howland loosened his grip. Oliver said, "Reverend True threatened me . . ."

"He was holding a pillow over Henry's face," said Victoria. "Trying to smother him."

At that point, Ellen appeared at the door, tying the belt of her plaid wrapper. "What's Ashpine done now?" she grumbled. Ocypete followed her.

Before anyone could respond, a deep male voice echoed down the hall. "Where's the Meadows-Rotch room? Anybody tell me where they're at?" and Lambert Willoughby shambled up to the door carrying an enormous basket of flowers. "Well, Miz Meadows, just the person I want to see."

"Leave them across the hall," said Ellen, waving toward their room.

Before Lambert could leave, Ocypete pulled an envelope out of the bouquet and opened it. "How sweet. Look at this, Ellen. From Selena."

"Out of the way, please!" Doc Jeffers strode into the room and scowled at the assemblage. "Out! All of you! Get out!" He peered at Henry, who was lying on his back, pale but breathing. "Get Hope in here, right away!"

"The reverend had a relapse, Doctor," said Mindy.

"It was no relapse," said Victoria. "Oliver was smothering him."

Mindy glanced with concern at Victoria. "I'll fetch Hope," and she hurried out of the room.

"It's all a terrible mistake . . ." said Oliver.

Casey referred to her notes. "Says here, Miss Sampson attacked her husband, Reverend True."

Henry gasped.

"Everybody clear out of here," ordered Doc Jeffers.

Oliver perched on his bed. "I've got to lie down."

Doc Jeffers held his stethoscope against Henry's chest. Henry's breath wheezed in and out.

Light footsteps raced down the hall, and Hope entered. Doc Jeffers pulled the earpieces away from his ears and turned to her. "Get them out of here. Now!"

"Right." Hope herded everyone into the hall.

"Can we be of help?" asked Ellen.

"Stay out!" said Doc Jeffers.

When they were out in the hall, Casey asked Hope, "How sick is Ashpine?"

"He was to be discharged today."

"I want to talk to him. Is there a room with some privacy we can use?"

"The nurses' lounge. Follow me."

"Hope! I need you here," Doc Jeffers bellowed.

"I'll take them," said Victoria. "I know

where the lounge is."

"Thanks, Auntie Vic."

"I've got to get back to bed," said Oliver.

"I don't think so," said Hope. "You go with them." She returned to Henry's bed-side.

Victoria led the way down the hall to the lounge. Oliver, with Casey and Junior Norton on either side of him, trailed after her with Howland following.

The nurses' lounge was off a long corridor, a small drab room with a gray-and-black speckled linoleum floor, no windows, several armless plastic chairs in yellow and orange, and a brown tweed couch. A table on the other side of the room held a coffee-maker with an inch of dark liquid that smelled like road tar, bubbling on a hot plate.

Victoria perched on one of the yellow chairs.

"Sit," said Casey to Oliver.

He slumped onto the couch. "I'm sick." He lifted himself up slightly and tucked in the sides of his gown.

Casey ignored him. "What are you doing here, Victoria? Reverend True claimed his wife tried to kill him."

"I'm not sure what happened," replied Victoria. "I got to Delilah's house after the skirmish was over."

"What was all *this* fuss about?" Casey indicated Oliver, who was looking aggrieved.

"When I entered Henry's room, Oliver was trying to smother Henry with a pillow."

Oliver squirmed on the rough couch cushion. "I was trying to make him more comfortable."

"He was smothering him," said Victoria. "Trying to kill him."

Oliver struggled to his feet. Junior Norton pushed him back. "Don't you touch me!" Oliver cried.

"I think it's likely that he killed Tillie, the pilot, and Lucy Pease. It's sheer luck that Henry wasn't victim number four."

"No!" shouted Oliver. "Never! I never killed anyone! I didn't even know those people."

"He wanted Tillie's job," said Victoria. "An audit will show you how lucrative her job was. Once Oliver got himself hired, he set up his own scam the assessors didn't even know about."

"I didn't even know Tillie! I didn't know any of them." Oliver was almost sobbing. "I was making the reverend comfortable, that's all. Adjusting his pillow."

"Mr. Ashpine, I want to hear what Mrs.

Trumbull has to say," said Casey. "You'll have your chance to talk." She turned to Victoria. "Care to comment?"

"I had nothing to do with any scam," Oliver sobbed. "Delilah Sampson's bill was a perfectly honest mistake. I'll correct it. I'll apologize."

"Please, Mr. Ashpine. Let Mrs. Trumbull talk."

"She's lying!"

"Enough!" snapped Casey. "Sit down!"

"Delilah Sampson wasn't the only person to get an inflated bill," said Victoria.

"I'm new at the job. Honest mistakes, all of them!" cried Oliver.

Junior Norton eased Oliver back onto the couch. Oliver leaned forward and dropped his head in his hands. He looked up suddenly. "I'll sue you for false arrest!" Oliver cried. "Undue force!"

"You're not under arrest, sir," said Casey. "We'll listen to what you have to say, and you're entitled to have a lawyer present, if you want."

"I don't need a lawyer! I haven't done anything!"

Casey turned away from him. "We need to talk in private, Victoria." She glanced at Junior Norton, who raised his hand in acknowledgment.

Victoria and she went into the hall and closed the door to the lounge behind them.

"It's your word against his, Victoria. You claim Ashpine was smothering Henry, he claims he was fixing the pillow. Let's hope Henry recovers. If he does, he can speak for himself."

"Don't let Oliver back in the same room with Henry," Victoria insisted.

"I'll have Henry switched to another room and one of our guys will be on duty until we sort this out."

CHAPTER 33

Victoria usually slept soundly through the night. But tonight, after witnessing Oliver Ashpine's attempt on Henry's life, she woke up a little after three feeling uneasy. He was an embezzler. The files she'd copied from his office proved that. But because of technicalities, the police would have to obtain a search warrant to get access to his files. An embezzler who could smother a helpless invalid in a hospital bed could easily have killed three other people. He was a cold-blooded killer, she was convinced. The hospital would release him. He wasn't really sick.

If Henry were to die . . . She didn't even want to think about that.

She got out of bed and stood by the west window overlooking Doane's pasture on the other side of the lane. Her room was bright. Pale moonlight cast a shadow of the window frame on the floor. A dog barked in the village. A rooster crowed, and she thought about Jordan Rivers and Lambert Willoughby, and how angry the two had been over something as simple as a crowing rooster.

The early-morning chill worked its way through her thin nightgown. She pulled the down comforter off her bed, tossed it over her shoulders, and sat by the window in her grandmother's rocking chair and gazed out at the peaceful view of the pasture, the village beyond, and the moonlit church steeple.

In the wood lot next to the pasture an owl cried, an eerie who-oooo, who-oooo. A car went by on the Edgartown Road. At this time of night there were few cars, and the only other sounds were the sounds of her childhood — barking dogs and crowing cocks.

She'd been up more than an hour and was feeling sleepy enough to go back to bed when she heard a car slow down on the road and turn into her drive.

Hurriedly, she slipped on wool socks and her shoes with the hole cut out for her sore toe, buttoned her sweater over her nightgown, and went into the study that adjoined her bedroom. Through the south-facing window she could see the car pull up next to Elizabeth's convertible and stop.

Victoria decided to wait until she knew who'd come calling this late before turning on the lights. She found her flashlight and, shielding its beam, went down the front stairs, holding the banister tightly.

From the dining room window she saw the car more clearly. Moonlight glinted off something reflective on the side of the car. Strips of fluttering duct tape. Lee's ancient car.

Something had to be seriously wrong to bring Lee out so long past midnight. She switched on the kitchen light, filled the teakettle, set it on the stove, and waited.

She waited for several minutes. A car door slammed. Moments later there were heavy footfalls on the stone steps leading to the entry, much heavier than she imagined Lee's could be.

Who would come to her house at this time? And in Lee's car? Darcy would drive Delilah's limousine. Howland would drive his station wagon. She couldn't think of anyone else.

Someone pounded on the door and Victoria stood up and reached for her stick.

"Who is it?"

"I've got to talk to you, Miz Trumbull," demanded a male voice she didn't immediately recognize.

"The door's not locked." Victoria held her stick by the end, ready to swing it, and backed up so the kitchen table was between her and whoever this was.

The intruder paused. Victoria could see only a silhouette through the glass panes of the door, backlit by moonlight.

The teakettle whistled. She'd overfilled it again. Boiling water bubbled out of the spout onto the hot stove. There was a blue flash and the kitchen light went out.

Victoria felt around for her flashlight. "Come in!" she called to the person at the door. She aimed at where she thought his face would be when he stepped up into the kitchen. As he opened the door, she switched on the light.

The intruder shouted, "Goddamn!" and shielded his eyes with his forearm. He was wearing a red baseball cap with "Red Sox" stitched in bright blue.

The beam cast eerie shadows on his lower face, and it took Victoria a moment to recognize who it was. She reached for her chair and sat down, holding her stick in one hand, the flashlight aimed steadily at his face in the other.

It was Lambert Willoughby, brother of the murdered Tillie, son-in-law of the murdered

Lucy Pease, and owner of the rooster named Chickee.

"What are you doing here? And why are you driving Lee's car?"

Willoughby shut the door behind him. "What happened, you trip the circuit breaker?"

"Why are you here?"

"Where's the breaker box?"

"Why are you driving Lee's car?"

"It's my sister's car. Tillie. She loaned it to Lee. Can I talk to you?"

"Do you know what time it is?"

"After four. Could you stop shining that damned light in my eyes?"

"The circuit box is on the cookroom wall." Victoria pointed with the flashlight.

"How about giving me the light?"

Victoria sighed and keeping the table between them, pointed the flashlight beam at the breaker box, and Willoughby opened it.

"Expect me to fix it by feel, do you?"

"That should be simple enough," said Victoria, keeping her distance.

Willoughby muttered something she didn't understand. There was a click, and the kitchen light came back on.

"Thank you," said Victoria, blinking in the sudden brilliance. She pointed to one of the gray-painted chairs and told him to sit. "What are you doing here?" she demanded, once he was seated. And then, "Would you like a cup of tea? The water's hot."

"Yes, ma'am." He took off his hat, smoothed the bright blue letters, and put the hat back on. "Sox are looking pretty good this year."

Victoria looked blank. "I've got several kinds of tea," she said.

"Herbal tea, if you've got it."

Neither spoke until after Victoria brewed the tea in the blue china teapot and poured it into mugs.

"You got honey or something?"

"On the counter under the window." Victoria could hear a car and then a truck on the Edgartown Road, and saw a glow in the eastern sky. "There are spoons in the drawer."

She sat again and waited. "Well? What's so important you had to come by in the middle of the night?"

"It's morning. I'm on my way to work. You seem like a smart woman," said Willoughby, squeezing honey into his tea. He returned to the gray-painted chair. "I gotta tell you some stuff that's been bugging me, but it's in confidence, okay?"

"That depends," said Victoria, puzzled.

"I trust you not to blab, Miz Trumbull."

"I don't blab," said Victoria.

"You told the cops about the assessors' scam, but they're not doing anything, right?"

"They're looking into it."

"You know better than to believe that, right?"

"Go on," said Victoria.

"You know what you're talking about. Those old biddies skimmed off I don't know how many thousands over the years. Nice investments they got stashed someplace."

"Did Tillie know about the scam?"

"My sister wasn't all peaches and cream," said Willoughby, "but she was some smart. She knew, all right. She went along with them, happily taking her share, saving it up. She wanted to be a movie star ever since she was a little kid. Gonna move to California one day. She figured she needed money for a couple of years' living expenses." He looked down into his tea and stirred it absently. "Plus acting lessons. She had it all planned out. That's where I thought she'd gone, when everybody figured she'd run off with that Edgartown man."

"I think I see where this is leading," said Victoria. "It's leading to Henry True, movie producer."

"Exactly right. He had her bamboozled. Me and the wife told Tillie the reverend was a phony, but she didn't believe us. Tillie talked with the wife's mother . . ."

"Lucy Pease?"

"Right. They was close, Lucy and Tillie. She told Tillie that what the reverend was filming was art and would look great when she got to Hollywood."

"I found the DVD Tillie showed Lucy," said Victoria.

He looked up. "Is that right? Where? We searched every place we could think of."

"In a metal box, buried under your chicken coop. Oliver Ashpine's Jack Russell dug it up."

"Bertie. Yeah," said Willoughby. "Damn mutt."

"Did you want to see the DVD?"

"I don't know that it would do any good. Pretty bad?"

Victoria thought before she answered. "Suggestive. Not really bad. Howland Atherton tracked the recording to a company that Henry True owns."

"Bastard — 'scuse me, ma'am."

"Quite all right," said Victoria. "I feel the same way about Reverend True."

"Would that stand up in court? What you found out?"

"You mean about Henry True producing pornographic films? I think so," said Victoria, sipping her own tea. She looked at him over the steam. "Would you be willing to testify, if this ever goes to court? About the assessors' embezzling tax money and about Henry True luring young women into posing for his films?"

"It's more than Henry True getting my sister to do porn videos, Miz Trumbull." Willoughby set his mug on the kitchen table. "He killed my sister."

Victoria took a deep breath at the same time she swallowed a mouthful of tea and coughed.

"You okay, Miz Trumbull?"

Victoria nodded and coughed a few more times. "Henry True didn't kill your sister, and I can prove it. Oliver Ashpine did."

"No, ma'am. Beg to differ. You just look at the timing. Knowing my sister, she put the touch on the reverend." He continued in a falsetto, " 'Reverend True, sir, if you could advance me a little money, say, plane fare to California, I won't tell my brother about the dirty videos you made of me.' " He dropped back to his normal voice. "He knew if she told me, I'd beat the shit out of the son-of-a-bitch — excuse me, ma'am."

CHAPTER 34

Victoria cleared her throat a few more times. "Whoever killed your sister killed Lucy and Henry's pilot."

"Seems that way," said Willoughby. "Only possible suspect is the goddamned Reverend True."

"The night the pilot was killed, Henry was with Delilah."

"Thought she'd kicked him out."

"When Chief O'Neill and I arrived, the chauffeur had to wake up Delilah. He saw Henry hurry back to the guesthouse. They apparently had a temporary reconciliation."

"Sneaky bastard. He could've slipped her a sleeping pill and snuck out to do the dirty deed. She'd never know, and he'd have an airtight alibi."

"No one knows exactly when your sister died, only that it was about five months ago."

"And what have the cops done? Nothing,

that's what."

"They're doing everything they can," said Victoria, feeling that she ought to defend the police. "In five months a lot of evidence disappears. I'm convinced that Oliver lured her up to the attic and killed her there, knowing it would be some time before she was found. He knew he'd get her job and the money that went with it."

Willoughby lifted his cap and scratched his head. "A lot of money, a lot. But not enough to kill anyone for."

"Some people kill simply to keep others quiet," said Victoria. "Had you heard that Oliver tried to smother Henry in his hospital bed last night?"

Willoughby looked interested. "Henry in the hospital?"

"His wife bludgeoned him with a lamp. I arrived as Oliver was holding a pillow over his face."

Willoughby laughed. "Dead?"

"Henry's alive but unconscious. I haven't heard whether or not there's been brain damage."

"Hard to tell with him. Send them both to prison."

"We can agree on that. Henry as purveyor of pornographic films and Oliver for embezzlement *and* murder. If the state de-

347

mands an independent audit, we can put the three assessors away, too."

Willoughby coughed and stood up abruptly, and Victoria suddenly thought of his large new house. He checked his watch. "Got to get going." He adjusted his hat. The sun had come up and was sending bright beams into the kitchen. "You're dead wrong about Ashpine. True killed the three of them."

"Why would he want to kill Ellen?"

"You mean the assessor? She wasn't killed."

"Lucy was killed in Ellen's house. Oliver mistook Lucy for Ellen."

"You got that wrong," said Willoughby. "You knew, didn't you, Lucy was my mother-in-law?"

"Yes, I know. I'm so sorry about her death."

"No great loss, the old biddy. Lucy and Tillie was close, like that." He held up two fingers. "Tillie always wanted to be a movie star, ever since she was a little kid. Told Lucy the reverend was giving her a chance to break into the big time, acting in his videos."

"Didn't Tillie realize what kind of movies they were?"

"No, ma'am. She didn't want to see them

as anything but art films. She'd only got as far as prancing around in her underwear, sticking her finger in her mouth and wiggling her butt. We told her, the wife and me, the reverend was making dirty movies, and the next one he'd film of her would be with her buck naked. She got all upset at that."

"And turned to Lucy, I suppose?"

"Shut us out completely. Tillie showed the DVD to Lucy and then bragged to us about how proud Lucy was of her art. She said me and the wife didn't understand 'culcha.' " He looked sideways at Victoria. "I don't know about you, Miz Trumbull, but I know a dirty movie when I see one."

After Willoughby left, Victoria went upstairs again. It was still early, not yet six o'clock, but there was no point in going back to bed. She dressed in her worn corduroys, made her bed, and returned to the kitchen. Elizabeth wouldn't be up for at least another hour.

McCavity stalked into the kitchen from his spot in front of the fireplace, rubbed against her legs, then seated himself next to his empty bowl and waited.

Victoria fixed her own breakfast, after her cat was fed, and settled herself at the cookroom table with her bowl of cereal and the latest edition of the *Island Enquirer.* The events at the hospital had happened only last night, so there'd be no coverage. She'd write something in her column about Henry's near brush with death without actually accusing Oliver. She took an envelope out of the wastebasket and jotted down notes while she ate.

While Victoria was writing up her notes, Hope went into Ocypete and Ellen's hospital room with the lab results.

"Elderberries?" said Ellen. "Elderberries? I've eaten elderberry jelly all my life and never had any trouble."

"Me, too," said Ocypete.

"Definitely elderberries," said Hope. "In the candy Miss Moon brought you. Here." She handed Ellen a paper. "I looked this up on the Internet and printed it out. I thought you might be interested."

" 'Uncooked unripe berries and to a lesser extent uncooked ripe berries may cause significant GI upset,' " Ellen read out loud. She held her finger at her place and looked over her glasses. "GI?"

"Gastrointestinal," said Hope.

Ellen moved her finger along the page of fine print. "This sounds exactly like what hit us. 'Nausea, vomiting, and diarrhea. The leaves, roots, stems and bark are also GI irritants.' "

Ellen passed the printout to Ocypete.

"I spoke to Miss Moon," said Hope. "I feel responsible. I shouldn't have allowed her to bring candy into the hospital."

"She'd have taken it to us at our homes and we'd have eaten all of it there," Ocypete said. "You probably saved our lives."

"What did Selena have to say for herself?" asked Ellen.

"She said she'd made up her own recipe and wanted to retain the vitamins by not overcooking it," said Hope. "She ground up the berries in her food processor, strained out the seeds and stems, and used the juice, sugar, and unflavored gelatin to make the candy."

"She wanted to kill us," said Ellen. "No wonder she wouldn't eat any herself."

"I don't think elderberries have ever been fatal," Hope said. "She was terribly upset."

"Not as upset as we were," said Ellen.

"The candy tasted wonderful," said Ocypete. "You'd think poison would taste like poison."

"Miss Moon had no idea the berries could be a problem," said Hope. "She's made elderberry jelly and wine for years."

Ocypete sighed. "Thank goodness it

wasn't a disgruntled taxpayer. I was so afraid . . ."

Hope checked her clipboard. "If you're feeling okay, Doc Jeffers said you can go home this afternoon."

"I'm starving for a rare steak," said Ocypete.

"You're to eat a bland diet for the next week, no rare steak, no hot salsa. Sorry." Hope tucked her pen into the holder on the top of her clipboard and left.

"Morning, Gram." Elizabeth greeted Victoria before she poured herself a cup of coffee.

"You heard what happened yesterday?" asked Victoria.

"How Delilah brained her husband and Oliver tried to finish him off?" Elizabeth set down her coffee mug. "I almost feel sorry for the guy. How is he?"

"Howland's taking me to the hospital this morning to see how Henry is. They intend to discharge Oliver today, over my objections."

"Anything I can do before I leave for work?"

"I don't think so, thanks. I want to finish my column before he gets here."

■ ■ ■ ■

After Elizabeth left, Victoria took out her typewriter. She had finished most of her column when Howland arrived.

"More coffee, Victoria?" He held up the coffeepot.

"Thank you."

He seated himself across from her and she told him about Lambert Willoughby's early-morning visit.

"What did he want?"

"He wanted to convince me that Henry is the killer."

"But you think Oliver's the killer."

"I think the killer is Oliver, Lambert thinks it's Henry, and Henry insists that Darcy is guilty. He's not, of course. Darcy wasn't even here five months ago when Tillie was killed."

"Perhaps one of the assessors is the killer."

"I can't picture any of those three elderly women as the killer."

"Elderly?" asked Howland.

"It's a state of mind," answered Victoria.

"I'm not sure there's a standard for identifying a killer," said Howland. "Every one of us would kill, given the incentive."

"Never," said Victoria, shaking her head.

"Suppose someone threatened one of your daughters or your grandchildren?"

"I'd outthink him."

Howland laughed. "Let's get to the hospital."

The West Tisbury Police Bronco was parked in the hospital lot when Howland and Victoria arrived.

"Why didn't Casey call me?" Victoria said as they passed through the automatic doors into the emergency room.

Hope was doing paperwork at the admissions desk. "You're just in time, Auntie Vic. Reverend True is conscious, and the police hope to get a statement from him. You and Mr. Atherton can go on in."

Casey and Junior Norton were standing in the hall outside Henry's room. "Tried to reach you, Victoria," Casey said. "The hospital called when he regained consciousness."

"I was probably out in the garden," said Victoria.

Nurse Mindy was standing by Henry's bed. She bent down to him and whispered, "Hon, we've got visitors. They have some questions to ask you."

"Raise the bed, will you?" mumbled Henry. He put his hand up to his bandaged

354

head. "Still pretty groggy," he said to the group assembled around the foot of the bed.

"A few questions, sir," Casey began. "Are you up to it? We don't want to tire you."

"I'm okay."

"First of all, we understand you accused your wife, Miss Sampson, of trying to kill you."

Henry started to laugh, then held his head again. "If I said that, I must have been out of it."

"But she did try to kill you, sir, right?"

"My wife?"

"Yes, sir. I understand she tried to kill you."

"Of course she didn't try to kill me." Henry tried to sit up straighter, and Nurse Mindy fluttered around him. "We have our little spats, the wife and me, like most happily married couples. She has a temper. Redhead, you know?"

Junior was taking notes. Victoria pulled up a chair and sat. Howland stood by the door, arms crossed.

Casey continued with her questions. "Would you explain, sir, how you got injured?"

"She was upset about some little thing I said and banished me from our bedroom. Next morning, I went to apologize, and she was still pretty hot. Threw a lamp at me, didn't actually mean to hit me."

"And that's it, sir?"

"Perfectly ordinary spat," said Henry.

"Do you intend to press charges?"

"Good heavens, no," said Henry, again putting his hand to his head.

Junior Norton continued to write.

"You had a roommate, sir," said Casey, referring to her notes. "Oliver Ashpine. We have a witness who claims Mr. Ashpine tried to smother you with a pillow, is that right?"

"I don't even know Ashpine," said Henry, wrinkling his brow. "Why would he do that?"

Victoria stood up and started to say something. Casey warned her with a look and Victoria sat down again.

Casey continued. "He held a pillow over your face. Do you recall that?"

"First you accuse my wife of trying to kill me, now this Ashpine person." Henry snorted. "Sounds as though I'm on someone's hit list."

"Sir, we're quite serious. We have reason to believe Mr. Ashpine was trying to smother you, and if someone hadn't come into your room just then, he might have succeeded."

"I think the visitor misinterpreted Ash-

356

pine's intentions. He was putting another pillow behind my head, that's all."

Victoria watched his expression. He was lying.

Casey's expression didn't change. She said, "You deny, sir, that Mr. Ashpine deliberately put the pillow over your face?"

"Categorically."

"And you don't want to press charges?"

"Certainly not."

Victoria stood up. Her cheeks were pink. Her eyes glittered. Her lips were pressed tightly together.

"Is that all?" Henry moved his head to the side. "You can lower my bed, again, nurse." Then, with a sigh, he said, "I'm glad to have cleared up that little misunderstanding."

"Reverend True is tired, now," chirped Nurse Mindy. "Time to go."

"If you change your mind, sir, please contact me." Casey handed Nurse Mindy her card.

As soon as they were out in the hall, Victoria sputtered, "The idea! The very idea!"

Casey shrugged. "Your word against Ashpine's and Reverend True's. What can you do?"

Victoria turned to Howland, who'd been standing silently by the door. "Please, take me home."

CHAPTER 35

On the way back to Victoria's, Howland made a couple of unsuccessful attempts to calm down Victoria, but she was steaming mad.

"What's wrong with him? I can understand his defending his wife, but why should he defend Oliver? He was lying. I feel like a fool. Henry would be dead, if I hadn't yanked that pillow off his face. And he denies it ever happened. Why?" Victoria slapped her knee. "And Oliver Ashpine is free. To kill again. With impunity!"

Howland glanced over at her. "Impunity is an excellent weapon."

Victoria ignored his attempt at humor. "Nobody believes me. Nice, kind, thoughtful Oliver was simply making Henry more comfortable, according to both of them. He was trying to kill Henry!"

"I believe you. So does Casey."

"Bah!" said Victoria.

Delilah's limo was blocking the drive when Victoria and Howland returned from the hospital. She let herself out of Howland's car without his help and without thanking him and marched up to the limousine. Delilah lowered her window with a pleased smile.

"You're blocking my drive," Victoria said. "No one can get in or out."

"I'm sorry." Delilah emerged from the backseat without waiting for Darcy to open her door. Victoria stood, hands on her hips, annoyed with the world in general. Darcy glanced at her, drove around the circle, and parked under the maple tree. Howland took off without looking back.

Victoria led the way into the kitchen, with a begrudging attempt to be civil. She plopped down on a kitchen chair. "What do you want, Delilah?"

"I'm embarrassed about yesterday, Mrs. Trumbull. I was so angry at Henry about his porn videos I intended to kill him."

"He's not pressing charges," said Victoria.

"He wouldn't dare. The nerve of him, telling Lee she was going to be a movie star. Lee's only a kid. She believed him. She actually trusted him."

"Tea?" asked Victoria.

"I can't stay, but thanks. Did you ever find that deed Mrs. Danvers said I needed?"

"It slipped my mind," said Victoria. "Give me a ride to Town Hall and I'll look for it right now."

"I don't mean to take you from your writing," Delilah said. "But . . ."

"That's quite all right," said Victoria. "I need to take my mind off things. Howland and I located most of the files before we found Tillie's body."

"Awful. Just awful!" Delilah held her crimson fingernails against her lips.

"It won't take me more than a few minutes."

"Are you sure you won't feel, you know, uncomfortable up there? I mean, after finding what you did? The body?"

Victoria marched down the stone steps. The fat buds of the double daffodils by the cellar bulkhead were showing streaks of bright yellow, but Victoria didn't even notice. Every spring, hers were the first in town to bloom.

Darcy brought the limo around and they headed to Town Hall. There were signs of spring all along the road, clumps of daffodils on Brandy Brow were about to burst into a cloud of sunshine.

At Town Hall, Mrs. Danvers greeted Victoria with her wintry smile.

"I'd like to go up to the attic," Victoria said.

"Don't find any more bodies," said Mrs. Danvers, with a rare burst of humor.

Delilah gave out a small nervous laugh. "Shall I go up with you, Mrs. Trumbull?"

"You needn't. It will take me only a few minutes, ten or fifteen at the most. I know where the folder is."

"I'll wait here, then, if you don't mind. I'm not sure I can . . ." Delilah didn't finish.

In the morning light, the attic no longer seemed sinister. Victoria found the file box marked "1910," found a folder inside marked "Deeds," and carried it downstairs. Delilah was sitting at the long table where the selectmen usually met, examining her nails. Victoria set the folder in front of her on the table.

"You know you can't take that out of the building," said Mrs. Danvers, looking over the top of her glasses, her hands poised above her computer keyboard.

"We're looking for that deed *you* asked for," said Delilah. "You don't need to be so, so . . ."

Victoria interrupted. "We'll only be a few

minutes, and then, if you don't mind, I'll make a copy and take the box back upstairs."

Mrs. Danvers sighed. "I'll take it back. I suppose I ought to see what the attic looks like," and she turned again to her computer.

Victoria found the deed, made sure it was what Delilah needed, and went to the copier.

Mrs. Danvers untangled herself from her ergonomic chair. "I'll copy it for you." She took the deed and fed it into the copier.

"Thank you. How much do I owe you?"

"Forget it," said Mrs. Danvers. "Everybody in this town pays too much in taxes. I'm not going to charge you for five sheets of paper." She stapled the copy together and handed it to Victoria, who gave it to Delilah, who was examining her face in a small mirror, smoothing her lip liner with her pinky finger.

Delilah put the mirror away in her purse and picked up the deed. She leafed through it, then read until she came to the end. And then she started at the beginning again and studied each sentence, following the words slowly as though she couldn't understand what she was reading. Her face had paled.

"What is it?" asked Victoria.

Mrs. Danvers paused in her typing and

looked up.

Delilah dropped the deed on the table, pushed her chair back, and stared out the window at the church across the road.

"What is it?" Victoria asked again. "Let me see the deed."

Delilah didn't move.

Victoria picked up the copy and sat down at the table across from Delilah. The first four pages seemed to be a straightforward transfer of property from Josiah Hammond to his son, Israel, with specific boundaries spelled out. One read, "From the great oak two hundred paces in a southwesterly direction to the rock shaped like a toad . . ."

Delilah was slumped in her chair as though her bones had dissolved. Her color had gone from white to a greenish gray hue, and she continued to stare out of the window. Victoria turned to Mrs. Danvers. "I don't suppose the oak and toad-shaped rock are still there?"

"That property has been surveyed to a fare-thee-well," said Mrs. Danvers. "Cement bounds with metal plates." She smiled. "I don't think that's her problem." A nod to Delilah.

Victoria read on. And there it was. On the last page, in a list of restrictions that carried solemn penalties, was what had stricken Delilah.

Victoria glanced at her. "The house was never to be torn down, was it?" she said.

Delilah was silent.

"If it were to be torn down," Victoria said as she set the deed to one side, "the property, in its entirety, reverts to the town to be used as a park."

Delilah spoke in a small voice. "I've got lawyers who will break that." She seemed to get a spark of courage. "That deed will never hold up."

"I wouldn't be so sure about that," said Mrs. Danvers. "When you bought the place, I warned you not to tear down the old Hammond homestead and told you what would happen if you did. Told you it was a historic building. Didn't listen to me, did you?" Mrs. Danvers pushed her glasses back into place and returned to her computer, with a grim smile.

Darcy came into Town Hall and spoke softly to Delilah. "The hospital called, Miss Sampson. Reverend True has been released from the hospital, and is ready to be picked up."

"Then do it," said Delilah. "Take Mrs. Trumbull and me home first."

"Will you be all right?" asked Victoria.

"I'll survive."

CHAPTER 36

In an attempt to clear her mind, Victoria went outside to watch the vivid sunset colors flare and die. The clouds turned a dark purple, wind clouds, she called them. As she was about to go indoors again, Howland drove up. He was carrying a large box of Chilmark Chocolates.

"To cheer you up, Victoria. A cure for almost everything."

Victoria smiled. "Thank you. I'm afraid I was being difficult earlier today."

"Understandable."

"Would you like tea?"

"Please."

While they were waiting for the water to boil, the phone rang. Victoria answered, listened, then put her hand over the mouthpiece. "It's Lambert Willoughby. He's calling from Oliver's house and he wants me to get there right away."

"Did he say what it's about?"

"He sounded upset. Will you take me there?"

"Of course."

Victoria spoke into the phone. "Howland and I will be there in ten minutes."

When they arrived at Oliver's house, they heard a dog's frantic barking. Bertie, Oliver's Jack Russell, was standing inside the open door, quivering, his feet apart, head up, yapping insistently.

Willoughby lumbered to the door. "Thank God you got here, Miz Trumbull. Ashpine's down."

"Dead?" asked Victoria.

"Almost. I called the Tri-Town Ambulance after I called you."

"What happened?" asked Howland.

"I was trying to take a nap and that goddamned mutt was barking his head off. I came over with a baseball bat to shut him up and found Ashpine there." He pointed to Oliver, who was lying on his back on the floor near his computer. A blanket was draped over him.

"Heart attack?" asked Victoria.

"Dunno. The mutt is really bullshit about something. I figured since you fingered Ashpine as the killer, you oughtta be the one to collar him."

Willoughby was interrupted by a loud crowing from across the lane.

"Damn, sounds like Chickee's got out."

"Have you given Ashpine first aid?" asked Howland. "Is he breathing?"

"He's breathing, kind of. I didn't move him in case he broke something. Put a blanket over him, is all."

The ambulance siren sounded in the distance.

Chickee crowed. Bertie's barking was more frenzied.

The ambulance turned into the lane that ran between the Willoughby and Rivers properties, pulled up in front of Oliver's house, stopped, and let the siren die. Erica and Jim, the same EMTs Victoria had seen at Delilah's the day before, hurried up the steps.

"There's your man," said Willoughby, pointing.

"Any idea what happened?" Jim asked

"Nope. His dog alerted me, and I came over to shut him up. Found him on the floor. Just like that."

Chickee crowed again, closer, and the crow ended in a strangled croak. Bertie continued to yelp.

Erica knelt by Oliver's head and felt the left side of his neck for a pulse. "Jim?" she said. "Look here." Victoria looked, too, and saw a red, thumb-size bruise. Erica pulled the blanket away from his neck and Victoria saw the same red mark on the right side of his neck.

"Someone tried to cut off his circulation," said Victoria.

"Looks that way," said Jim. "A way to deprive the brain of oxygen."

"I'll call the police," Victoria said.

"I called them," said Erica.

Bertie, in constant motion, hustled over to the cellar door, scratched at it, and continued to bark. He looked around, and barked still more insistently.

"Probably smells a rat," said Willoughby. "Jack Russells is ratters."

Chickee squawked and Jordan Rivers entered, holding the rooster, wrapped in a clean T-shirt, against his chest. "What's going on?"

A second siren sounded in the distance, and in a short time the West Tisbury Police Bronco pulled up behind the ambulance. Casey emerged, hand on her holstered gun. Junior Norton followed behind her.

"Okay, everyone, what's the trouble?" Casey looked down at Oliver and the two EMTs working over him. "Heart attack?"

Jordan handed Willoughby the rooster.

"Look at the marks on his neck," said Victoria. "Bertie must have frightened off an attacker. He can't be far away."

"I'll call the state police." Junior slipped outside, radio in hand, and was back shortly. "They're on their way."

"Bertie is telling us someone is in the cellar," said Victoria. "Is there an outside entrance?"

"Yes, ma'am," said Willoughby. "Bulkhead door out back."

"Watch the exits, Junior," said Casey, unsnapping her holster. "I'll check the cellar."

"No, ma'am. Better let me do that," said Willoughby, passing Chickee on to Victoria. "Could be dangerous."

Casey started to protest. "Too much testosterone around here," she muttered.

Victoria smoothed the T-shirt around the rooster's ruffled feathers.

"I'll go with you," said Jordan, pushing his glasses into place.

"That's my man." Willoughby held out his hand for Jordan to shake. "Miz Trumbull thinks we've finally cornered the killer. Ready?"

"Ready," said Jordan, hitching up his bicycle trousers. "Is there a light down there?"

■ ■ ■ ■

Junior Norton helped the EMTs load Oliver into the Tri-Town Ambulance. The ambulance took off, red lights flashing.

Victoria set Chickee on an overstuffed chair. The rooster struggled out of the T-shirt, tucked his head under his wing, and dozed off.

Time passed. There was no sound from the cellar.

"What's taking them so long?" asked Victoria.

"I'll check," said Casey.

Before she could open the door, Willoughby and Jordan Rivers came up from the cellar. Willoughby was breathing heavily.

"Clean got away," he said between puffs.

"Could he still be hidden somewhere in the cellar?" asked Victoria.

"Nope. Cellar's clean as a whistle. The bulkhead door was open, though. Must've got out that way while we was dealing with Ashpine."

"Where's Bertie?" asked Howland, who was sitting at Oliver's computer studying what he had been looking at.

"Bertie took off after him," said Jordan. "We followed him for a short way, but it's too dark to see anything. He's a gutsy little dog."

Casey turned to Victoria. "I'm going to the hospital to check on Oliver. Wait here for the state cops."

"And I'm going to my place and get a six-pack," said Willoughby. "Want a Bud, Miz Trumbull?"

"That sounds lovely," said Victoria.

"I'll take care of Oliver's dog while he's in the hospital," said Jordan.

Howland moved his chair, and in doing so, knocked over a box that was next to the desk. A dozen or more cards spilled out. Howland picked one up. "Property cards," he said. "What was Ashpine doing with these?"

"They belong in Town Hall," Victoria said.

A terrific scratching and growling sounded at the front door, and Victoria opened it. Bertie stood there with a scrap of dark cloth between his teeth. He laid the scrap down at Victoria's feet, and looked up expectantly at her. She picked it up and let the dog in. The cloth was bite-size and black. She smoothed it out. Cotton sweatshirt material, fuzzy on one side, smooth on the other, and clearly torn from sweatpants.

"Good pup," said Victoria, patting his sturdy flank. The dog wriggled, stumpy tail wagging.

"About the only good thing I can say about Jack Russells is they're smart," said Willoughby, who came in after Bertie, carrying the beer. "He went after the guy. Have a beer, Miz Trumbull." He wrenched up the pop-top and handed the can to her. "Want a glass?"

"No, thanks. This is fine." Victoria tucked the scrap of fabric into her pocket without thinking and took the cold beer.

"Guess this proves you're wrong about Ashpine being the killer, Miz Trumbull. Leaves us with Reverend True, just like I told you." He held his can of beer up. "Cheers!"

"Cheers!" said Victoria, and took a few sips. "It can't be Henry. He got out of the hospital only a few hours ago. He could hardly run through the woods in the dark."

"Told you, he's a sneaky bastard. How about a Bud, Atherton?" he called out. "One with your name on it."

"No, thanks," said Howland. "Victoria, want to see what Ashpine was looking at when he was attacked?"

Victoria was still engaged in the Henry versus Oliver debate. "Henry was weak, extremely weak, when I saw him in the hospital this morning. I'm surprised they discharged him."

"Don't believe anything he says or does," Willoughby said.

"That's true." Victoria nodded, recalling Henry's refusal to press charges against his would-be killers. "But he wasn't faking his feebleness."

Howland turned again to Victoria. "Ashpine was looking up appraisals, including the assessors' and Willoughby's houses."

"Mine? The dirty rat," said Willoughby.

Victoria went over to the computer and Howland moved aside to give her room. The screen showed a photograph of a house and listed the address, owner's name, a description of the buildings and land, and the appraised value.

"Interesting," said Victoria, shifting to a second screen, then a third.

"Trying to squeeze more taxes out of us," said Willoughby. "That's what he was doing."

After studying a fourth screen, Victoria turned to Howland. "Would you please take me home?" She handed him her unfinished beer.

"Sure," said Howland, setting her beer on the table.

"You can take that Bud with you, Miz Trumbull," said Willoughby. "Something for the road."

"Not right now, thanks," said Victoria.

"Hadn't you better wait for the state police?" asked Jordan.

"You deal with them, Jordan. Come, Howland."

Outside, Howland held his car door open and Victoria got in.

"What's the hurry, Victoria? Are you okay?"

"I think I know where the intruder went after escaping from the cellar. There's an ancient way behind the Willoughbys' that leads to State Road across from the New Ag Hall. He must have known about it. The attack on Oliver was all planned out."

"He must know the area pretty well," said Howland. They jounced over the washboard surface of Simon Look Road, turned onto Old County Road, passed Whippoorwill Farm and the school, and turned onto Scotchman's Lane.

"Hurry!" said Victoria. "If we're lucky, we may be able to intercept him."

Scotchman's ended at State Road, and Howland stopped at the stop sign and waited. A blue pickup truck passed, heading toward Vineyard Haven. "Which way, Victoria?"

Victoria was trying to decide whether to

turn right or left when a light-colored SUV whizzed past them, well over the speed limit.

"I've seen that car around Town Hall," said Howland, as the taillights disappeared around Deadman's Curve. "Subaru. I'm pretty sure it belongs to one of the town employees."

"Follow him," said Victoria. "Don't lose him."

"There's only one way he can go until he gets to Brandy Brow."

They were well behind the Subaru when it turned right at Brandy Brow. The car slowed in front of Alley's and turned into Ellen's driveway.

"I should have known," said Victoria.

"Want me to park behind him?"

"Her," said Victoria. "Park behind her and call Casey. Tell her to meet us here with the state police."

"Right," said Howland. "I'm going in with you."

"Wait here. There won't be any trouble now. Keep an eye on things, in case I'm wrong."

CHAPTER 37

Victoria climbed the steps to Ellen's side door, brushing past the lilac bushes that grew on either side. It was a little over a week ago that she'd climbed those same steps and found Lucy's body. It seemed much longer. She took a deep breath and knocked. She waited, then knocked again. When there was still no answer, she tried the door. It was unlocked and she peered into the neat kitchen.

"Ellen?" she called from the doorway.

No answer.

She went hastily through the tidy downstairs rooms, the dining room, the unused parlor, feeling very much the intruder. Hesitantly, she climbed to the second floor. There, she heard a flurry of activity. A door slammed. Drawers opened and shut. In the front bedroom someone was breathing in heavy, labored gasps. Victoria headed that way. Through the half-open door she saw a suitcase on the bed with clothing being hurled into it.

"Ellen?" she called.

The activity stopped abruptly.

"Mrs. Trumbull?"

Ellen was standing, her arms full of clothing. Perspiration trickled down her forehead. Her normally neat hair straggled out of its pins in disorder. She wore a rumpled and soiled black sweat suit.

"No!" she said, and dropped into the chair next to the bed. She held up her hands as though to protect herself. "No, no, no!"

Victoria remembered Bertie's gift and pulled the scrap of black fabric from her pocket. "This is yours, isn't it?"

Ellen looked down at her left pants leg where there was a ragged tear. "The dog attacked me."

"Did he hurt you?" asked Victoria.

"Merely a scratch. If he hadn't gone after me . . ."

"Better put some antiseptic on it. Can I get it for you?"

Ellen took a deep breath and let it out. "In the bathroom cabinet."

Victoria returned with a brown bottle of peroxide and a handful of cotton balls.

Ellen held out her hand for the bottle. "I'll take care of it, Victoria. If only that dog . . ."

"It was more than Bertie," said Victoria. "We were closing in on you." Victoria gestured at the open suitcase. "You can't run, you know. More than anyone else, you must know that."

Ellen's eyes darted from one side of the room to the other, from the strewn clothing on the floor, to the suitcase on her rumpled bed, and back to Victoria. She took another deep breath, as though to store up as much free air as she could. She held the peroxide bottle, unopened. "I made one mistake too many," she said.

"Your mistakes go back a long time," said Victoria. "An avalanche you couldn't stop once you'd set it in motion."

"You know, now, that I killed them, don't you."

"Yes," said Victoria.

"Aren't you afraid of me?" Ellen looked up. "Knowing what I've done? What I'm capable of doing?"

"You won't harm anyone else," said Victoria. "You've come to the end and you know it. You can't escape."

Ellen sighed, and tossed a sweater she'd been holding onto the bed.

Victoria sat down on the end of the bed. "You surprised Oliver while he was looking at your property card, didn't you," she continued. "Oliver had taken the cards home with him, including yours."

Ellen looked away.

"I saw what was on your card."

"Then you know," said Ellen.

"Yes. You no longer own your house."

Ellen looked away.

"You'd better treat that dog bite," said Victoria, indicating the wound. "Even a scratch can become nasty."

Ellen twisted the bottle cap and stopped.

"How did you lose it?" Victoria asked softly.

"An unwise, stupid investment." Ellen closed her eyes.

Suddenly, everything made sense to Victoria. "TruArt Productions?"

"Fine-art films. A sure thing, he told me. A risk-free moneymaker. A cultural asset." She laughed without humor. "The Reverend True showed me a slick, bound prospectus, and I fell for it."

"You had a lot of money to hide, didn't you?"

"Not only mine, but the other girls', too."

"Ocypete and Selena?"

"I talked them into sinking their money into TruArt. I had more than a hundred thousand dollars of my own I'd saved in cash . . ."

"Cash!?" said Victoria.

"Yes." Ellen smiled. "I was trying to avoid a paper trail to cover up for having so much cash. I even 'sold' my house to him with the understanding that the transaction was in name only. He assured me that the house was still mine. I trusted him, and he cheated me. He lied and sold my house out from under me to pay his bills."

Victoria whistled softly. "You've lost everything."

Ellen nodded.

Victoria said, "Henry is paying huge sums to the mob for so-called protection. Far more than his company is taking in. He doesn't dare not pay. Do you want me to dress your wound?"

"No. No, I'll do it." Ellen unscrewed the cap the rest of the way and poured peroxide onto the cotton balls. She pulled up the torn leg of her sweatpants.

Victoria frowned. The wound was not a mere scratch. It was a jagged slash above her ankle, flesh torn to the bone. Blood had poured into Ellen's running shoe and the wound was still oozing blood.

"That needs stitches," said Victoria. "And you'll have to get a tetanus shot."

"It doesn't matter."

"We've got to stop the bleeding. Now. I'll

bind up your ankle until we can get you to a doctor." She went to the bathroom and returned with a roll of gauze. She pulled a chair over for Ellen to set her foot on, and knelt beside her.

"I can understand your anger at Henry," Victoria said as she wrapped gauze around Ellen's ankle, "but why didn't you kill him, rather than the pilot? Not that I condone any killing."

"I intended to kill Reverend True." Ellen winced as Victoria pulled the gauze tightly over the wound. "I thought the pilot was the reverend. Another mistake."

"How could you possibly mistake the pilot for Henry? They weren't at all alike."

"I'd never met Reverend True. I'd only talked to him on the phone and corresponded with him."

"I'm not hurting you, am I?" asked Victoria.

"That's all right. Someone told me Reverend True was on Island, so I called him, disguising my voice. I told him I was an admirer of his television show and I wanted to meet him and get his autograph. I never gave him my name, of course."

"Didn't he seem suspicious of you?"

"In retrospect, he must have been. I think he sent the pilot in his place, sensing something was wrong." She looked down as Victoria finished wrapping the gauze around her ankle. "Thanks, Mrs. Trumbull."

Victoria got to her feet again. "I suppose after that Henry was very careful."

Ellen nodded. "I didn't get another chance."

"He thought Delilah's chauffeur had killed the pilot, you know. I don't think he suspected you for a moment."

"When I called him, I said I was visiting the Island and would love to see his grounds. He agreed to meet me around sunset by his pond, one of his favorite times." She lifted her foot off the chair. "I realize, now, that he wanted it dark, in case I'd seen pictures of him."

"As an assessor, you must know that property well," said Victoria.

"I had walked every inch of it, long before Delilah Sampson bought it. That evening, I hid in the underbrush. When the person I thought was the reverend showed up, I strangled him. And it wasn't my intended victim after all."

Victoria shivered.

Ellen noticed the shiver. "I know it seems cold-blooded to you, Victoria, but I was trained to kill."

"You were in the military, weren't you?"

"Intelligence."

"Do you think you can walk all right?"

"You're really a pretty good medic, you know," Ellen said, examining the bandage. She got slowly to her feet. "I suppose the police are waiting for me?"

Victoria nodded. "I'll ask them to take you directly to the hospital. But before we go, I have a few other questions. Sit down again."

"I think I know what you're about to ask," Ellen said, as she slumped back into her chair. "I moved to West Tisbury after a twenty-year career in the military, still in my forties. I wanted to do my bit for my community. I ran unopposed for assessor, a job nobody wanted, and naturally I won. Selena and Ocypete were already in office. We three hit it off, early on. What we called our 'setting-aside account' started entirely by accident. We'd overbilled a taxpayer by mistake, and fully intended to refund his money. But he never questioned the over-payment." She paused for several moments. "That's how it started. After that, we targeted only a few people each year."

"Did anyone ever question the bills?"

"A few. Not many. It was quite a modest scheme until Oliver Ashpine indulged in his over-the-top scam."

"How did Tillie get involved?"

"Once we saw how easy it was to skim off a few thousand here and there, we decided it was a foolproof way to supplement our incomes." She got to her feet again. "I suppose I should change my clothes." She looked down at her torn, blood-stained pants and muddy, blood-soaked shoes.

"Do you need any help?"

"I think I have everything that I need right here." She indicated the heap of clothing on the bed. "Actually, this is all I have left." As Ellen changed her clothes she continued to talk. "We realized, as we got more ambitious, that we needed the support of the tax collector, as well as a trustworthy clerk. Lambert Willoughby, who works in Town Hall, suspected what we were doing, so we had to cut him in. Lambert recommended Tillie, his sister, and she worked out perfectly. She couldn't have been more trustworthy."

"Trustworthy, I see," Victoria repeated. "When did that change?"

"With Reverend True. Tillie wanted to be a movie star, and the reverend told her that his videos would be a sure entree into Hollywood. She decided she needed money to go to California, to buy a wardrobe, to take lessons, to rent an apartment. She started to pressure us for a larger share of the setting-aside account. Then she threatened to tell the selectmen what we were doing. We couldn't tolerate blackmail, so she simply had to go."

"Did the other assessors know you'd killed her?"

"They may have suspected. I don't know. When Selena's candy poisoned us but not her, I thought she'd caught on. She hadn't, of course."

"How did you lure Tillie up to the attic?"

"That was easy. During lunchtime when everyone was gone, we went up there together to look up some records. She had her back turned. I put my hands around her throat and throttled her. It's quite easy, you know. I thought her body would mummify in that dry environment, and it did." Ellen untied her shoes, slipped them off, and eased her torn sweatpants over her bandaged ankle.

"Why did you kill Lucy, Lambert's mother-in-law?"

"Like most people in town, she thought Tillie had run off with that Edgartown man. When she ran into him at the Stop and Shop a couple of weeks ago, she asked about Tillie, and he had no idea what she was talking about." Ellen selected a pair of slacks and slipped into them, then gently pulled on clean socks and shoes.

"We understood you were off Island at the dentist's when Lucy was killed."

"That was the only tricky killing to work out." Ellen sat back in her chair. "I actually did have a dental appointment. I told Lucy I had an emergency dental appointment, and would be staying overnight in Falmouth. I asked her to take care of Adolph. I took the early ferry to Woods Hole, but returned to the Island on the very next boat. It was still early when I arrived home. She was in the pantry. I don't think she even heard me. I strangled her with her own scarf. Then I took the next ferry to Woods Hole, went to the dentist, stayed overnight, and you know the rest."

"If you're ready," said Victoria, getting up from her chair, "we'd better go, Ellen. They're waiting outside for us."

CHAPTER 38

A week later, Victoria and Howland were in the cookroom, drinking coffee and talking about the murders. Victoria sorted her mail and was slitting it open.

"Sad, isn't it." Victoria put the letter opener down and stirred her coffee. "Ellen Meadows got caught up in a scheme too good to pass up. As a result, three people are dead."

"I'll never understand how one human being can kill another," said Howland.

"She was trained to kill. She was awarded medals for killing the right people. Now she'll spend the rest of her life in prison." She showed Howland a bill from the tax collector. "How can anyone afford to live here?"

"I think they'll be adjusting the bills downwards, thanks to you, Victoria."

She set the bill aside. "Whatever good reputations Selena, Ocypete, and Oliver had are gone forever. No one will ever trust them again. They, too, will go to prison for a long time. What will become of Lambert Willoughby?"

"He has to return all the money plus interest, and he'll be on probation until he does," said Howland.

"You knew Darcy from your work, didn't you?"

"I knew who he was," said Howland. "Emery Meyer. I suppose everyone in clandestine operations knows of him."

"Darcy told me Senator Hammermill sent both him and the pilot to get evidence of Henry's chicanery." Victoria removed a check from an envelope and laid it next to the tax bill. "Another one of my poems was accepted. I'll need to write a few more."

"Why didn't she tell Darcy up front?"

"That's what Darcy said. Apparently she wanted them to work independently."

"Henry thought Darcy was from the mob, here to kill him. He'll feel safer in prison," said Howland. "Have you talked to Delilah lately? What's she going to do now that her property's been repossessed?"

Victoria tossed a catalog into the trash. "This company sends me one every month. I refuse to do business with them. Waste, waste."

"Delilah?" asked Howland.

"She'll be fine. The town is leasing her house back to her at a fair rate," said Victoria. "She's opening a bed and breakfast with help from Lee, and the planning board approved a petting farm with chickens and fainting goats." She tore up a sheaf of checks from her credit card company and tossed the pieces toward the trash. "Jordan gave her some honesty seeds. He told her honesty was invasive, so she had Darcy scatter them in front of Town Hall."

"Has Darcy left yet?" asked Howland.

Victoria raised her head and listened. She could imagine his voice. "We have a lot in common, you know. He'll be back," she said with assurance.

"You and your bad boys." Howland got up from the table. "Let me have your mug. I'll put it in the sink."

Victoria followed him to the door. The sun was shining. Daffodils and forsythia were in bright, full bloom. A hundred or more blackbirds caroled from the maple tree. Spring had come to the Island.

Howland and she stood at the top of the stone steps admiring the fresh new world.

"Elections are coming up in a couple of weeks," said Howland, turning to her with a grin. "We have vacancies for three assessors and a tax collector. How about running for office, Victoria? You're a shoo-in."

ABOUT THE AUTHOR

Cynthia Riggs, a thirteenth-generation Islander, lives on Martha's Vineyard in her family homestead, which she runs as a bed-and-breakfast catering to poets and writers. She has a degree in geology from Antioch College and an MFA in creative writing from Vermont College, and she holds a U.S. Coast Guard Masters License (100-ton).

Visit her Web site at www.cynthiariggs.com.

The employees of Thorndike Press hope you have enjoyed this Large Print book. All our Thorndike, Wheeler, and Kennebec Large Print titles are designed for easy reading, and all our books are made to last. Other Thorndike Press Large Print books are available at your library, through selected bookstores, or directly from us.

For information about titles, please call:
  (800) 223-1244

or visit our Web site at:
  http://gale.cengage.com/thorndike

To share your comments, please write:
  Publisher
  Thorndike Press
  295 Kennedy Memorial Drive
  Waterville, ME 04901